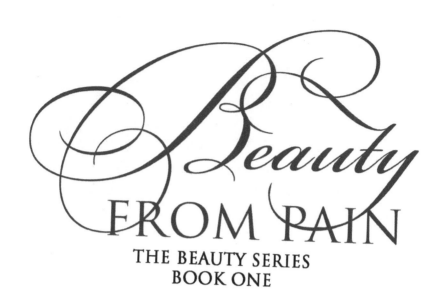

Beauty FROM PAIN

THE BEAUTY SERIES
BOOK ONE

GEORGIA CATES

GEORGIA CATES BOOKS, LLC

Published by Georgia Cates Books, LLC

Sign-up for Georgia's newsletter at www.georgiacates.com. Get the latest news, first look at teasers, and giveaways just for subscribers.

Interior Formatting by Indie Formatting Services

Editing Services provided by Jennifer Sommersby Young

Photograph by Brett Jackman, Polar Impressions Photography

Cover Model Samantha Dionisiou

ISBN-13: 978-1482348736 (CreateSpace-Assigned)

ISBN-10: 148234873X

To J, F, and M. You are my dream come true.

"But this had been a sin of passion, not of principle,
nor even purpose."

—*THE SCARLET LETTER* BY NATHANIEL HAWTHORNE

CHAPTER ONE

LAURELYN PRESCOTT

I AM SICK OF BEING ON THIS PLANE. THE FOUR-AND-A-HALF-HOUR FLIGHT from Nashville to Los Angeles was fine. The layover was tolerable, thanks to the airport bar. But the last leg of our flight to Australia is becoming more and more unbearable with each passing minute.

I try to calculate how much longer it is until we land in Sydney. My exhaustion makes it difficult for me to do the simple equation in my head, but it looks like it's still almost two hours until I will feel solid ground beneath my feet again. I sigh and tell myself to be patient. I've made it this far. I can take another two hours. I mean, I don't really have a choice at this point, right?

I look at my best friend sleeping in the seat next to me and I'm irritated. Addison has slept most of the flight, leaving me to entertain myself. She offered to share her Valium, but I declined, certain I wouldn't need it. Wrong.

I climb over Addison and take a walk up and down the aisle to stretch my legs, which helps me feel better. Upon returning to my seat, I decide reading will help pass the time, so I grab my e-reader and pick up where I stopped on the slutmance I'd started earlier. Only at chapter six and of course, the woman is in love with the hot new guy but is in denial. How typical.

Chapter twelve is winding down when the pilot announces that we'll be landing in Sydney in ten minutes. Addison doesn't stir, so I put my naughty tale away and nudge her, knowing it will take the next ten minutes to get her out of her drug-induced slumber.

"Wake up, Addison. We're almost in Sydney."

She barely stirs so I nudge her again. "Addison. Get up. We're in Sydney. You need to get buckled for the landing."

She lifts her head and stares at me with unfocused eyes. She straightens in her seat and takes a moment to get her bearings. "Wow, that went faster than I expected."

"I guess so since you were in a freakin' coma. It was the longest thirteen hours of my life. I didn't sleep a wink the whole flight because I was too busy wondering if we were going to end up being shark food." That came out a little pissier than I'd intended.

"Well, there's no reason to be miserable when you don't have to be. You should've taken a happy pill and then maybe you wouldn't be so cranky right now." She won't have to offer twice on the flight home three months from now. Lesson learned.

Buckled into my seat, I squeeze my eyes as the plane's wheels screech against pavement. Our fellow passengers erupt into cheer and clapping when we're safely on the ground. I'm not the only one glad to be getting off this plane.

We collect our three months' worth of luggage and take a seat in the terminal to wait for our last flight. With an hour layover, I decide to visit the airport bar. "I'm gonna grab a much-needed and well-deserved toddy."

Addison's phone rings and I recognize her brother's ringtone. Before she answers, she gives me a warning. "Be back in thirty minutes or I'm sending security for you." I don't reply in words but make sure she sees the hand gesture I have for her.

The airport bar isn't far from our terminal and I plop down on a stool. "What can I get you?" I might not be able to tell by my surroundings, but I know I'm in Australia when I hear his accent.

"I'd like something from a local brewery. I tend to favor lighter flavors."

He serves me a pale ale from a Sydney brewery. It's stout, but good.

2

I sit at the bar enjoying my ale. The bartender doesn't try to talk about where I'm from or where I'm heading. He appears to be in his fifties, so I can only assume he's heard more shit than he'd like over the years and thus isn't interested in mine. Works fine for me.

When I finish, I go back to where Addison is guarding our huge pile of luggage. "Was Ben calling to check on us?"

"Yeah. He was making sure our flight was running on time. I told him to expect us to arrive around three. He said he's bringing a friend to help with our luggage."

I see how many bags we have and I swear we look like a traveling band of gypsies. Most of it is Addison's, but I have my fair share—there's no way to pack lightly for a three-month stay. "That's not a bad idea."

"He's my brother. He knows how high maintenance I am." I sit and prop my feet on the suitcase in front of me. "He didn't say it, but he's really excited to meet you."

He's really excited to meet me. This is a huge red flag. I hope she isn't thinking of playing matchmaker.

"Don't you dare even think about encouraging him." I'm not interested in dating anyone right now. She knows this better than anyone. This whole Australia gig is about getting away from all that shit, not finding another pile of it.

"He hasn't dated many Aussies while he's lived here. I'm just saying you shouldn't be surprised if he tries to start something with you."

Oh, hell no. We're not even there yet and she's already trying to hook us up. "It's not happening, Addison."

"You'll be living in the same apartment with him for the next three months. Who knows what could happen?"

Okay. Now, I'm getting pissed because it feels like I'm being ambushed. "I might not know what will happen, but I know what won't, so forget it."

"Fine, fine, I won't mention it again. Ben wants to take us out tonight, but I know you haven't slept much. I told him you might not feel like it."

"Maybe I'll feel up to it if I can catch a power nap on the flight to Wagga Wagga."

❦

THIS TIME IT'S ADDISON NUDGING ME WHEN OUR FLIGHT IS PREPARING TO land. "Laurelyn. Wake up. We're finally here."

I sit up and fluff my long brown hair. I look terrible when it's flat and I'm sure it's lying against my head after my nap.

I couldn't have slept more than forty minutes, but I welcome the overall refreshed feeling it brings—except for my mouth. The combination of mouth breathing, beer drinking, and lack of oral hygiene during our travels has skunked things up. I don't want to meet Addison's brother for the first time and have him question which end is my face. "I need some gum. Do you have any on you?"

Addison reaches into her purse and holds out the lime-green pack in my direction. "Doublemint work for you?"

I take two pieces because I'm fairly certain it's going to take two shots of Doublemint to do the job. "Thanks."

We walk out of the jet bridge with our carry-ons and I see two great-looking guys standing in the terminal watching the disembarking passengers. I know Ben as soon as I see him. I could pick him out of a crowd anywhere, even if I'd never seen his picture. There's no way to miss him; he's the perfect male version of Addison. His blond hair is darker than hers (her monthly date with the hairdresser helps those playful highlights). Their olive skin presents a striking contrast with their light hair. He is stunning, just like his sister, but in a masculine way. It's too bad I'm not interested in dating because he is hot.

He puts his arms around his sister's middle and squeezes as he lifts her from the floor and spins several times. "I can't believe my little sister has come all this way to see me." He lowers her feet to the floor and looks at me. "And you must be Laurelyn."

"Indeed I am."

Addison and I have been best friends since we met our freshman year at Vanderbilt, but my path has always failed to cross Ben's for one reason or another. Now that we're meeting after four years, I'm not sure if I should extend my hand for a shake or lift my arms for a hug, so I wait for his cue.

4

He goes for the hug. "It's good to meet you, Laurelyn. I've been hearing about you for years, so I feel like I already know you."

"I hope my best friend hasn't ruined your opinion of me."

"Never." His crooked grin shows off one of his deep dimples. It's not a friendly nice to meet you smile. He's flirting with me already, so I'm wondering what my good pal might have told him.

Addison clears her throat. "Are you going to introduce us to your friend?"

The vibe I'm getting from Ben makes me uncomfortable, so I'm happy to shift my focus from him to his buddy. Zac is tall with an athletic build. His dark hair is buzzed close to his scalp except for the spiked tuft on top, and long, sooty lashes frame his almost-black eyes. He's wearing a fitted black T-shirt and I spy the tribal art tat wrapping around his bicep. His whole exterior screams trouble and that means one thing: my bad-boy-loving pal is going to be all over him.

He offers his hand to Addison first. "It's very nice to meet you."

Oh, swoon. I'm not into guys like him, but I could listen to his smooth Aussie accent all day.

I think I hear a sigh from Addison, and I know she's thinking the same thing. "It's great to meet you. Love your accent."

He offers his hand to me, but not his attention—that still belongs to Addison. "I hope your trip has been a pleasant one."

The trip here wasn't a damn bit pleasant, but it's rude to complain to someone I've just met. Addison replies, so I'm neither forced to lie nor complain because she is eager to keep Mr. Dark and Handsome's attention. "We had a super trip."

"Do you ladies feel up for hitting a club tonight?"

I feel like hitting something, but it's called a bed.

Addison is well rested from her snooze on the plane, so that means I'll be the party pooper if I decline, which I've never been labeled as, and I don't intend to start now. "I'm like an Energizer bunny, ready to go."

I'll sleep when I'm dead, right?

CHAPTER TWO

JACK MCLACHLAN

I SIT IN THE DARK CORNER AND SCAN THE ROOM LIKE A STARVED PREDATOR searching for prey. I haven't chosen her yet, but the woman who will share my bed for the next few months is in this room right now.

I watch a lovely blond approach my table. "What can I bring you?" Hmm. A waitress—not at all my usual taste.

I have a type. Attractive. Mature. Refined. This barmaid meets the attractive requirement well enough, but she's void of refinement or maturity as displayed by her choice of apparel—a white, barely there tank top and frazzled cutoff denim shorts. She doesn't do it for me. Plus, my last two companions were blond. I want a different flavor this time, but no redheads. I want a brunette. A beautiful one.

I remind myself I'm not in Sydney where I have an endless variety of sophisticated women from which to choose. My choices are more limited in the small town of Wagga Wagga, but that doesn't mean I have to settle for the first attractive woman I see.

"I'll have a Shiraz."

I'm prepared for a more prolonged relationship this time—three whole months instead of the usual three or four weeks. I'm looking forward to keeping this one around a little longer, and that's all the more reason to be certain I make a wise choice.

I begin my search of the club with the first table toward the front of the room. A brunette beauty sits with a group of women. I watch her for a while, but decide she's too friendly with the woman sitting next to her. Lesbians aren't in my repertoire.

I spend the next hour scanning the club and come up empty-handed. I'm discouraged. No one stands out as the one and this club is by far my best bet for meeting single women in this town. Maybe I should consider coming back another time when it's not open mic night. Tonight, the place is crawling with boozed college students.

Tonight's search has been a failure, but at least the karaoke was entertaining.

I'm finishing off the last of my wine before I leave when an announcer from the club takes the stage and asks for the next singer to step forward. A small group of people across the room nominates one of its own. My view of the poor bastard is blocked by the crowd of intoxicated kids standing between us, but I'm certain this is going to be another delightful train wreck.

The club erupts into cheer and chants. "Do. It. Do. It. Do. It." A young woman walks onto the stage and stands with her back to the crowd as she takes a guitar from its stand. She lifts its strap over her head and then tosses her long brown hair over one shoulder. When she's finished settling the guitar into place, she circles around and sits on the stool in the middle of the stage.

She's beautiful. And somehow overlooked during my search.

She's wearing a short ivory dress and a denim jacket with brown cowgirl boots. She bares her thighs as she lifts her feet to rest on the bottom rail, but she's careful to push her dress between her legs so she doesn't provide a peep show to the crowd.

She strums the borrowed guitar a few times and then leans into the microphone. "Is everyone having a good time tonight?"

She's American. I think. Her accent sounds different—not like what I've heard in the past.

The crowd erupts into a drunken cheer and I hear a man's voice yell over the crowd, "It's better now, sweet thing!"

She smiles and adjusts the mic. "I'm not from around here. It's my first night in Australia."

"Leave with me and I'll make you feel right at home!" a man shouts from the back of the room.

She ignores the fat, ugly bastard yelling at her. "I don't know what kind of music Australians like, but this has been one of my favorites for as long as I can remember." She strums a few more chords. "This is 'Crash Into Me' by the Dave Matthews Band."

She sings it slower than the original, putting her own twist on it. Her voice is raspy and sexy, her eyes closed. She oozes eroticism. She tilts her head and opens her eyes when she begins to sing the chorus. I swear it feels like she's looking right in my direction, singing to me.

The stage lights shine in her face and common sense tells me she can't see me sitting in the dark corner at the back of the club, but that doesn't stop me from hoping.

She finishes the chorus and shuts her eyes again. Her long legs bounce against the rail of the stool to keep rhythm and I fall victim to her siren's song. She has bewitched me. And I want her. She's the one.

She opens her eyes and looks in my direction again as she sings about hiking up a skirt a little more. Man, she can show me her world if she so desires.

The waitress returns to my table, but I don't glance in her direction when she speaks. I can't take my eyes from the beautiful brunette on stage for even a second. "Can I bring you another Shiraz?"

My plans have changed. "Yes, please."

The American girl finishes her song and the crowd is all cheers and whistles. She smiles as she pulls the guitar strap over her head and then leans forward to the mic. "Thank you."

I watch her leave the stage and return to a table where she is sitting with a blond woman and two blokes. Damn! A boyfriend, perhaps?

My waitress returns with my wine and places it on the table in front of me. "Excuse me, do you know the girl who just performed?"

"No. She said it was her first night in Australia."

I take my wallet from my interior jacket pocket and remove a hundred-dollar bill. I slide it in her direction across the table. "What about the people she's sitting with?"

She sees the money on the table and picks it up to deposit in the pocket of her black apron before turning to see who my songstress is sitting with. "The blond guy is Ben Donavon and his friend is Zac Kingston. They're regulars in here, two or three times a week."

Why is this American here with those blokes? "She sounds American. Do you know why she would be with them?"

"Ben is a Yank. His family owns a vineyard in California and he's here to study wine at the uni. I think she'd have to be someone he knows from home."

I hold up a second hundred-dollar bill between my fingers. "See this? It's yours if you can find out what she's doing here and how long she'll be in Wagga Wagga. And find out if she's dating either one of the blokes."

She smiles and I see she's interested in playing my little game. "I'll be back to collect that in a minute."

I sit back and enjoy my Shiraz while the waitress does my detective work. A visiting American couldn't be more perfect for my next companion. Once our relationship is over, she would be on an entirely different continent, which ensures we won't have any accidental future run-ins.

My stay in Wagga Wagga is becoming more promising.

I finish my glass of Shiraz as my waitress returns. "Her name is..."

I cut her off before she can finish her sentence. "No, I don't want to know her name."

I can see this stumps her, but money is money. "Ben's sister is her best friend and they've come to spend the summer with him. She met Ben and Zac for the first time today."

Good. That means she isn't dating either of them.

If the guys are students in the wine science program at the university, I'm guessing they will be at the vintage dinner at the school on Friday night. They'll be anxious to showcase their wines. I wonder if she'll be there as a guest.

I pull another bill from my wallet and hold it up for Blondie to see. "This is yours if you can find out what their plans are for the vintage dinner at the university on Friday night. I want to know if the brunette will be there."

She smiles again. "I could play this game all night."

Ten minutes later, she returns with another Shiraz and an update.

"The guys will be presenting their wines at the dinner, and both girls will be guests."

I slide the well-earned bill across the table. "Perfect. Thank you."

"It's been my pleasure. Would you like me to keep the Shiraz coming?"

"Yes."

I spend the next hour stealing glances at the beautiful American through the crowd of people between us as they shift. I'm disappointed when the foursome gets up to leave, but I see the perfect opportunity for a convenient face-to-face encounter when she moves toward the restrooms.

I migrate in that direction and wait for her to emerge for our chance meeting in the hallway. When the door to the ladies' room opens, I walk toward her, but she's looking down into her purse. She attempts to dodge right, so I move with her. "Pardon me."

Her accent is so unusual. And endearing.

She steps to her left and I move with her like a mirror image. "So sorry, Miss."

Look up at me.

"Wanna dance?" she laughs as she lifts her eyes from her purse.

"I'd love to." Her smile spreads with my reply. We lock eyes and I try to identify the color of hers, but I can't. It's too dark in the narrow hallway.

I was right. She is the one.

She seems embarrassed. "I'm sorry. Asking someone to dance is an expression we use where I'm from. You know? Like when two people try to get around one another as we just did."

"I'm familiar with the expression, but one can always hope." I step around her toward the door to the men's room. "I think I would have enjoyed a dance with you."

CHAPTER THREE
LAURELYN PRESCOTT

How do you decide what to wear to a vintage dinner at an Australian university when you aren't really sure what a vintage dinner is?

I stand at the sink brushing my teeth while Addison showers. Man, this sharing a bathroom with two other people is no joke, especially when one of them is as high maintenance as Addison.

I rinse and wipe my mouth. "You never told me what this thing is that we're going to tonight."

"It's a vintage dinner." Awesome. That tells me everything I need to know.

I grab my makeup bag and begin applying my foundation. The lighting in our bedroom is terrible and the bathroom isn't much better, but who am I to complain when I'm staying here as a nonpaying guest. Besides, Addison complains enough for both of us. "Can you give me a little more to go on? Like, what's going to be happening and what I need to wear?"

"It can't be too formal if it's hosted by a university, so I think a sundress should be fine. What about that black strapless with the wide white band around the waist? It's a chameleon and will fit in if this shindig is on the dressier side. Didn't you bring it?"

I remember hanging it in the closet when we unpacked. "I did."

"Ben says the event begins outdoors with hors d'oeuvres where we'll try the first round of new vintages. When we finish that, we'll go inside for dinner and have more wine. There'll probably be a band, so expect some dancing."

Eating, drinking, and dancing. Slow dancing. It sounds fun and innocent enough, except I suspect Ben considers me more than a simple guest.

After I finish my hair and makeup, I slip into the black strapless. When Addison comes into our bedroom, she has me make a complete spin and gives me a whistle. "Looking good in the neighborhood."

"Thanks."

She's wearing an ivory halter dress I don't recognize. The ivory against her blond hair and olive skin is gorgeous. "I don't think I've seen this before."

"It's new. I bought it before we left. Think Zac will like it?"

"I think Zac would like you in anything. Or nothing at all."

She laughs but knows it's true. He wants her bad. "I think he likes me."

"Being reserved doesn't suit you, Addie. Of course he likes you. I don't know how you could question it. He's been here constantly since we arrived."

"I know, but he hasn't said anything or made a move."

"It's only been three days. Not every guy tries to get you in the sack thirty seconds after you meet."

"I know. I guess I'm second-guessing myself because he hasn't tried."

"Watch his reaction when we walk out. You'll know where his head's at."

The eyes tell it all when Zac sees Addison. He is hot for her. Unfortunately, Ben's reaction to me is very similar. What the hell am I thinking? It's a huge mistake for me to attend this event as Ben's guest wearing this dress, but it's too late now.

Luck is with me the first half of the night as I'm able to avoid Ben. He's busy presenting his vintages, but like always, my luck runs out. We finish dinner and he takes my hand to pull me from my chair. "Come dance with me."

I smile and follow him onto the dance floor, mostly because I don't have a reasonable excuse not to. One dance. I can do that.

I glance over at Addison dancing with Zac. She's giddier than a pig in shit and I'm happy for her. Her relationship luck hasn't been much better than mine. "She seems to be having a good time."

"Zac doesn't appear too unhappy, either. If I had to guess, I'd bet you and I have officially been dropped for the rest of the night."

Shit! That means we'll be alone when we get back to the apartment. "It's all right. I still have jet lag. I'll probably go straight to bed anyway."

A young man walks up beside us. "Mr. Donavon, I'm sorry to disturb you, but we're having trouble finding your merlot."

Ben stops swaying, but doesn't release me from his embrace. "I'm sorry. Who are you?"

"I'm Greg, one of the servers for tonight's event."

Ben looks puzzled. "All of my vintages were stored together."

Greg appears apologetic as he shrugs. "We've searched everywhere and can't find it with the others."

He releases me. "I'm sure it's been shuffled around in all the chaos. Will you excuse me for a moment?"

"It's fine. This is your special night. You need to do whatever it takes to make this successful."

He strokes his hand down my arm. "I won't be gone long."

"It's okay. No hurry." Really. Don't hurry.

I walk to the dinner table feeling a little guilty that I'm relieved by the interruption. I eye Addison and Zac on the dance floor and recognize her signature moves. When they circle around and his back is turned to me, she points to him and mouths, "I'm fucking him tonight."

I've heard that before and I have no doubt she will. That's Addison. She's been on a different continent for all of three days and she's already found her next hookup. I put my hand in the air to mimic that of a tigress claw and mouth a silent roar.

I'm giggling at her doing the same gesture behind his back when a man's voice startles me. "Enjoying the wine this evening?"

I look up at the person speaking and I'm not prepared for whom I see. A feather could knock me over. It's him, the beautiful man from the club.

I didn't get to study him for long the other night, but he's even better looking than I remember. He's tall with broad shoulders, the kind I'd like to run my hands across and glide down his strong arms. His dark hair is unruly in contrast to his businesslike attire, and I wonder if he purposely fixed it that way or if a woman has just finished running her fingers through it. If it is the latter, then damn, what a lucky woman.

He's dressed in another suit, this one dark platinum with a pinstriped shirt beneath. His coordinating blue and platinum tie makes his azure eyes even more intense.

Did he say something? Wait—he asked if I was enjoying the wine? At least that's what I think he said. "I am. Very much."

He shifts his attention to the glass in front of me. "What are you having?"

Oh, shit. I don't know what kind of wine it is. There are only two kinds in my book: good or bad. I give it a once-over and decide there's no reason to pretend I know. "Honestly? I don't have a damn clue. It's red and it's good. That's all I know."

He smiles as he takes the glass from my hand. He lifts it for inspection before tucking it under his nose. "It's Cabernet Sauvignon." He tilts it upward and takes a small sip. "Not bad."

Oh, double swoon. His lips are where mine were. Lucky glass. "I'll have to take your word for it because I know nothing about wine."

His brow wrinkles as he looks at me. Damn. His eyes are mesmerizing, the kind you can get lost in with very little effort. "If you don't know wine, then how did you come to be at a vintage dinner?"

"I'm the guest of one of the students showcasing his vintages."

He gestures to my glass of wine he's still holding. "Is this one your friend's?"

Is it Ben's? They'd started running together several glasses ago. "I think so."

"It's good. As for most of the others I've tried tonight, I can't say the same."

"I'll tell Ben you said so. Or perhaps you'd like to. He stepped away, but he should be back any minute." I silently pray he won't return and ruin my conversation with this man I haven't stopped thinking about since our prior meeting.

14

He has a crooked grin. "If I recall correctly, I think you owe me a dance."

"Yes, I believe I do." He reaches for my hand and leads me to the dance floor where the band is playing a fairly decent version of Van Morrison's "Someone Like You." We begin to step with the tempo.

"You're American?"

"Every day and twice on Sunday."

He laughs. "What brings a funny Yank like you to Wagga Wagga?"

I glance over his shoulder and see Addison noticing us, so I give her a smile. "My best friend invited me to spend the summer."

"Your accent sounds different from the other Americans I've met."

I had taken a lot of flack from Addison over the years about my strong twang. "That's because I'm from the South," I explain.

"I like it," he says. "So, how were you were able to put your life on hold for three months?"

"I needed to step away from my career for a little while so I could clear my head about some decisions I need to make."

He peers over my shoulder and an irritated countenance appears on his face. "I have somewhere to be in a few minutes, so I have to cut our dance short, but would you join me for dinner tomorrow night?"

How could I tell this man no? "Yes, I would like that."

"I have a meeting tomorrow evening and I expect it to run late. May I send my driver to pick you up around seven?"

He has a driver? "Umm, okay."

He takes his phone from his pocket. "Where are you staying?"

It takes a moment for me to recall the unfamiliar address, but he puts it into his phone as I call it off. "452 Stanton Street."

"My driver's name is Daniel and you can expect him to be prompt."

"Okay. I'll be ready." As he walks away, I remember we never introduced ourselves. "Wait. I didn't get your name."

He smiles as he walks backwards away from me. "It will be more interesting if you don't know. See you tomorrow night."

More interesting? What the hell is that supposed to mean? He tells me his driver's name, but not his? That's weird. I should know his name if I've agreed to meet him for dinner.

I'm about to chase him when I feel a warm hand on my arm. "Hey,

15

what are you doing standing out here on the dance floor by yourself?" Ben asks.

"I wasn't alone. I was dancing with someone, but he had to leave." I search for Nameless, but he is already gone. Like a phantom.

Ben gives me a bewildered look, as if I made up the whole thing. "Okay. Would you like to finish the dance?"

"Sure."

As I dance with Ben, I can't stop thinking about the phantom or the way he disappeared without giving me his name. Shit! I bet the good-looking bastard is married and that's why he wouldn't tell me who he is.

That isn't going to work for me. If there is one thing I don't do, it's married men.

I need to talk to Addison, but she is in the middle of her presex show with Zac. That means she's sending me home alone with Ben. I'm not in the mood to deal with that. "I'm not feeling well. I think I'm going to catch a cab back to the apartment."

"I'll drive you."

I put my hand on his arm. "I can't ask you to do that. This is your big night. Stay and show off what you've accomplished."

"I don't mind. Really."

Yeah, I know. He's such a nice guy, but I'm not interested. "I know, but I'd feel worse if you didn't stay to promote what you've worked so hard for."

He concedes and I catch a cab back to the apartment. I make a point to be in bed when he comes home. I pretend to be asleep when he taps on the bedroom door because I'm not sure what he wants.

Well, that's not true. I know what he wants, but I've chosen the coward's way. I should be brutal and tell him to back off, but I don't. I dodge him, only prolonging the inevitable.

❦

I JERK AWAKE WITH THE SHIFT OF THE BED BESIDE ME. WHAT THE HELL? THE adrenaline surging through my veins makes my heart take off like a helicopter. It's throbbing erratically in my neck, my chest, my head. Even my hands.

"Addison?" I pray I hear her voice answer me.

"Yeah." She whispers like she's afraid she'll wake someone. Too late.

I'm relieved to hear her voice instead of Ben's, but I'm madder than hell. I look at the clock on the nightstand. It's 3:18 in the morning. "You scared the shit out of me. What are you doing climbing into bed at this time of the morning? I thought you were at Zac's place."

"I was."

Yeah, and now you're not. "Why did you come back? Did something happen?"

"No, but you know me. I don't want to be that girl, the one who wears out her welcome."

Right. Because Dude doesn't owe you anything after he gets in your pants. "Let me get straight on this. You don't want to be the girl to wear out your welcome, but you'll be the girl who lets him wear out your vagina?"

She slaps my arm in the dark. "That's just crude, Laurie." She giggles. "But oh so true. He did wear it out like a champ."

Ugh! I was joking. She's not.

"It's a game, Laurelyn. Trust me. I know what I'm doing. He'll want me more if he has to lie in bed thinking about me from across the hall. He'll wish he'd asked me to stay, but there's another reason I came home. I don't want Ben to know I locked loins with Zac."

Good grief. That's what we're calling it these days. "Why would Ben care?"

"You're an only child so you don't get it. Brothers don't care how old you are. They're weird about their friends screwing their sisters."

What about a sister freaking out over her brother trying to lock loins with her best friend? Shouldn't she be trying to dissuade Ben or something?

"So, I saw you dancing with a good-looking suit last night. What's going on with that?"

Good-looking suit. I can roll with that. "That was him, the man I ran into at the club on our way out the other night. The same one I haven't been able to stop thinking about for three days."

"Oh, wow. What a coincidence." She doesn't have to tell me. I thought I'd never see him again.

"I know. He asked me to dinner tonight." I let out a high-pitched squeal that shouldn't come from a twenty-two-year-old woman. "He's sending his driver to pick me up because he has an afternoon meeting. Is that weird?"

"I guess not, unless he's calling the man behind the wheel of a taxi his driver. He must be rich. What does he do?"

"I don't know. We didn't get that far."

"What's his name?"

I opt to not tell her he said it would be more exciting if I didn't know. "Umm, we didn't get that far, either."

"Well, that's fucked up. You're going out with a guy and don't know who he is? Who am I going to report to the police if you go missing because he's another good-looking serial killer? You know, Ted Bundy was terribly charming too."

Oh, hell. I hadn't thought of that. What if he is some kind of weirdo? "I guess tell them it was the good-looking suit who did it."

CHAPTER FOUR

JACK MCLACHLAN

DANIEL MESSAGES ME WHEN HE IS PULLING UP TO THE FRONT OF THE Ashford Hotel, so I leave our table in the hotel restaurant to meet her. When I walk out of the hotel to greet my American girl, Daniel is circling around to open her door, but I stop him. "I have it, Daniel. Thank you."

After opening her door, she steps out onto the sidewalk. She's wearing a satiny floral one-shouldered dress belted at the waist and mile-high heels that stretch her legs even longer than they already are. She's beautiful and I ache to reach out my hand to touch the exposed skin on her shoulder.

She looks up at the hotel and then back to me. "Seriously? You brought me to a hotel?"

Her face tells me she's pissed off, but it's easy to see why she might jump to conclusions. "The meeting with my sales team was in the hotel's conference room. I thought we might have dinner at Ash. It's the hotel restaurant. I'm told it's the best in town."

Her cheeks pink. "I'm sorry."

"Don't give it another thought."

She takes my offered arm. "You're not from Wagga Wagga?"

"No." That's all I give her and she doesn't push further.

allow her to walk ahead of me through the revolving door into the lby. "Are you staying in this hotel?"

"No. I'm staying at an estate in the country."

"Oh."

I escort her toward the back of the restaurant to our table. I pull out her chair and slide it under her when she sits. "Are you hungry?"

She smiles and I find myself wanting to know all the secrets she hides behind it. "Very. I'm not one of those girls who's scared to eat in front of a date. I hope you don't mind that."

"Not at all."

She's quiet as she reads the wine list and our server arrives to take our drink order. "I'll have a Sauvignon Blanc."

She lifts her eyes from the list. "I have no idea how to order wine. I'll have what you're having."

"Two Sauvignon Blancs."

She holds the menu in front of her and I can't see her face. She's studying it like there could be an exam later. "I don't know what I want. Everything looks good."

"My business associate recommended anything seafood."

A moment later she places the menu on the table. "Seafood sounds good. I'll have the stuffed prawns."

After the server brings the wine and takes our order, we continue our safe, generic conversation. "How did your friend's vintages fare last night?"

"Ben did well, but I never expected anything less. Wine is his family's business."

I remember the waitress mentioning that. I believe she said he was from California. "I understand that. You're much more passionate about it when it's your livelihood."

"You say that like you know from experience." She's a sharp one.

"I do. I'm employed in the wine-making business as well." It's a half-truth since I neglect to tell her I own a large number of the wineries across South Australia and New Zealand.

She smiles and I see her make the connection. "So that's why you were at the vintage dinner last night?"

"Yes. My employer donates money to the wine program, so he is given an automatic invitation to the event. I was sent in his place as a representative."

We talk about nothing in particular and I feel the mood of our conversation shift when we finish eating. "I've spent the last hour having dinner with you and you still haven't told me your name. Maybe it's an Australian thing, but where I come from, that is one of the first things you tell someone. Is there a reason you haven't told me?"

I'm interested in picking her brain, hearing her possible explanation. "Why do you think that could be?"

She studies my face and for the first time I notice her unusual eye color. I thought they were brown, but now I see I was only half-right. They're lighter, more like caramel than chocolate. And her hair isn't a single shade of brown; it's full of honey-colored streaks.

Her back stiffens. "I think you're married with a wife and two-point-five kids waiting for you to come home."

I almost forget her question, I'm so caught up in watching the windows to her soul. I see something there, but I can't put my finger on what it is.

I hold up my empty left hand and point to where a wedding band would be if I had one. I smile because the thought of me being married is such a polar opposite from the truth. "No wife. No two-point-five kids."

She sits back in her chair and doesn't appear as though she's buying what I'm selling. "The lack of a wedding band doesn't prove anything."

"I am secretive, but it has nothing to do with being married."

Our server returns to remove our dishes and we fall silent until he walks away. "Why are you secretive?"

"For lack of a better answer, it's just how I am."

She frowns. "Well, that explains everything."

These are dangerous waters I'm treading. This girl is different from the others. If I don't handle her the right way, she'll run. Of this, I'm certain. "You and I will both be in Wagga Wagga for the next three months. I'd really like to see you while we're here."

"Would I finally get to know your name?" She's laughing but has no idea that withholding real names is my number-one stipulation for dating.

Hell! She's got me off my game and feeling like I've never done this before.

I draw a breath to clear my head before I begin. "My life is complicated for reasons I won't discuss. When it comes to dating, I need it to be simple and undemanding. Disclosing my identity complicates things, so you wouldn't know my real name."

"You're not joking."

I can't read her reaction. I have no idea if she's on board or freaking out. "When the three months is over, so are we. I'll move on and you will too. Because you won't know my name or any identifying information about me, you'll have no way to contact me. Ever."

This face I can read, and it's full of confusion. "But why?"

I have reasons, but I won't explain them. "Because that's the way I need things to be."

She's clearly pissed off as evidenced by the scowl on her face. "If you never wanted to hear from me again, that wouldn't be a problem on my end, Jack."

I smile because she has no idea she just used my real name. "You'd have the same courtesy. You don't have to tell me your real name and you choose how much or how little you want to tell me about yourself."

She puts her elbows on the table and leans forward. "You're crazy as hell, but you already know that, right?"

I feel her slipping through my fingers, so I'm forced to use my last line of defense. "I'm a very wealthy man. The three months we spend together would be the best of your life. You'd never be able to top what you'd experience with me."

She sits back and laughs. "Well, at least you're not egotistical."

I wasn't finished. I had one more card up my sleeve. "I'd make your fantasies a reality."

She licks her lips and then draws the bottom one into her mouth. God, I'd love to do that for her. "You want me to have sex with you."

Now she's catching on. "Yes, I would like that very much."

"Sounds like you need an escort or a prostitute, and I'm neither of those things."

Oh, shit. I've fucked up royally now.

I reach for her hand to calm her. "I wasn't suggesting you were either.

Sex wouldn't be the only part of our relationship. There would be much more to it than that."

She jerks her hand away. "I don't sleep with strangers and apparently that's what you'd continue to be since you won't even tell me something as basic as your name."

I pull my hand back. "You have a very reasonable argument, but it wouldn't be like that. We would come to know each other in our own way."

"To hell with this shit. I'm outta here." She pushes away from the table. "Please call your driver and ask him to take me home."

Way to go, Jack. Way to go.

I pull my phone from my pocket and call Daniel. "Front of the hotel, now."

I watch her face as she stares off, refusing to look at me. I regret we didn't have more time together. I wish I could take it all back and handle it differently.

"He'll only be a minute. Please, allow me to walk you out." She doesn't agree or object as I stand to walk her toward the exit.

The car is at the curb as we move through the revolving doors. I open the back passenger door for her and her caramel eyes meet mine before she gets inside. "Have a nice life, whoever you are."

Wow, that's final.

She climbs in and I stand, my hand on the door, waiting to shut it. I don't want to let her go like this. I fight the urge to get into the backseat with her but I know it's useless. I've insulted her, and she's made it clear she wouldn't accept my proposition. But dammit, I don't want this to be the last time I see her, so I stop arguing with myself and get into the car.

She regards me with narrowed, suspicious eyes. "What are you doing?"

I close the door. "I'm riding with you."

She scoots as far from me as possible. "My answer is no, so what's the point?"

Great question. "I don't know."

We ride in uncomfortable silence as Daniel drives us to where she is staying. I rack my brain trying to think of an alternate approach, but come up short.

After the car stops, Daniel opens the door and she gets out. I follow, walking by her side toward the apartment's entrance, and I can't fight the urge to make another plea. "Please, think it over and reconsider my offer."

She stops dead in her tracks. "You arrogant jackass! You rode with me so you could try to talk me into going along with this crazy-ass idea of yours."

I'm not sure why I feel like I have the right to touch her or why I think she'd let me, but I reach out and place my finger over her lips. "Shh. Don't say no again right now. Wait until you've had time to think about it. This is a new idea, and you might find you feel different about it once you've thought it over."

I trail my thumb to her bottom lip and rub it as I remember the way she sucked it. "If you say yes, you'd spend the next three months having the time of your life."

I take my hand from her face. "I'll be in the hotel restaurant tomorrow night at eight o'clock if you decide you want to discuss it further."

CHAPTER FIVE
LAURELYN PRESCOTT

I UNLOCK THE DOOR AND ALL BUT FALL INSIDE THE EMPTY APARTMENT. Addison is out with Zac for their first postcoital date. I have no idea where Ben is, but I'm glad to be alone. I don't want to explain why I've returned from a date with a man I can't name.

It's still early but nothing is on television, so I change into my pajamas and go to bed. Sleep doesn't find me easily because my mind keeps racing with thoughts of what Mr. Nameless has asked me to do.

It's shocking. It's bizarre. It's interesting.

It's a fascinating idea. At least I know how things would end. There would be no chance of a broken heart. He said it would be the best three months of my life. I'd experience new and wonderful things. He'd make my fantasies come true.

Why choose me?

I've known from the time I was a small child something was wrong with me. I've never been able to have a normal relationship with a man —neither romantic or nonromantic. Maybe my problems stem from my father—or lack thereof—or my mother's unrequited love for him. Neither have been much of a positive influence on my feelings regarding romantic relationships. Whatever the cause, I'm damaged goods. Maybe I should consider this. It's not like I have a better offer on the table.

It takes hours for me to doze off because I can't stop thinking about the things Nameless said. But I do fall asleep, only to be awakened by Addison sneaking into our bedroom again. Does she think that Ben is stupid? He has to know what she's doing with Zac.

I look at the clock: 6:27 a.m. this time. She almost made it to a reasonable hour.

She slides into bed next to me. "Tell me I'm not going to wake up to this for the next three months," I say.

"I make no promises. I see you're here so the good-looking suit must not have been a serial-killing weirdo. How did it go?"

She was dead wrong about the weirdo part. "It was a bizarre date to say the least."

"I'm finding out Aussie guys are different."

I can think of many words to describe Nameless, but none do him justice. There needs to be a new word for what he is. "Different doesn't even begin to cover what this guy asked me to do."

"Ooh, that doesn't sound good."

"My first thoughts were that it was crazy, but now I'm not sure. I've had time to think about it… and it might be sort of hot."

Addison sits straight up in the bed. I have her full attention. "What did he do? Ask you to give him a hand job under the table at dinner?"

I can't bring myself to tell her the part about how he wouldn't tell me his name or anything personal about his life. "He asked me to date him for the next three months and then walk away without any further contact."

She lies back on the bed. "So, the guy isn't into long-distant relationships? Seems pretty reasonable since you'll be nine thousand miles away. Zac and I sort of have the same arrangement."

No, it's not the same, but I can't tell her the rest. "I guess. He told me he was rich and he would make the next three months of my life the best I've ever had. He said he'd make my fantasies come true."

"Umm, the best three months of your life and fantasies coming true? What's holding you back?"

"It just seems pointless to date someone when I know it's going to end in three months." And then there's the whole issue of having sex with someone I don't love. I'm not sure I can do that.

"You're overthinking it, Laurelyn. The guy's rich and he promises you the best three months of your life. It's a no-brainer."

I can't believe I'm considering it. "You think I should do this?"

"If you don't, will you go home and wonder what you might have missed?"

The answer is clear. "Of course I would."

There's a knock at our bedroom door. "Come in," Addison says. Ben opens it.

"There's a delivery in here."

Addison's face lights up. "What kind of delivery?"

"It's flowers and a catered breakfast."

"Awesome!" she says, throwing back the covers. "See? I told you I knew how to play the game." It looks like Ben is going to find out about Zac sooner than she'd planned.

We walk into the kitchen and there's a floral arrangement on the counter next to a basket of breakfast pastries. Addison holds a bottle of champagne in one hand and orange juice in the other. "Mimosas for breakfast. Can you believe that? And this isn't cheap champagne. It's expensive. Very expensive."

She takes the card from the blank envelope and her smile fades after she reads it. "Oh. This isn't for me."

I feel a surge of hope. Could all of this be for me? From him, the man with no name? "What does the card say?"

She holds it up. "'You won't regret saying yes.' It's signed, 'from Lachlan.'"

I smile, but bite my lip in a failed attempt to hide my pleasure. His name is Lachlan.

I'm confused by this unexpected confession. He said names weren't part of the game, so what has changed? Maybe he decided he is more interested in a normal relationship than the bizarre one he proposed last night.

I pluck the card from Addison's hand because I want to read it for myself. I rub my thumb over his written words. The penmanship is masculine. I'm sure he signed it personally.

I hear a pop as Addison opens the champagne. "Laurie, this guy is jockeying hard for you, girl."

Ben's arms are crossed and he looks pissed. "Come on. You just met this guy. Doesn't this seem like a little much?"

"I'd love it if a guy did this for me." Addison tops up her champagne with some orange juice. "This is a guaranteed panty-dropper in my book."

"Addison!"

Ben storms out of the kitchen and slams his bedroom door. "You shouldn't have said that in front of him, and we both know why."

Addison reaches for a pastry. "Oh, he'll get over it. So, what are you gonna do?"

There's nothing wrong with trying it. If it doesn't feel right, I can always back out. "He asked me to meet him tonight if I wanted to discuss it further. I think I'm going to go."

"That's my girl. I love that he has to wait all day wondering if you'll show tonight. He'll be so hard up by the time he sees you walk in. You have to show up late. I have the perfect little black dress that will knock his socks off. The back of it is so low, you can almost see your ass crack."

She runs into our room and returns with a next-to-nothing black minidress. Wow, she's right. It is low. And short. Maybe even too short. I hold it up and have no doubt it is going to hit me high thigh since I'm taller than she is.

"Isn't this gonna be too short for me?"

"What do you mean too short? Have we met?"

⚜

It's a lazy Sunday so we spend the day hanging out in the apartment after gorging on quiche and Mimosas. Ben is sullen the rest of the day, his attitude suggesting he is unhappy about the prospect of my new acquaintance. He doesn't speak to me all day, but that's all right. I may be staying with him, but I don't owe him anything. And his behavior is making it a lot easier to not feel guilty about meeting up with another guy tonight.

It's six o'clock and I decide to start getting ready to meet Lachlan. Addison wants me to be late so he'll sweat it out, but if I'm tardy, it won't be because I wasn't ready on time.

I jump in the shower and shave my legs and pits twice, just in case, but in case of what, I don't know. I apply my makeup as I stand with one towel wrapped around my hair and one around my body. I decide to go with smoky eyes—the sultriness will go well with the sensual dress and tall heels Addison has chosen for me.

It's twenty minutes until eight and I stand in front of the mirror studying the final product. Hmm, not bad if I do say so myself. The smoky eyes and scarlet lips are definitely going to get his attention but my upswept hair makes my bare back call out to be touched, and quite possibly, kissed. I have never felt so alluring in all of my life—or so much like a ho—because I know why I'm going.

Addison surveys me and instructs me to do a spin. "Laurelyn, you're smokin' hot."

She is my best friend so it's her job to say stuff like that. "It's the dress."

"Hell no, it's not. It's all you, and he'll know it when he peels that dress off you."

Someone's awfully anxious for me to get it on with this guy. "He's not peeling jack off me tonight. I'm just going to talk."

She takes my hands and looks like she's going to give me some serious advice. I prepare because this isn't something I would expect from her. "Listen to me, Laurelyn. The best way to get over somebody is to get under someone else."

Well, her record stands unblemished. She's yet to blow my mind with deep, philosophical advice. I'm laughing when I hear my cab blow for me. "Cab's here."

She hugs me before I leave. "Have a great time. Text if you see you'll be late so I won't worry."

"Yes, Mom."

It's uncomfortable, but I look to where Ben is sitting on the couch. He doesn't make a move to even glance in my direction, so I leave without speaking to him. It's probably better that way.

It's a short drive to the hotel and I'm almost hyperventilating by the time I walk up to the hostess. "I'm meeting someone."

"The name?"

I smile as I say it. "Lachlan." It's ridiculous that I feel like I've won some sort of battle by knowing his name. Laurelyn, one. Lachlan, zero.

She doesn't look happy about my arrival. "Oh, yes. He left word he might have a guest joining him. Right this way." She leads me to a table for two in the same dimly lit corner we occupied last night. As I walk toward him, he looks up from the menu. His gaze follows my body from my feet up to my eyes. He smiles.

I can't wait to see his reaction to the back of this dress.

He stands and walks around to slide my chair out for me, just as he did the prior evening. "I didn't know if you'd..." He trails off and I know he's giving his full attention to the back—or lack thereof—of my dress. He clears his voice. "I didn't know if you'd come or not."

Yeah, I think he likes the dress just fine. "I didn't intend on coming, but here I am all the same."

"I'm very glad you did. You look lovely."

"Thank you, Lachlan." His light blue eyes lock with mine and I give him a smug smile, letting him know I'm happy I won.

The smile he gives me in return is complacent. "Did you like the Sauvignon Blanc last night?"

"I did."

"Would you like to have that again or try something else?"

I shrug. "That's fine."

He orders our wine and then sits back in his chair, seemingly pleased with himself. "I assume you're here to discuss my proposal."

I sit up straighter when I take notice of myself slouching. I can't show any sign of weakness if I'm going to keep the upper hand. "It would seem so."

"Ask me anything." He's so beautiful and confident. Dammit, it's unnerving.

I lace my fingers together and prop my elbows on the table. Yes, I know that's considered rude at dinner, but I like the confidence it gives me. "You have no qualms about asking me to do this. I assume you've done this before?"

"Yes, but never for more than three to four weeks. Three months would be new for me, but I'm excited about trying something different."

I'm anxious to point out how he has already tried something new by giving up one of his biggest stipulations for me. "You told me your name, so that's different. Does that mean your issue with being anonymous has changed?"

He takes a big drink of wine. "Lachlan isn't my real name. You needed something to call me, so that's what I chose."

"Oh." I feel my silly girlish hope deflate. "How many times have you done this?"

It could be in the hundreds. Or worse, maybe he has no idea.

"Is that really important?" He's stalling, so knowing the number becomes crucial to me at this point—a make-or-break kind of significance.

"It's important to me."

His brow wrinkles and I think he's doing the math in his head. "I guess there's been twelve."

I admit twelve is far fewer than I'd imagined, but he has to guess? We're not talking a hundred and twelve, so is it really that hard to be sure? "When did you start doing this?"

"The first time was four years ago. I did it on a whim and I liked it. It works for me, so I haven't had any other type of relationship since."

Twelve women in four years. That wasn't... terrible. "And you didn't tell any of those women who you are?"

"No."

Here comes the biggie. "Do you always have sex with the women who agree to a relationship like this with you?"

"Yes." That's what I expected him to say, but hearing him admit it gives me more of a reality check. I would be added to a list occupied by twelve others before me.

He sees the reality of it all registering in my head. "Don't think about the others. I don't."

And he wouldn't think of me either three months from now when he moves on to the woman after me. I'm surprised by how that bothers me. "I don't know if I'm cut out for this."

He reaches across the table and puts his hand on top of mine. "I won't feel like a stranger to you for long. You'll come to know me quickly. And it'll be the real me, even if you don't know my name."

I'm attracted to this man, but I'm not sure I can ever feel comfortable enough to have sex with him when I don't know his name.

"You'll be surprised how quickly our relationship will progress when there are no silly pretenses. We come together knowing what the other's expectations are, so it makes things easier, more relaxed. Our time together is so much more enjoyable because our only motives are to enjoy each other's company. There's no pressure and it's... fantastic."

I guess there isn't any pressure when he knows I'm a sure thing.

"Are you on birth control?"

Damn, he's no nonsense and doesn't hesitate in getting right down to business, although I haven't agreed to any of this. "Of course."

He smiles. "Good. We'll still use condoms. I'm more comfortable with two forms of birth control since none of them are a hundred percent. I don't want you leaving here with my ankle-biter in your belly."

Damn, he's presumptuous.

As the child of a single mother, I neither want nor need a child. I catch a rigor thinking about it. "Definitely not."

Casual sex. Can I do this? At least when I was sleeping with Blake, I thought I loved him. As beautiful as he is, I don't know if I can be intimate with Lachlan when I feel no love for him. Hell, I don't even know him, but he says I will. And soon, it seems. "Is it difficult to end the relationship when it's over?"

He's so casual about the whole thing. "I've never had a problem with it. There's no kind of attachment because we're not together long enough, and we're both aware of how things will end."

But we wouldn't be together for three to four weeks like his other relationships. We'd be together for three months. That seems like a big difference to me, but what do I know? I'm not the one who has done this before.

"So, in all that time, I wouldn't meet your friends or family?"

"No. Meeting those people who are closest to me is too complicated. It would be impossible for you to meet them without learning who I am, and I don't want the task of lying to them about what we are to each other."

"So, they'd never know I existed. Of course, that makes sense." I swallow hard. Am I really thinking of agreeing to this total madness? To becoming someone else's secret? Haven't I played that part enough already?

"Are you accepting? Because it sounds like you are." His intense blue eyes smolder, begging me to tell him I will be his for the next three months.

"I'm not saying yes yet."

"But, you're not saying no."

He wants this badly. "The only thing I'm agreeing to do is spend time with you. We'll see how things go from there."

He beams. "I need something to call you besides Yank or American girl."

If I don't know his real name, he doesn't deserve to know mine. I try to think on my feet, but it's hard to come up with an alias I'd like to be called for the next three months. I go with my middle name and my sperm donor's last name. "Paige Beckett."

He reaches across the table and strokes my fingers with his, igniting a swarm of butterflies low in my gut. "It's very nice to meet you, Paige Beckett."

CHAPTER SIX

JACK MCLACHLAN

I ALREADY SEE PAIGE BECKETT ISN'T GOING TO MAKE THIS EASY FOR ME. THE others never made me wait for an answer. This is something new, but I like the thrill of not knowing. I don't need to hear her say yes tonight because working to win her over is going to be so much more fun.

"And you are Lachlan who?"

Everyone knew me as Jack, but my mother called me Jack Henry my whole life, so I go with something that feels familiar. "Lachlan Henry."

I've never used a name so similar to my real one, but I know why this is a first. Being coy with myself is useless; I don't want to hear her shout another man's name when I make her come. I want to hear her say my name, or at least some semblance of it.

I smile as I think about the things I will do to hear her call out my name. "And how old are you, Miss Beckett?"

"Seventeen."

"What!" There is no way she's seventeen. I inspect her face, studying it intently, but don't know what it is I hope to find. Laugh lines maybe?

She watches my face. "Is my age a problem for you?"

"Hell, yeah, seventeen is a problem." I throw my napkin on the table. All of this has been a waste. "Forget it all. This whole thing is off."

"I don't act seventeen. I'm very mature for my age."

"No way. You're not even old enough to be drinking that wine." I lean in and whisper so no one will overhear. "I'm almost twice your age."

"I don't mind. I have daddy issues." She breaks into a huge grin and I hear a girlish giggle. That's when I realize she's fucking with me and has the ability to lie with a straight face. I'll have to remember that for future reference.

I'm not amused. "I see I have a comedienne on my hands."

She's still smiling, seemingly pleased by my sharp reaction. "I'm not really, but you walked right into that one and I couldn't resist. Relax, I'm twenty-two, at least until the groundhog comes out in search of his shadow. How old are you?"

None of the women I've been with have been playful like she is. Since I always choose older women, she's quite a bit younger than what I'm used to. At least fifteen years. Maybe twenty. Will she wonder if I'm too old for her the same way I'm wondering if she's too young for me? "I'll be thirty next month. Is that a problem for you?"

"Nope. I hope to be thirty in about eight years."

All right, Jack. You could have your hands full with this one. Are you ready for her and what she could bring?

"Are you in school or do you have a profession?"

"I'm a musician."

Oh, that explains why she sings and plays the guitar so well. "I heard you at the club the other night."

"I didn't know if you were there when I sang."

I decline telling her I was the guy sitting in the corner being a creepy stalker. "You're very good. I've never heard 'Crash Into Me' sound quite like that before. I won't forget it anytime soon."

She blushes like she's not used to hearing compliments. "Thank you. It was a pretty big coincidence that we ended up at the same vintage dinner after running into each other at the club."

Should I tell her how I worked everything out so I could see her again? Oh, why not? "I don't think it can be called a coincidence since I already knew you were going to be there. I paid my waitress to find out if you'd be accompanying your friend's brother."

She gawks at me. "So, that's why that waitress was so damn nosy?"

35

I smile with pride. "Yes, and I arranged for your friend's wine to be temporarily misplaced so I could lure him away from you. You do realize he's quite smitten with you?"

"You're a master of manipulation."

I notice the way she chooses to not acknowledge my comment about her roommate's attraction and I wonder if she is well versed in the game of manipulation as well. "I prefer to call it determination."

"And are you always that determined to get what you want?"

I go to extreme measures to have my way, but I think I'll keep that to myself. "Within reason."

"I'm not certain I want to hear anymore about the tactics you use to get what you want." That's probably a wise choice.

I decide to let her choose our new topic of conversation. "So, what would you like to hear about?"

She shifts her attention to the glass of wine in her hand. "Tell me more about what you do in the wine industry."

That is an easy one. I can recite this in my sleep. "My employer owns a vast majority of the wineries across Australia and New Zealand. You can call me his right-hand man. I travel from vineyard to vineyard to oversee everything from the books to the harvest."

She nods. "I see. Do you have family?"

"Yes." She's waiting for more of an answer, but I don't budge.

"Do you see them often?"

"I visit when I'm in between vineyards."

She gives me a quizzical look. "This is like pulling teeth with you. I just want to understand you better. I'm not asking you to tell me anything identifying."

None of the other women were interested in knowing about my family, so I'm not well prepared for how to answer. "My oldies live outside Sydney. I have a younger brother. He's married and has two little girls. I also have a younger sister still living at home. She's a year younger than you and studies at a culinary institute." That's all she's getting from me. "What about your rellies?"

"It's just my mom and me."

She doesn't have a father? "What about your old man?"

"That's a long story."

Maybe it's not fair of me to ask since I'm unwilling to share much about my family, but I want to know her story. "I don't have anywhere to be."

She looks like she's settling in for a long explanation. "My mom was a rising musician when she got pregnant with me. My sperm donor was a famous country music star. They met when my mom signed with his label." She shrugs. "He was married so they started having an affair. His wife didn't take too well to finding out about her husband's pregnant mistress, especially since she was pregnant too. I have a half-brother I've never met and he's almost the exact same age as I am. Isn't that charming?"

She lifts her wine glass to her mouth. "So, as you can see, I wasn't joking when I said I had daddy issues."

"That's why you immediately asked me if I was married."

She's pushing food around her plate. "It's only one of the reasons."

"You didn't eat much. I thought you weren't scared to eat on a date."

She shrugs again. "Nervous stomach, you could say."

"If you're finished, you want to get out of here?"

"Sure."

We leave through the same revolving doors we used the previous night, but under very different circumstances. We stand on the sidewalk in front of the restaurant and Daniel pulls to the curb from across the street where he's been waiting. He gets out to open the door, but I don't have a clue where I'd have him drive us since I'm unfamiliar with Wagga Wagga. "It's a beautiful night. Do you feel like walking?"

"Sure."

I tell Daniel, "I'll call when we're ready to be picked up."

He shuts the door. "Of course, sir."

"Which way? Lady's choice."

She glances in both directions and shrugs as she points to her right. "Always go right and you'll never go wrong."

We start walking and I remember the shoes she's wearing. She looks great in them, but there is no way they will be comfortable for walking. "Those heels are sexy as hell but don't they hurt your feet?"

She laughs. "I'm used to wearing high heels. I'll be okay. But it's very considerate of you to think of my feet."

I'm not sure if she's being honest. "I wouldn't want you to be uncomfortable, so please tell me if they hurt and I will call Daniel to pick us up."

"I will." She surprises me by looping her arm through mine. "Thank you for the beautiful flowers and breakfast you sent. Addison and I were almost drunk by ten o'clock. It was great."

Flowers and breakfast were nothing compared to what I would give her if she agreed to be with me. "You're welcome. I'm glad you liked the champagne. What about Australia? Are you enjoying it?"

"I like it very much, but I can't get use to the idea of Christmas during summer."

I had forgotten December is winter in the US. "I've never thought of it being any other way."

"Will you spend Christmas with your family outside of Sydney?"

Her questions aren't identifying, but they still make me uncomfortable. "Yes. Everyone gathers at my parents' on Christmas Eve and we spend Christmas Day together. It makes for an interesting night with my brother's kids waiting for Santa to come since the oldest is three now."

"Oh, that sounds like fun."

I can tell she's an only child. "It is fun for about two minutes, and then everyone is sick of each other."

She stops dead in her tracks and places her palms against the glass window of a store. "Look at that. I think it's a Martin D-45."

I inspect the guitar on the stand in the window and see nothing special about it. It just looks like any other to me. "I take it that's good?"

I think she might be amused by my question when I see her grin. "Yes, that's very good. I've dreamed of having one forever."

"Why haven't you gotten one?"

She gazes into the window and reminds me of a child wishing for a toy at Christmas. "Because a D-45 costs about twelve grand."

"Shouldn't you have one if you're going to be a successful musician?"

"Sure, I need one, but that doesn't mean I can afford it. I have my mom's guitar to get me by until I can afford one. It's older than I am, but it's still good." Her hands are still splayed against the storefront glass. "She's never told me so, but I think the sperm donor gave it to her. Sometimes I catch her playing it and she looks like she's been crying."

She wasn't kidding about having daddy issues.

"I'll have a Martin one day," she sighs as she steps away from the storefront.

We continue our walk until we come to the next street and I see the sign for Stout Avenue. "The Blues Club shouldn't be far from here. You want to swing by and see what's happening?"

"Sure. Which way do you think it is?"

"One way to find out." I pull out my phone and use an app to find it several blocks to the north. "It's six blocks that way."

She lifts her foot from one of her shoes and inspects it. "I don't know if I can walk six blocks. My heels are starting to rub."

"You said you would tell me if they hurt. I don't want you to be in pain. I'll call Daniel."

She lifts the other foot and inspects it. "Would you think I was weak if I let you?"

"I don't think for one minute there's anything weak about you." I spot a bench on the sidewalk. "We'll wait for him here."

While awaiting Daniel's arrival, we sit on the bench and I reach for her feet. "Let me see what we've got going on here."

She resists as I try to pull her feet into my lap. "What are you doing?"

"What does it look like? I'm going to rub your feet while we wait for Daniel."

"You don't have to do that."

"I know I don't have to. I want to."

She gives in and twists on the bench to put her feet in my lap. I slip off her shoes and begin rubbing the first foot. "If you say yes, I will pamper you everyday like a princess."

She laughs, clearly not realizing how serious I am. "That certainly sweetens the offer and makes it more tempting."

I slide my palm from her foot up her calf. "I don't want my offer to be tempting. I want it to be irresistible, so tell me what it will take for you to say yes."

She studies me and grins. "I need time, and I need to know you better."

She's always guarded, but I'm impatient, so the time she needs for getting to know me is the one thing I don't want to give her. Doesn't she understand we can do that after she agrees?

In a fine example of Daniel's impeccably wrong timing, he pulls up as I am trying to warm Paige to the idea of us. I slip her shoes back onto her feet. When she stands, I scoop her in my arms and carry her to the car where Daniel is waiting with the opened door.

Her arms are around my neck and she gives me a disapproving look. "I think this is a little over the top."

"I tend to be that way, and you'd do well to remember that. I meant it when I said I didn't want you in pain and I'd pamper you like a princess."

She giggles again like that seventeen-year-old girl she pretended to be earlier. "I think I could've managed the few steps it would've taken me to get to the car."

We slide across the backseat. "This is me trying to persuade you to say yes, Paige."

"I thank you, but it's quite unnecessary. And I hope you don't think you're carrying me from the car into the club because that's not happening."

"We'll see."

Daniel stops on the street in front of The Blues Club. "I'm not getting out unless I'm walking on my own. No sneaking to scoop me up again. Got it, Jack?"

I whirl around before I get out of the car. She has called me Jack for a second time. "Yes, ma'am."

I get out of the car and offer my hand. "Thank you."

She's standing in front of me and I can't resist asking, "Why do you call me Jack?"

"I don't know. It's something my mom has always said, so I say it too. Sort of like when I asked you if you wanted to dance when we were trying to dodge around each other."

"Oh."

We walk into the club and sit at a table close to the stage. There is a full band tonight and I recognize "Every Breath You Take" by The Police.

Paige pecks the tabletop with her fingertips to the beat and a waitress comes to our table. We're sitting right next to the speakers, so she yells out over the music, "What can I get for you?"

Paige smiles and winks at me when she places her order. "I'll have a screaming orgasm, please." Hell, yeah. She'll have plenty of those over the next few months if I have anything to do with it.

"And for you?"

Interesting drink choice. Interesting enough that I think I might need to try one. I stare at Paige as I call out my order. "I'll have a screaming orgasm also."

I slip out of my jacket and toss it across the empty chair next to me. "Do you always wear a suit?"

"I do when I have business meetings."

"I didn't realize you had a meeting tonight."

"It was a brief one." She watches as I loosen the knot of my tie and unfasten the top button of my shirt. I unbutton my sleeves and roll them up on my forearms. "You don't like the suit?"

"I like it very much, but I'm curious to see what else you wear."

"Then I guess you'll have to see me again so you can find out."

Our waitress returns with our drinks and I pass her my card to start a tab. "I'll be suitless for the next few days. Would you like to come out to the estate where I'm staying for a visit tomorrow? I'd love to give you a tour of the vineyard."

She takes a drink of her screaming orgasm as she watches me over the rim of her glass. "Okay."

Another yes. It isn't the one I want, but it's a start and could lead to the one I'm desperate to hear. "Perfect. If I pick you up around ten, that will give us time to drive back for lunch. Does that work for you?"

One-on-one time is what I need to persuade her to accept, so tomorrow I will get the yes I so desire.

CHAPTER SEVEN

LAURELYN PRESCOTT

FOUR SCREAMING ORGASMS LATER, WHICH IS TWO MORE THAN I USUALLY have, Lachlan and I slide into the backseat of his car. I only make it to the middle of the seat as I glide across, so our legs are touching when he gets in beside me. The only thing separating our skin is the fabric of his trousers, but his touch sends a thrill of excitement throughout my body.

Daniel peers at Lachlan through the rearview mirror. "Where to, sir?"

He surveys me for an answer. I think he's hoping I'll tell him I want to go home with him tonight, but I don't. I haven't agreed to this insanity yet.

"To Miss Beckett's," he tells Daniel.

I'm feeling the effects of my four cocktails. Liquid courage pulsates through my veins. I feel brave. And flirty. I put my hand on Lachlan's thigh and use my fingertip to trace an imaginary infinity symbol. I feel the muscle in his thigh grow taut through his pants. "Mr. Henry, does Daniel have any idea what it is you do with the women you keep in your company?"

Without being asked, Daniel reaches for the control on the radio and increases the volume of the music in the front of the car. I hear "Talk Dirty To Me" for a brief second before he changes the station to classical. Or maybe opera. I'm too buzzed to tell. Either way, I don't care for it.

I lean forward. "Daniel. Change it back to Poison."

I see him eye his employer in the rearview mirror. Lachlan gives him a curt nod and I hear Bret Michaels singing again.

"I love this song."

"I do too, but I'd like it much better if you were singing it to me instead of Poison."

"I've been known to take requests."

"Me too. I can talk dirty by request anytime."

I become hypersensitive to everything about this man. His breathing sounds louder and his scent stronger, so masculine. I love the feel of his leg beneath my finger. "You didn't answer me. Does Daniel know what you do with women?"

It's dark and I can't make out his expression. "I pay Daniel to be available when I need him. He isn't my confidant, so we don't discuss what I do with the women I date."

"The women you date," I whisper as I turn to stare out the window. The streetlights flash like strobes as we pass. If I say yes, I will be number thirteen. I can't imagine that going well. Thirteen is always unlucky.

He puts his hand on my knee and heat radiates up my thigh. "I want to know what you're thinking."

His intimate gesture gains my full attention. "I would be number thirteen."

I'm not certain, but I think he's amused by my observation. "I suppose you would be."

I'm superstitious. I always have been. "It's an unlucky number."

"I don't think it is. I was born on the thirteenth."

If I do this, something will go wrong and this man will hurt me. I know it as sure as I'm sitting here next to him feeling how much he makes me want to say yes. "How can you think it's possible to have something this hot without one of us getting burned?"

I see him grin in the darkness. "You think this thing between us is hot?"

Daniel pulls to a stop in front of Ben's apartment building. I don't reply to Lachlan—it's never wise to throw fuel on a fire already raging out of control.

Daniel opens the door and I get out of the car behind Lachlan. We walk up the sidewalk to the building's entrance and he shocks me by reaching for my hand. It's such a sweet and intimate thing to do. "Do you have your own bedroom?"

"No. Addison and I share the guest room."

"Good."

What? Did he think I was sharing a bed with Ben? What if I were? He didn't have a claim on me. Yet. "Where did you think I was sleeping?"

"I had no idea since these apartments are so small. However, I do know your friend's brother would like nothing better than to have you in his bed. Then again, so would I, so I don't guess I have room to say much."

There he goes again, saying whatever is on his mind. I'm not sure if I should appreciate his honesty or brace myself for whatever might come out of his mouth next. "Are you missing your filter, or is it an Aussie thing to blurt out every inappropriate thought you have?"

We're standing at the entrance to the building and I sense what's coming next. I feel it in my bones. And my groin. He's going to kiss me. And I want him to. Badly.

But then that isn't what he does.

He pushes me until my back is against the building. He pins me with his hips so I'm trapped. There's no escape—not that I would try. His eyes dart from mine to my mouth, then back up to my eyes. "I say exactly what's on my mind because I don't have time for silly games. I told you I don't do pretenses, and this is me showing you what I mean. I want you to know exactly what's on my mind."

It's unnerving the way his eyes pierce mine. "And what's on your mind right now?"

His mouth is so close to mine, I feel his warm breath on my lips. "Right now, all I'm thinking about is how I'm going to get you in my bed so I can show you all the ways I can make you come."

Umm… yes, please and thank you.

He makes me want to get on all fours and crawl like a tigress. I'm burning from the inside out, and he hasn't even kissed me yet. This man is talented. I wonder what he'd be able to do if we weren't standing in a very public place.

He takes my mouth with his hand and squeezes my jaw inward

before he rubs his thumb over my lips. "I've been wanting to devour this mouth since the first time I saw you."

"Then, why don't you?" I feel audacious so I issue a challenge. "I dare you."

I watch his face as I wait for him to take me up on my invite. Come on, I want you to do it. My chest heaves up and down so hard, I can see it moving in my peripheral vision, and my breathing is embarrassingly loud. I'm stunned by my sudden and unexpected urgency for him. I shove the bells and whistles I hear aside—the ones alerting me to how wrong this is—because I don't want to heed my subconscious warnings. I only want to feel what this man is offering—to make my fantasies come true.

The next moment, his lips are on mine and my mouth opens to invite his tongue inside to play. His hand slides from my face to the nape of my neck and pulls me hard against his body, holding me prisoner. Through the thin material of my dress, I can feel how hard he is for me.

His tongue finds mine and begins a slow, seductive dance. This man knows how to kiss. He has the ability to weaken my knees, and my body is no longer my own to control. It belongs to him, to do with as he wishes. He's my puppeteer.

I moan against his mouth and he slides his hands up the bare skin of my back through the opening of my dress. His mouth leaves mine and he drags it across my face to hover over my ear. "I can't wait to have a naughty with you. You know it's only a matter of time, and when I do, I'm going to make you come so hard."

I hear the catch in my own breath. No one has ever said anything like that to me, even Blake, and Lachlan's promise pools like pure liquid seduction between my thighs.

His mouth is hovering over my ear when I hear his husky voice again. "You want that, don't you?"

"Yes." I don't know whose voice I hear, but it sounds nothing like mine—it's that of a desperate woman.

"There's no reason you have to be in my bed for me to make you come." He takes his hand out of the back of my dress. I feel it slide around my waist down toward the spot where I want his touch most. I pant with anticipation.

I hear the sound of someone clearing his voice and I jump because I'm startled. But Lachlan isn't—he's annoyed as he drops his hand from its southern destination. He sighs heavily and inspects the person interrupting us.

It could have been anyone in the building—or the world—but of course, it isn't. It's Ben. His voice drips with contempt as he walks past us to the door. "Excuse me. I didn't mean to interrupt."

I'm embarrassed and don't know what to say. "No, it's fine. You weren't interrupting anything."

Liar, liar. My pants are so on fire. And so is the rest of me.

Ben interrupted Lachlan at the very moment he was about to stroke my slut button. Oh, dammit, the timing couldn't have been worse. "I'd like to introduce you to Lachlan Henry. This is Ben Donavon."

They stare at each other for a few seconds and I wait for them to whip out their dicks and start a pissing contest. Wow. The silence isn't awkward at all.

Lachlan extends his hand first. "Nice to meet you, Ben."

Ben takes his hand but doesn't appear at all pleased about doing so. "I don't recognize your name, but your face is familiar. Have we met before?"

Lachlan releases his hand and shakes his head. "I don't think so."

Ben continues to study Lachlan. "I'm pretty certain we have."

Lachlan rubs his chin with his palm. "I was at the university's vintage dinner. That must be it."

"No, that's not it."

Lachlan shrugs and puts his hands in his pockets. "I don't know what to tell you, mate."

Ben makes no attempt to hide that he wants me away from the opposition. "If you're done here, I'll walk you up."

I'm so not done here. Not even close. "Umm, I'll be up in a minute."

He doesn't say anything as he slings the door open with more force than is necessary.

Lachlan doesn't wait for the door to shut before he brings up Ben's attraction to me again. "That bloke wants you in a bad way."

I don't want to talk about Ben. I want to get back to Lachlan sliding his hand under my dress, so I move closer and put my arms around his shoulders. "Where were we?"

He brings his mouth back to mine and tugs on my bottom lip with his teeth. "I will spontaneously combust if we are interrupted again. How about I make good on my promise tomorrow when you come out to the vineyard with me?"

I want to tell him I'm willing to take the risk, but he's right. Being interrupted again would blow. "Okay."

He kisses my forehead and it's unexpected because it feels affectionate—not at all like the arranged relationship we're entering into. "I'll be here to pick you up at ten o'clock."

"I'll be waiting." Breathless and aroused.

"There's no pressure, but my schedule is clear through Thursday evening. I'd really like for you to stay a few days with me at the vineyard. I'm eager to get our stranger anxiety behind us so we can move on to the fun stuff."

"I haven't said yes." That's me playing hard to get.

He pulls me close and whispers against my ear. "But you will."

He is one cocky son of a bitch. But an accurate one. Still, I'm not ready to let him in on that little secret. I want him to work for it a little longer. "I'll think about it."

"And I'll think of you until tomorrow." He kisses my forehead again and I watch him walk to his car.

This beautiful man has a dark side that draws me in, yet makes me want to run. I've never been more certain of anything in my life, and I wonder how I've allowed myself to be pulled in.

When I walk into the apartment, Ben is nowhere in sight. I guess he's in his bedroom avoiding me, which is fine. I refuse to feel guilty about having a relationship with someone else. I never led him to believe there was anything between us.

I go into the bedroom and Addison isn't home, so I check my phone. She's sent a text to let me know she's staying at Zac's. Good. I hope she stays all night this time.

CHAPTER EIGHT

JACK MCLACHLAN

AFTER ENJOYING A VERY PLEASANT EVENING WITH MISS BECKETT, I'M IN BED no more than an hour when I get a call from my right-hand man at the Chalice Vineyard. I immediately sit up, knowing something serious has happened if he's calling me at this hour. "Clyde, what's happened?"

"I'm sorry to wake you at this hour, Jack, but there's been a fire at Chalice tonight. It's under control now, but there's damage on the south side."

Chalice is my favorite vineyard. My father owned it when I was growing up and I spent a lot of time there as a child with its workers, who are now my employees. As such, they are almost family—their safety is priority. "Was anyone injured?"

"No injuries."

Thank God no one is hurt. "Have you been able to assess the damage?"

"It's hard to tell because it's still dark, but it appears to be minimal. We were lucky to catch it when we did. John was awake and saw the blaze from his bedroom window." It helps that the vines are still green and there's moisture from a rain we had a couple of days ago. At least we had that in our favor.

"Can you tell how it started?"

"The fire chief will be back to inspect it in the morning, but he told me he has reason to believe it was arson. He said he should be able to give us a definite answer tomorrow."

Arson? That isn't good.

I call Daniel to let him know I will be leaving for Sydney within the hour.

I don't have Paige's number, but I'll need to let her know of the change in plans. I go into my library and take out the phone I've already chosen to give her. I write a quick note and insert it inside the package.

My next call is to my personal assistant, Jonathan. "It's Jack. I'm sorry to call at this hour, but I have a job for you that must be done first thing in the morning. When you come into my office, you'll find a small brown box on my desk. I need you to deliver it to the recipient by eight in the morning and not a minute later. It's personal and very important to me."

"Of course, sir. No later than eight."

There's little to no traffic on the road so I drive my black Fisker Karma coupe convertible faster than I should as I race toward Chalice. The businessman in me should use the drive to think about how I plan to handle the problem at Chalice, but I have something else on my mind. This something else has long brown hair, big golden-brown eyes, and a body that makes me hard just thinking about it.

CHAPTER NINE
LAURELYN PRESCOTT

I WAKE THE NEXT MORNING TO AN ARM SMACKING ME ACROSS MY FACE. UGH! She's back again. My vacation from getting smacked around in my sleep is short-lived. I give her a stout shove. "Knock that shit off, Addison."

She grunts and flops away from me. Good. I'm safest when she's facing away from me.

I hear a loud knock on my bedroom door and Ben's irritated voice on the other side. "You have another delivery from him."

Addison's eyes pop open. She stretches like a cat and moans like a porn star. "Another delivery? Maybe he sent breakfast again. I'm starving."

I look at the clock and see that it isn't quite eight o'clock. It was late when he brought me home last night, so how has he managed to have something delivered to me this early?

I put on my bra because I won't go free-boobin' in front of Ben. My robe provides added protection over the pajamas before I investigate what my three-month fling has sent me.

A small brown package is on the table. I use the scissors to cut into it. Inside I find a new iPhone with a personalized card:

I have an emergency at one of the vineyards. I'll be gone most of the day so I'm forced to cancel our plans for today. This phone is your direct line to me. My number is already programmed in. I'll call you later when the situation is under control and we'll make plans for a rain check soon.

— LACHLAN

I'm surprised by the disappointment I feel. "Lachlan has a problem at work, so it seems I'm free for the day."

"Great. Zac and Ben are tied up with some kind of project, so I think we should have a girls' day out and go shopping."

I don't have money for shopping, so I guess I'm browsing. "That sounds like a great idea."

Addison picks up the new iPhone. "Why did he send you another phone? Doesn't he know you already have one?"

The iPhone isn't a gift. It's a booty-call device—his means of communicating with me about hooking up while he holds all the control. This is one way he remains untraceable. He'd never give me his real number, so I predict he has one just like this designated only for my calls. That's what he means when he says it is my direct line to him.

It's also a reminder that this relationship isn't romantic and won't ever be. It is arranged and temporary. I'd do well to not forget that any time soon.

"My phone's been acting up since we got here. It won't hold a charge so I guess he thought I needed a new one." I lie to my best friend because I can't bring myself to confess the terms of Lachlan's arrangement. She'll think he's bat-shit crazy. And that I am, too, for agreeing to it.

CHAPTER TEN

JACK MCLACHLAN

I TURN THE FIVE-HOUR DRIVE TO CHALICE INTO A LITTLE MORE THAN FOUR. When I arrive, I see Clyde standing outside the office building, waiting for me. "Jack, it's been too long. I'm glad to have you here, but I'd be happier if it wasn't under these circumstances."

Clyde began working for my father at Chalice before I was born and now he works for me. I've known him my entire life, so I trust him. "I'm sorry I had to drag you out of bed in the middle of the night for this."

"It goes with the territory, Clyde. The good, the bad, and the ugly. This just happens to be a dose of the bad and ugly at the same time."

"The fire chief said he would be here at nine, so I expect him any minute."

I'm anxious to see the burned area. "Can we go out to survey the damage?"

"Not until he's finished inspecting it in the daylight. There were a lot of people working to put out the fire, so he doesn't want any further contamination of the scene."

That seems reasonable. I check my watch and see it is a quarter to nine. Paige has gotten my package by now and I have a few minutes before the fire inspector will arrive, so I try out our new means of communication.

I take out the phone meant only for Paige's calls and dial her number. She must have had the phone in her hand because she answers on the first ring. "Good mornin', Mr. Henry."

"Good morning, Miss Beckett."

"Are you wondering how I knew it was you?" I could hear the amusement in her voice.

"Could it possibly be because I'm the person who sent you the phone and I'm the only person with the number? Or because my name came up on the caller ID?"

She laughs. "None of the above."

"No, huh?" Though I'd been in a hurry before leaving this morning, I had taken the time to program a personalized ringtone. "Maybe it was the 'Talk Dirty to Me' ringtone."

"That's the more likely reason."

"Liked that, did you?"

"Very much so. You deserve extra points for that."

So, she's keeping score? "I was unaware of the extra point system. What does a personalized ringtone earn me, Miss Beckett?"

"I haven't chosen a reward system yet, but I'll let you know once I decide."

She has another decision I am way more interested in than a points-and-reward system. "Please do. I might want to work harder on earning extra points if the reward is worth the work."

"My prize is always worth the effort, Mr. Henry. Have you solved your problem at the vineyard yet?"

"Yes and no. There was a fire last night so the imminent danger is over, but I'm waiting for the fire inspector to come out so he can tell us what happened. I'll be tied up with this mess most of the day. Since it's a four- to five-hour drive, I won't be back until late. I was hoping to get a rain check on our plans, possibly tomorrow?"

"Hmm, I'll have to check my social calendar. It seems to be pretty full at the moment." She hesitates. "Looks like I can work you in."

I wonder if I'll ever get used to her playfulness. "Same plan? Pick you up at ten?"

"I'll be waiting."

I see a vehicle coming up the drive and assume it's the fire inspector.

Good. He's early. I'm ready to be done with this so I can get back to Avalon. Back to Paige. "Okay. I'll see you tomorrow."

We end our call and I meet the inspector outside my office. He explains the evidence he'll be collecting and how it'll be used in the investigation. I follow him to the site and stay out of his way as he gathers the proof of someone trying to burn my vineyard.

Seeing the damage is painful, but I remind myself of how it could've been much worse if any of my people had been injured.

"I'm sending this evidence for testing because I have to, but I don't need the results to tell you this was arson. There's accelerant all over the scene, so you might want to be thinking about who your enemies are. They could try this again."

I don't have to think about it; I know who did this. "I'll do that."

I walk the investigator back to his car and then go into my office where Clyde is waiting to hear the verdict. He's sitting in one of the chairs across from my desk, so I walk around and fall into an exhausted slump in my leather chair. "He said he didn't need to see the results from the evidence to know it was arson."

"Do you have any idea who would want to do something like that?"

We went back a long way, but I couldn't tell Clyde about the knee-deep shit I'd gotten myself into, so I lie to the man I thought of as a second father. "No. You have any suspicions?"

"The only thing that pops into my head would be a competitor, but they wouldn't have struck this early in the season or after a rain. That is amateur work."

Or the work of a sociopath trying to get my attention.

CHAPTER ELEVEN
LAURELYN PRESCOTT

During our girls' day shopping spree, Addison and I visit a lingerie shop at a plaza of boutiques near Ben's apartment. They have everything from naughty to nice, including a wide variety of sex toys.

Addison couldn't be happier as she admires a Santa-themed bra with matching panties and garter belt complete with the red and white candy cane-striped thigh-highs. She stands in front of a mirror and holds it up to herself. "Damn, Zac would have a very merry Christmas if I were wearing this."

"Speaking of Christmas, what are the plans? Are we cooking at the apartment?"

She twists so I can't see her face and it's my first clue that something is going on. "Umm, about that."

There's my second clue. When she stutters and stalls, it's never good. "What exactly does 'umm, about that' mean?"

She has this please don't be pissed off look on her face. So, what do I do? I get pissed off. "Don't freak out, but Zac wants to take me home with him for Christmas so I can meet his family."

Worst. Friend. Ever. "Addison! You're not leaving me by myself with Ben. You know how he's been with me since I met Lachlan."

"I wouldn't leave you alone with him. Both of you are invited to Zac's."

No freakin' way. "You and Ben can go without me. I'd rather spend Christmas by myself than be uncomfortable around a bunch of people I don't know." She knows I hate feeling like I'm imposing. I can't believe she's asked me to do this.

"You don't think Lachlan will invite you home with him?" This is Addison's way of trying to feel better about ditching me.

That would be a negative. "Definitely not. We just met."

She puts her hands on her hips as though I've offended her. "Why do you say it like that?"

Maybe because I don't even know his real name—that would be my first reason. "We don't know each other well enough to spend the holidays together."

"I haven't known Zac much longer than you've known Lachlan."

Maybe not, but she'd been banging him since the day we arrived. Okay, it was day three. "You and Zac are different. You've spent almost every minute together since we got here. I've only been out with Lachlan on a couple of dates. It's apples and oranges."

She holds the sexy Santa lingerie out for me. "Wear this for him and I guarantee you'll get an invite to his family's for the holidays. Maybe even a marriage proposal."

I've gotten all the proposals I need from Mr. Lachlan Henry. I'm still debating the one currently on the table. "I'm not looking to get an invite to his family's house. Or a marriage proposal." I take the red and white furry lingerie from her and admire it in the mirror. "He's asked me to spend the next few days with him. And nights. Maybe I need this. What do you think?"

"You didn't tell me you'd be staying over at his place. That sounds more serious than a couple of dates."

I hang up the Santa outfit and pull a naughty-elf set from the rack. "I don't know. He asked, but I haven't decided yet." That's another lie. I know I'm staying with him, but I don't want to sound like a ho, so I pretend I'm unsure. And I pretend like I don't know if I'll buy this lingerie. But that's a lie too.

❧

I HEAR FEAR IS A GIFT. IN THE EVENT THAT IT'S TRUE, I'M VERY GIFTED TODAY. I'm almost shaking as I wait for Lachlan to arrive.

My phone starts singing "Talk Dirty to Me," so I answer and try to sound like I'm not a bundle of nerves. "Good morning."

"Good morning to you. I'm almost at your place. Do I need to come to the door to challenge lover boy for your hand?"

That might be the case if Ben were here, but he's not. Thank goodness. "I'm the only one here. I'm ready so I'll come down and meet you." I hang up and slip my Lachlan issued cell into my purse next to my own. I grab my floral duffle and lock up.

As I come out of the apartment building, Lachlan steps out of a fancy-ass convertible wearing faded jeans and a khaki button-up. It's not dressy; it's rugged, more like what I'd expect someone to wear in the outback. And I'll be damned if he's not wearing an Indiana Jones hat. Even out of a suit, he's hotter than the devil's ass.

This is going to be a great couple of days.

He meets me halfway on the sidewalk. "No suit today, I see."

"As promised."

One promise kept. We'll see if he keeps his other.

"I see you have a bag." He grins and kisses my cheek as he reaches to take my bag from me.

"It doesn't mean I'm staying." That's such a lie. I wonder if he can tell by looking at me.

He cocks his head. "An overnight bag doesn't mean the same thing in the US as it does in Australia?"

"This one means I like to be prepared just in case."

"It feels heavy to me, like you're prepared to stay a couple of nights." He reaches for my hand and holds it as we walk to the car. This is him getting an early start on ridding us of our stranger anxiety.

"We'll see how things go."

He pops the trunk and puts my things inside the sporty, and very expensive, black convertible. "I've never seen a car like this before. What kind is it?"

"A Fisker Karma Sunset."

"I've never heard of that before. It's... stunning."

"I know." He opens the door for me. I get in and watch his beautiful form walk around to the driver's side. Let's be honest. Who wouldn't agree to a three-month fling with this man?

I know I'm going to agree. And he knows it too. He's said as much, but I can't let him think I'm giving in so easily.

He starts the car. It has a deep roar. "Top up or down?"

"Down, but let me grab a ponytail holder out of my purse."

"There's some in the glove compartment."

It's only a ponytail holder, but there's no way I'm wearing anything belonging to number one through twelve. He reaches over to open it and notices my expression. "I didn't ask you to wear another woman's undies. My little sister has long hair and she likes to ride with the top down. She keeps a stash in there."

Nice recovery.

I take the holder from him and pull my hair up, wondering if he's bullshitting me about his sister. "Ready."

The drive to the vineyard outside Wagga Wagga is beautiful. We pass mile after mile of grapes on the way to the house and as we get closer, I see a traditional old-world-style mansion in the distance. It looks Italian, not Australian, but then I'm not really sure what I think constitutes Australian architecture. "Miss Beckett, this is Avalon Vineyard."

Wow. It's incredible. "Your boss must think a lot of you if he puts you up in a place this nice."

"You could say that."

When we get out of the car, Lachlan walks around to the trunk. He lifts his brow as he asks, "Since you don't know if you're staying, does your bag go inside or remain in the trunk?"

He is dying to hear my confirmation, but I'm not finished having fun with this little game. "Umm... I think it's fine to take it inside to one of the guest rooms."

"I don't know why you're pretending you might say no."

Because this is his game. These are his rules. I need to feel like I have control over some aspect of it, even if it's only for a little while.

Our first stop is the kitchen. It's beautiful and fitting for the house, like one of those grand Italian kitchens from a luxury home magazine. At least, that's the only time I've ever seen anything like it.

There's a basket of goodies on the counter, so I walk over and peek inside. It's filled with an assortment of food, and of course, a bottle of wine. "Very nice."

"I can't take the credit. Mrs. Porcelli packed the lunch for us."

"Who's Mrs. Porcelli?"

"She does my cooking and housekeeping."

How odd. His employer pays him enough to employ someone to do his cooking and cleaning. "Will I meet her or does she fall into the friend/family/identifying information category?"

"I haven't decided, but it won't be today because she's already gone."

"Because of me?"

"No. She's gone home for the holidays."

That's right. Christmas is only a few days away. "So she doesn't live in Wagga Wagga, either?"

"No. I employ her the same way I do Daniel. They go where I go."

They go everywhere with him. How much does it cost to have employees like that? I can't imagine it being cheap. "Daniel is on holiday as well?"

"Yes. All the vineyard employees are gone until Monday, so it's just the two of us. Alone."

Was that supposed to scare me? "So, no one's around to hear my screams?"

"Now you're catching on. Come with me and I'll show you the rest of the house."

We enter the living room and there is a beautiful black baby grand in the corner. I'm in love. "You play?"

He laughs at my assumption. "Not a note."

I walk over and stroke the ivory keys. "It's beautiful."

"The interior designer thought it would be a pretty piece to take up some of the void since the room is so big."

I toy with the keys, playing the chorus of a song I'd been working on before I left home. Its tune is perfect.

"It's a shame it never gets played. I'm hoping it will get some use over the next few months." The piano isn't the only thing he hopes will get some action. "I'd love to hear you play."

"We'll see," I say as I run my hand down the keys and walk away, even though I'm dying to sit down and put it to use. There'll be plenty of time for that later. Three months to be exact.

"The bedrooms are this way." I follow him down the hall and he uses the tour to inform me that the previous owner, who died in a freak accident, now haunts the room I will be sleeping in.

Nice one. He wishes he could pull one over on me like that.

"I usually get along with ghosts and poltergeists pretty well, so I should be fine."

He takes me across the hall. "If you decide to stay in the guest room and get scared in that big lonely bed all by yourself, this is where you'll find me."

His bedroom is gender neutral and contemporary. The bedding is a modern geometric pattern of mostly gray and white with yellow and black accents. Everything from the flooring to the ceiling coordinates. The bedroom is aesthetically appealing, but there's nothing romantic about it, so it matches our relationship perfectly.

Every room in the house is spotless, and I wonder if it is Mrs. Porcelli's doing or if he likes things orderly because he is some kind of neat freak.

I think we are finished with the tour of the house, but he takes me to one more room we haven't visited. "Last stop."

He opens the door to a room with wall-to-wall mirrors. The floor is covered with different kinds of exercise equipment, some I've never seen before. "Gee, someone likes to see himself while he works out."

"The previous owner had a ballerina in the family and this was her studio."

"Okay. That's a little more acceptable."

"You're welcome to use this gym any time you want. It has surround sound for music or you can watch the idiot box." He points to a cabinet against the wall. "The flat screen and receiver are in there. It has Bluetooth so you can play your own music or you can stream anything you like."

There he goes assuming again. "You think I'm going to stay long enough to need a workout?"

"Since you've not given me an answer, that still remains to be seen."

I walk over to an elliptical and step up. I make a few strides. "I exercise at home, but this isn't what I do. Exercise equipment bores me."

He wiggles his eyebrows. "So what is your kind of workout?"

I slow the speed of my stride on the machine. "If you're going to be like that, I don't think I'm gonna tell you."

"Please."

I think for a minute, trying to decide if I want to tell him. "I dance."

"Dancing is great exercise."

I pick up speed again and stare straight ahead. I don't want to see his face when I tell him. "I pole dance."

Yep. That got his attention. "Pole dance? You mean, like a stripper?"

"Yes, but I don't do it the way you're imagining. It's a beautiful art form when it's done tastefully. I do it because I like it, and it's a hell of a workout. Very strenuous. You use muscles you didn't know you had. You'd be surprised what's sore the next day." I didn't look at him, but I knew he was smirking.

He walks around to stand in front of me and I look down at him from the elliptical. "You only do it for exercise?"

I nod. "Yeah. No one knows I take lessons except my instructor and classmates. And now you."

He licks his lips and rubs them together. "Just when I thought you couldn't get any hotter, you go and tell me something like this and prove me wrong."

I lift a brow at him. "There's a lot you don't know about me."

"How long have you done it?"

Hmm, I started my first year of college. "I guess it's been about... four years."

"You must be pretty good if you've done it for that long."

I shrug because I've never been one to brag, but I'm damn good at it. "I guess. My background in gymnastics doesn't hurt, either."

"Gymnastics too," he laughs. "So you've never danced on a stage in fuck-me pumps for a bunch of horny bastards?"

I think I just threw up in my mouth a little. "You say that like you're pretty familiar with the scene."

He holds up his hand. "I'm pleading the Fifth."

"That's an American amendment. It doesn't work for Australians."

"You didn't answer my question."

"Neither did you."

He has a huge grin. "I may have seen a stripper on a pole once. Maybe twice."

Damn liar.

I stop the elliptical and sigh loudly, as though he is wearing me down. "Yes and no."

"Yes to what and no to what?"

"No, I've never danced on stage for horny bastards. But yes, I wear fuck-me pumps when I dance on the pole."

"Now, you're bloody hot in my book. What am I going to do with you?"

"I believe the answer to that question still remains to be seen, now doesn't it?"

CHAPTER TWELVE

JACK MCLACHLAN

I'M INSTALLING A POLE IN THIS GYM. ASAP.

We have to stop talking about pole dancing and anything containing the term fuck me in it before I bend her over my weight bench. I put my hands in my pockets to disguise the hard-on our conversation has triggered. "Are you hungry? Good. Me too. Let's go."

She laughs as she steps down from the elliptical. I suspect she knows what she's done to me. "Is something wrong, Lachlan?"

"Nothing's wrong. I'm a bit peckish and ready for a bite of lunch."

My hands are still in my pockets when we start to walk out of the gym. She loops her arm through mine as we walk toward the door. "Me, too. Where are we going for our picnic?"

Her touch only adds fuel to the flame in my jeans. "I haven't decided. I thought we'd ride out on the ATV and pick a spot together."

"That sounds like fun."

We swing back through the kitchen to pick up the basket of food and wine before we head out across the vineyard. I drive out to the middle of the property and stop when I find a somewhat flat grassy area about a mile from the house. "What do you think of this spot?"

"The view is gorgeous."

We get off the ATV and spread a blanket across the ground. We sit next to each other with the basket between us and she helps me spread the food. "Tell me how you got into the wine business."

A little truth with a splash of lies on the side. "I guess you could say I was born into it. This is what my dad did for a living before he retired, so it's what I do."

"And it makes you happy? I mean, the traveling and being away from your family?"

The cork pops loudly from the bottle of Shiraz. I take a glass from the basket and fill it with wine. "I'm paid quite well to like it. Besides, I get to meet interesting people such as yourself during my travels, so what's not to like?"

Paige takes the offered glass. "But what about having a family? Don't you want a wife and children?"

I stifle my laugh. "I decided a long time ago I would never marry."

I watch her as she holds the glass up to inspect the color of the vino before she smells it. She's a fast learner. "Maybe the right woman hasn't come along and stolen your heart."

I hope she isn't suggesting she is the right woman because she'd be wrong. There is no right woman for this kind of life. "No wife wants to be the center of her husband's world on a part-time basis, and that's what a marriage with me would be like."

She takes a small drink, waits for the aftertaste, and then smiles. "It's good. At least I think it is."

I take a small drink. "I've had better and that's why I'm here—to make this vineyard one of the best."

She reaches for a cheese cube and cracker. "You shouldn't let your job keep you from having a family if it's what you want."

So we are back to that again. "I watched my mom raise three kids in my dad's absence. Don't get me wrong. My dad is great, but he was never home. I'm not doing that to a wife and kids. It's not fair." Wow, where did that come from?

"That's a very selfless way of thinking."

"That only proves you don't know me. I assure you I'm anything but selfless." I don't want to talk about myself anymore. She makes me afraid I will slip and say too much. I'm not used to so many personal questions. "What about Paige Beckett? Does she see a band of gold in her future?"

She gets that twinkle in her eye like most women have when they think about weddings and babies. "I want to get married and have children one day."

She finishes making a sanger from the fresh bread and deli meat and passes it to me. "Children? That must mean you want more than one ankle-biter, huh?"

"Oh, definitely. I want at least two because it sucks being an only child."

"That'll be hard to juggle with a music career."

"I didn't say I had all the details worked out, but there's plenty of time for that." She holds her arms out toward the rows of vines. "I want to know more about this."

I tell her about the vineyard, the grapes, and explain winemaking while we eat. She watches my face, truly interested and mesmerized by the process, which is unlike the other women I've been with. They weren't interested in me—only what I could do for them. Except for one.

She has no idea, but this is a huge stretch for me. It's the first time I've brought one of my companions to any of my homes on the vineyard. The remote distance from town doesn't leave me much choice, but I feel comfortable bringing her here since she isn't from Australia and won't be showing up on my doorstep six months from now.

After we finish eating, I stand and reach for her hands to help her up. "Come with me. There's something I want to show you. I think you'll like it very much."

We pack the remains of our picnic and drive toward the property behind the house. I park the ATV outside a pair of large ornate wooden doors leading to the storage area for the wine.

"Where are we?"

"This is a wine cave."

"I've never heard of that before."

"It's where wine is stored." I reach for her hand and help her from the ATV. "Come on. I can tell that you're going to appreciate this."

I open one of the doors to the cave and lead her inside to see the products of my livelihood. She's mesmerized as her eyes study everything from the stonework dome over our heads to the rows of wine barrels lining each room. "This is… incredible. How was it built?"

"It's dug out of the ground like a basement and a frame is constructed to keep it from caving in from the weight of the ground around it."

She notices the ceiling. "The stone arches are gorgeous."

The arches aren't the only beautiful thing in this room. The dim glow of the lanterns dances across her face as she studies her surroundings, and I have no doubt that the next three months are going to be spectacular. But first, she has to tell me yes.

She is going to say yes. I'm going to see to it.

I follow her into the next room where the special events are held and she explores like a curious child. She sees the tables and is about to ask for an explanation, but I don't want to talk anymore. I want to feel her against me again. I'm eager to finish what I started two nights ago.

She's surveying the long dining hall table when I creep up behind her. "Why is there a… oh."

I slide one of my arms around her waist and pull her back against me. With my free arm, I push her hair over one shoulder. I press my lips to the exposed skin on her neck and trail kisses toward her ear. "I can't stand it any longer. I need to touch you."

She leans against me and laces her fingers through my hand on her waist. This is her way of showing me that she'll welcome more of what I'm doing. I sneak my hand under the hem of her shirt and glide it upward until my palm finds her lace-clad breast. I feel her nipple grow hard through the lace as I slowly stroke it. I push my hand inside the cup of her bra from the top so I can free it from its entrapment.

She moans softly and grinds herself against my groin as I gently knead her breasts. "I think I have a promise to made good on, don't I?"

She doesn't answer but nods in agreement.

I slide my hand down her flat stomach and feel a piercing in her navel. I make a mental note to investigate that later, but I have other plans in mind for right now.

I tug on the button at her waist to unfasten her shorts. It opens after a light jerk and I slowly slide the zipper down. I put my hand flat against her stomach and rub it in a circular motion, each rotation bringing my fingers closer to the spot she so desperately wants me to touch.

I slip my hand inside the top of her lacy panties. I smile against her neck when I feel the smooth skin beneath. "You have no idea how much I like that."

She tilts her head up and back against me. Her breathing is deep and fast. I have her right where I want her, so I slide my finger down through her slickness and back up once in a slow, torturous stroke. She likes it and wants more because she's pushing her hips hard against my hand. "Paige, you haven't given me an answer yet."

I hear a sweet, delicate whimper from her mouth. "Huh?"

"You still haven't accepted my proposal." I slide my finger downward again and then slowly back up until I feel the little swollen button where I rub in a circular motion. "I want you to tell me yes."

"Ohh... what? I can't think straight right now."

I stop the circular pleasure I'm giving her and my fingers retreat because I'm determined to hear her say it. I don't want to wait any longer. "Tell me you'll be mine while you're here."

She reaches for my wrist and pushes my hand further inside her panties. "Don't stop."

I give her a few more soft strokes before I come to a standstill again. "Give me the answer I want to hear and I'll keep going."

She rocks against my hand, riding it hard. "That feels so good. Don't stop."

She's desperate for my touch, so I use her need to get my answer a little earlier than she intended on giving it to me. She's trembling under my touch and I give her a few more strokes. "Tell me, Paige. Tell me you'll be mine."

"Yes."

"Yes to what?"

She's squeezing my forearm. Hard. "Yes, I'll be yours while I'm in Australia."

I smile against her neck again. "That's all I needed to hear."

I want to show her how happy she's made me. I pull my hand from her shorts and she whimpers at the loss of my touch, but it's only temporary.

I turn her around to face me. She watches my eyes as I place my hands on her hips and push her shorts and panties down to her feet. I lift her onto the table. "Lie back."

She knows what's coming and she welcomes it.

I put my lips against her inner thigh and place a kiss against her scalding skin. "Tell me again. I like hearing you say it."

I trail kisses up her inner thighs, waiting to hear her say it again so I can show her what being mine means.

"I'm yours," she moans and I reward her for her acceptance. I place my tongue flat against her center and give her one slow upward swipe before I find her small, engorged bump and begin circling it. She tastes so good, even better than I'd imagined.

I feel her reach for my hair and fist it, so I know I'm right where I need to be. I lick and suck her until her screams echo from every wall inside the cave. When she stops screaming, she's statuesque across the dining table.

Good thing everyone's gone for the next several days if she screams that loud every time she comes.

I crawl up her body, kissing it as I go until we're face to face. She's breathing heavily and appears dazed. She blinks several times to focus on my face. A smile spreads and I'm relieved to see that she's not angry with me about the tactics I used to get her answer.

I place a kiss against her mouth and smile because I know this is only the beginning. "You won't regret saying yes."

CHAPTER THIRTEEN
LAURELYN PRESCOTT

I LIE ON MY BACK, NAKED FROM MY WAIST DOWN, ACROSS AN ORNATE DINING table and stare up at the ceiling. I'm lightheaded and dazed during my postorgasmic bliss. Drunk almost. I'm no innocent virgin, but this is new for me. Blake never made me feel like that, not that he ever tried.

I don't want to think about him. I won't let him ruin anything else for me.

I feel Lachlan kissing his way up my body and it takes a minute before I'm able to focus on him when he hovers above me. I see his smile and I know he's pleased with my acceptance of his proposal. He didn't play fairly, but he got what he wanted from me. That's something I'll need to remember in the future.

I wait for the sound of his zipper sliding down, but it doesn't come. Instead, I hear him tell me how I won't regret saying yes and I can't argue because I know he's right. The next three months are going to be extraordinary.

I find my voice and whisper, "Caveman." That's going to be my nick-name for him.

He throws his head back laughing and I join in soon after. He's so beautiful when he smiles. The happiness in his dazzling blue eyes is unmistakable. I'm elated because it's all for me; I'm the one making him beam, and I couldn't be happier about that.

He lowers his face to my neck and nuzzles it with his nose. I know he's smelling me because I hear his long, deep intake of air followed by a sigh. "A caveman. You think that's what I am, huh?"

I feel the warm rush of his breath against my skin and chills cover my body. "You definitely have caveman tendencies."

He places a kiss against my neck and I lift my chin so he can have full access. "You don't like my tendencies?"

"I didn't say that."

"I was only helping you say yes," he reminds me, as if he's afraid I have forgotten my agreement.

"I was coerced by a caveman," I laugh. My laughter is cut off by my sharp intake of air when he runs his hand up my shirt to my naked nipple. He rolls it between his fingers and I feel it pebble from his touch all over again.

He sucks my earlobe and it's a reminder of how it felt to have his mouth between my legs. He whispers against my ear. "But you're not taking it back, are you?"

He's coercing me again, but in a different way. He doesn't realize it, but it's unnecessary. Paige Beckett already belongs to him.

I think about how much fun his persuasion might be if I tell him I recant. I don't mind his way of compelling me, but I decide it's better to not push my luck since he warned me he gets what he wants. He claims to use reasonable means, but I don't think that's true after what he just did to me to get a simple yes. "No, I'm not taking it back."

"Good. That's what I hoped you say." His mouth leaves my neck and he pushes himself up to stand. His touch is gone too soon and I suppress a whimper. He takes my hands in his and helps me from the table.

I stand wearing nothing from the waist down in front of him, and I feel vulnerable, even though I know this won't be the last time I'm naked with this man. The thought makes me want to do my happy dance, but I decide to save it for later when I'm alone.

He picks up my panties and shorts from the stone floor and holds them out for me to step into, like an adult dressing a toddler. I balance by holding his shoulders, and he leans forward and inhales deeply before he places a kiss against my smooth mound. He makes me want to fall back across the table to have a second round, but I resist because I know he has other plans for me.

He pulls my panties and shorts up, and I'm frightened by how well I know this place I shouldn't go. This man will be hazardous for my heart if I allow it. He'll use me up if I let him. I know this without a doubt and remind myself of a lesson well learned not so long ago. Never confuse sex for love.

Right now, we're black and white, but I vow that the second it becomes a hazy shade of cold steel gray, I will get out. No question about it.

He kisses my mouth as I fasten my shorts. I wonder if he does it because he's curious to see my reaction—if I'll kiss him back after he's had his mouth between my legs. I kiss him hard and he smiles.

"Take a walk with me." He clutches my hand and leads me through the maze of rooms toward the cave's exit. I'm a little disappointed to leave and I hope he brings me back here again soon. I'm quite fond of his caveman ways.

We walk between two rows of vine-covered trellises that stretch as far as the eye can see. He's quiet, but simply walking next to him is peaceful. My mind isn't spinning in search of our next topic of conversation—for some reason, not talking is okay. Simply being next to him is enough to keep me content and that's when I realize what is happening. He is right about this relationship. We feel relaxed with each other because there are no pretenses.

I'm his for the next three months and I'm prepared for what that means. It's clear he has boundaries, and he's told me what he expects from me. I'm stoked about my sudden epiphany and stop dead in my tracks. "This relationship... I get it now. I get why it works."

He smiles but still asks me for an explanation. "Tell me what you get."

I think he wants to hear me say the words, and I'm okay with that. "Because we have no pretenses and clear expectations, I don't feel pressured to be anything but me. I have no worries about what today, tomorrow, or next month means for us because I already know."

He reaches for my face and strokes his thumbs over my cheeks. He's

71

beaming as he watches my eyes. "You get it full circle now—what I want and need from you."

I see how delighted he is and I realize something. Pleasing this man brings me pleasure. Common sense tells me I should be frightened by that, but for some reason, I'm not.

We go back to the cave after our walk and he drives us back to the house. I think about the things he has planned for tonight. I know he has something in mind because this man doesn't fly by the seat of his pants. He's done this enough to be calculating, his every move premeditated.

We get to the house and he drops me off by the door while he parks the ATV. I take the picnic basket to the counter to unload it and put the dirty dishes and utensils in the dishwasher. Any other time, I suspect Lachlan would leave the mess for Mrs. Porcelli. Since she isn't here, I make it my job.

When he enters the kitchen, I'm loading the last of the dishes into the dishwasher. "You don't have to do that."

"I know, but now it's done and we don't have to worry about it."

He opens the refrigerator and takes out two bottles of beer. He twists the tops off and pushes one across the counter to me. It's an unexpected surprise, but I guess it's presumptuous of me to think he only drinks wine. "Have a coldie with me."

Wine drinking is a lot of work. Beer drinking is more my speed. I reach for the amber bottle and sip without holding it up to the light or sniffing it. I don't swish it in my mouth to judge its aftertaste. I simply drink and enjoy it because that's all you have to do.

I check out the label and see it's an Australian brand. I like it and it goes down smoothly. "Nothin' like an ice cold beer."

He reaches for my free hand and tugs on it. "Come into the living room with me so we can talk and relax." I follow him and we sit side by side on the couch. He's close enough that his leg brushes mine and I feel like a teenager all over again. The simple touch thrills me beyond belief. "I'm sorry about bailing on you yesterday."

"It's fine. I understand that it wasn't your choice."

He rests his free hand on my bare thigh and begins to work my muscle like a professional masseur. "What did you end up doing?"

"Addison and I went shopping, which was probably the wrong thing to do considering Christmas is in three days."

"Did you buy anything?"

"A few things." I smile when I think of the lingerie. I didn't know if it would get any use when I decided to blow my budget by buying it, but now I'm certain it will, and I can't wait.

"I haven't been in town long, but Wagga Wagga doesn't seem to have a lot of great places to shop."

He's right. The shopping choices aren't great. I'm used to Nashville. It's home to all the biggest country stars so places to shop are endless. "It's a little limited when compared to what I'm used to."

He's stroking my leg as he talks about Wagga Wagga, but I zone out for a minute because I'm remembering what he did to me in the cave. I hear him saying something about Sydney and I force myself back into the conversation just in time to hear his invitation. "I have tickets for Madama Butterfly in February in Sydney. Will you go with me and let me take you shopping?"

He's asking me to make plans with him two months from now, and I realize this relationship gives me the ability to accept his offer without worry about what will happen between now and then. "Sure, that sounds like fun."

He probably thinks I like opera because I'm a musician, but he'd be wrong. I'm not a fan, but I don't tell him this because he seems happy about taking me.

We finish our beers and have two more while we talk about everything and nothing at the same time. He tells me more about his life, but he's guarded and I wonder if he's telling me half-truths.

I hear "Jolene" by Dolly Parton playing inside my purse. It's my mom's ringtone and I'm not sure it's wise to talk to her after having a few beers, but I decide I should probably answer since I've only spoken to her once since I arrived in Australia.

I reach for my purse and apologize to Lachlan. "I'm sorry. This is my mom calling, so I should probably answer."

"Don't apologize."

I take out my singing phone and I'm reminded of the one Lachlan sent me. Neither of us has brought it up yet. I'm not sure if it's appropriate to thank him for it or not. It's a weird situation. Not thanking him feels rude, so I'll think that one over later. Right now, I have to talk to Jolie Prescott.

"Hey, Mom."

"Hey, baby girl. I haven't heard from you in a few days. I've been worried."

"Mom, you shouldn't worry. Everything is fine."

"Well, how am I supposed to know these things if I don't hear from you?"

"You're right and I'm sorry. I should have called already."

"Are you having fun in the land down under?"

Umm, yes. A lot. I delight in the source of my fun today and he holds up his empty beer bottle and waggles his eyebrows. He's asking me if I want another one, and I nod. He takes my empty bottle and I admire the incredible view as he walks away. He's been in a suit the other times we were together, so this is the first opportunity I've had to see how great his ass looks in jeans.

"I'm having lots of fun, Mom. Australia is great so far."

She gives me an update on the things I've missed in Nashville this week and then I hear her exhale a long breath. That's when I know there's a reason behind her call. "Have you thought any more about what we discussed before you left?"

I can't believe she's called me to bring this up again. She isn't going to take no for an answer. "No, I've told you, I'm not doing that and I'm not going to change my mind. Please stop asking."

Don't get me wrong. My mom is a good woman, but she is approaching the point of obsession with my career and it's exhausting. "Your father owes you, Laurelyn."

"Mom, I owe it to myself to make it on my own. When I look back on this years from now, I want to be proud of what I've accomplished."

"Laurelyn Paige, you are Jake Beckett's daughter and you should use that to your advantage."

"No, I'm Jolie Prescott's daughter, and I'll make my own way. I'm done talking about this. I love you, Mom, but I've gotta go. I'll call you next week."

I hang up as Lachlan reenters the living room. "Everything okay with your mum?"

Mum. It's so cute the way he says it. "As good as it can be. She can be difficult at times."

He passes me a beer. "Did she give you a hard time?"

A hard time is an understatement. "Yeah."

"Would you like to talk about it?"

No one besides my mother and grandparents know my father is a huge country music star. It's a secret I'm forced to keep from everyone I know, but I don't have to do that with Lachlan. He doesn't know my true identity so that makes him my one exception. "She wants me to threaten my sperm donor with going public about my paternity in exchange for him getting me a record deal."

That sounds so much worse when I say it out loud and I feel the need to defend her, even if she is wrong. "Please, don't think my mom is a terrible person. She's not."

Lachlan scoots closer to me and puts his arm around my shoulders. He props his feet on the coffee table and I can tell he's prepared to talk and listen as long as I want. "I don't think she's a terrible person. She only wants to see her daughter succeed, but the right way of achieving that has become blurred through her eyes."

We talk a long while and then go into the kitchen to continue our conversation over Mrs. Porcelli's reheated chicken casserole. I know nothing about her or their working relationship, but something tells me she has a soft spot in her heart for her employer. I picture a gray-haired woman who loves Lachlan like a son, but then a different notion strikes me. Perhaps she's younger than I imagine and is secretly in love with him.

We finish eating and thoughts of Mrs. Porcelli fade from my mind as we clear our dishes. When I finish, I'm drying my hands when he approaches me from behind and kisses my neck as he slides his hands around my waist. I think he likes doing that—surprising me—and I imagine him liking other things from behind.

He pushes my hair away from my neck so he can place kisses there and I tilt my head to the side. When he's done, he reaches for my face and turns it toward him so I'm peering at him over my shoulder. He presses his erection against my bottom and kisses the corner of my mouth. He wants me. Badly. "I've been thinking about getting you into my bed all day, and now I'm done thinking about it."

He takes my hand and pulls me toward the bedroom. I happily follow because I'm ready for this. I'm anxious to begin what he has predicted as the best three months of my life. So far, he hasn't disappointed me.

We walk into the bedroom and I see my overnight bag on his bed. I wonder when he moved it from the guest room, but I don't ask because it doesn't matter. We both know I was never going to sleep in any other bed than his. That isn't why I'm here.

We stand in the middle of the bedroom facing each other and he cradles my face with his hands as he kisses my mouth. His tongue moves slowly in a wave against mine and I melt against him.

He stops kissing me but doesn't pull away. I feel his mouth move against mine when he speaks. "Do you need a minute?"

His inquiry makes me question if he snooped in my bag and saw the lingerie, but I don't care. There are no pretenses here. We both know what's about to happen. The only question is which set of lingerie I'll be wearing when it does.

"Yes, please."

He gives me a quick kiss. "Don't be long. I'm anxious to get you under me."

We haven't spent a lot of time together but I can tell that he likes to say things like that. He's already proven he's a man who speaks his mind. I bet he talks dirty in bed. I hope so.

I grab my bag and head into the bathroom. I quickly undress and try to decide which lingerie to wear. The naughty Christmas set is on top, but I'm saving it for tomorrow night.

I go with the sheer black lace baby-doll and matching panties—it's naughty, yet somehow innocent at the same time. Something tells me Lachlan will like having it both ways. When I'm dressed and ready for him, I fluff my hair and finish myself off with body spray as I inspect the final product in the mirror. I feel every beat of my heart in my flushed face, but I'm not nervous. I want this man and everything he has planned for me.

I stop just inside the doorway. This no-pretense thing makes me brave, so I don't go to him right away. I feel playful, still a little buzzed from the alcohol. I want to tease him, so I put my hand on my hip and lean into the doorframe, supporting myself with a raised hand. The hunger in his eyes tells me everything his mouth doesn't. He's dying to have me.

He grins and sweet seduction oozes from him. I melt to a puddle on the floor because I know what he's about to do with that mouth; he's going to use it to make me come.

He watches as I walk to where he's standing by the bed. When I reach him, he twirls his finger in a circle. "Turn around for me." I'm not sure if he means all the way around because he wants to see the full view or because he wants my back turned to him. I know he likes to touch me from behind so I circle slowly, deciding he'll stop me if that's the way he wants me.

I make a full spin before he drops to his knees in front of me. He pushes my gown up above my hipbones. My panties are riding low and he kisses my stomach before he runs his tongue over the jeweled piercing through my belly button. "This was very unexpected today. I like it."

I put my hand on top of his head and run my fingers through his thick, dark hair as he kisses each of my hipbones above the elastic waist of my panties. No man has ever knelt before me and explored my body like this. On one hand, it's unsettling. On the other, it's hot as hell and has me drenching wet.

He hooks his fingers in my black lace panties and drags them down my legs. I have to use his shoulders to balance myself as I step out of them because my head is spinning so hard from everything he's doing to me.

He tosses them aside and runs his hands up the back of my legs, starting at my ankles until he cups my cheeks and pulls me against his face. His mouth is almost right where I crave it, and I'm ashamed to admit how badly I yearn for it to be on me.

He gazes up at me. He smiles when his eyes meet mine and we don't break contact as he leans forward to lick me in one long stroke. I'm shocked, but not by the feel of his tongue. It's the sight of seeing him do that to me. I think he wants me to watch the show.

"Sit on the bed." I do as I'm told because I'm afraid not to.

I sit farther back than he wants me to, so he grabs my legs behind my bent knees and pulls me until I'm barely on the edge. He takes my feet and places them on the rails and pushes my legs apart. "Don't lie back. I think you'll enjoy the visual."

Oh, fuck me running! Or on the edge of your bed using your mouth. I watch his head dip between my legs. He uses his tongue to lick me up and down before it circles the place throbbing with need for his attention. He pushes his thumb inside me and glides it in and out while his tongue works its magic. In little to no time at all, he takes me to that place—the one where a little is too much, yet never enough, and I'm close to coming undone.

It's that spot right there. As I'm sending him the telepathic message, he receives it and gives me exactly what I need to finish. Once the rush of pure pleasure starts, I can't stifle the incoherent garble escaping my mouth. I fist his hair and pull his mouth harder against me.

I feel a new sensation—tiny quivers deep inside as I spiral down from the place Lachlan has taken me. I come to my senses and realize I'm still fisting his hair. I let go and know I should apologize, but I can't find the coherency required to speak.

My legs are quivering, boneless appendages in the aftermath and I think my knees will buckle if I try to stand. I look at Lachlan to make sure I didn't smother him when I slammed his face between my legs. He's peering up at me. "You are so damn beautiful."

"Thank you," I whisper. I'm not sure if I'm expressing gratitude for the compliment or the supernatural orgasm he just bestowed upon me. I don't have time to iron it out because he kicks off his shoes and strips his shirt over his head without unbuttoning it.

He's the beautiful one—soft and hard in all the right places. He wastes no time in ridding himself of his jeans and boxer briefs. He's anxious to fuck me. And I'm anxious to be fucked, but first I want to return the favor he has gifted me with twice.

He sees me get off the bed and knows I'm about to drop to my knees, so he stops me. "Not this time. I need to be in control or I'll blow as soon as your mouth touches me." Yeah, I sort of know the feeling.

He spins us around and sits on the bed. He needs the control, but I see what else he wants, so I climb up to straddle him. He rubs his thumbs over my nipples through my nightie and I hear him suck air through his teeth when I grind against him.

"I can't wait any longer. I've got to have you right now."

He loops one arm around my waist and I hang on to him as he leans forward to get a condom from his nightstand drawer. When he sits on the bed again, he lets go of my waist and leans back. He tears the square package open with his teeth and rolls the condom on in one quick motion. I look down because I want to watch, but I'm too late because he's so fast.

I feel his hands on each of my hips and I'm flipped onto my back. He uses his legs to push mine apart and he positions his erection against the very wet center between my legs. He bites his bottom lip and shakes his head as he groans, "Paige, I'm about to fuck you so hard. You have no idea."

And then he drives into me with one smooth motion—hard, just like he promised. Or threatened. I suppress the surprise behind my lips and the noise I make comes out sounding like a moan. He pulls back with deliberate leisure and it feels like he's going to slide out completely, but then he thrusts into me again even harder. He does this several times and I realize what he's doing. He's pacing himself because he wants this to last as long as possible. And so do I.

I'm surprised when he reaches for my feet and brings them up to his shoulders so he can get deeper inside me. It's slow paced, but every stroke is deliberate. And oh so powerful. Nothing he does to me is unintentional.

He finds his voice between thrusts. "You. Feel. So. Damn. Good."

But all good things must come to an end, and this does too when everything inside my pelvis tenses and the sensation radiates down my thighs and curls my toes.

Literally.

CHAPTER FOURTEEN
JACK MCLACHLAN

WHEN I FEEL PAIGE SPASM AROUND MY COCK, IT SETS MY UNDOING INTO motion. I watch her face as I thrust into her one last time and I discover something about her. I already knew she was beautiful, but she's even more so when she comes.

I'm propped on my elbows and still inside Paige when I lower my face to kiss her. This is where I want to be right now. Inside her. And it's where I intend on being quite a bit over the next three months.

This is the part where things always get messy in regular relationships. This is when women want to talk about love and commitment, but not Paige; we aren't like that, so I can relax.

I kiss her again and then pull out. She frowns at the loss. "Don't worry. The caveman will be right back."

I hear her laugh as I go into the bathroom to throw the condom in the trash. I pull it off and tie it in a knot before I give it a toss. I hate them, but they're a necessity in any sexual relationship outside of a monogamous marriage.

I walk back to the bed and Paige has no reluctance about ogling me. There's no shame in her game and it's a turn-on to see her almost salivating as she gapes at my body. I work hard for it, so I enjoy the pleasure I see in her eyes as she's admiring it. "You might as well be the devil."

"Baby, you're the one holding the apple." I slide into bed next to her and she immediately climbs over and straddles me. She slides her hands from my pecs, down to my abs, and then up again. She leans forward and runs her tongue over each of my nipples before she glides down my body. Her legs move from my outer hips to between my thighs as she migrates south. She's slow about going down because she's giving me the time I need to get hard again.

I know she's about to take me in her mouth. I wait for it and then I feel a warm rush of breath on me. She runs her soft, wet tongue over my tip and I twitch in response. It's been a long time since anyone has done this for me. Too long.

When she finishes licking me from base to tip, I can't silence the groan that comes out when she takes me completely in her mouth. Damn. This isn't going to take long because this woman has mad oral skills.

I run my fingers through her hair while she sucks me off, and I tap the top of her head when I'm about to erupt. She doesn't stop and I wonder if Americans don't know about the universally known signal to stop, so I tap her again. "I'm about to come, Paige."

She sucks harder and that's when I realize she has no intention of stopping. It shocks me because no woman has ever let me come in her mouth. Damn, it's hot.

I'm about to explode and I hear myself grunt, "Ooh, shit," as I flex my hips up to Paige's mouth. When I'm done, she licks one last time and then peers up at me with a mischievous grin and laughs. "Mmm. Tastes like chicken."

I'm laughing after a blowjob. Those two things aren't supposed to go together, but I see they do with her. I think the odds of her killing me with sex are good, but what a way to go. At least I'll die happy.

❦

WHEN I WAKE THE NEXT MORNING, I FEEL VERY RESTED AND I KNOW IT'S THE great sex. It's always like a sleeping pill for me.

Paige is asleep on her stomach, the sheet scrunched down over her perfect little ass. I can't help but study the arch of her back. Some men love asses. Some, tits. I love the curvature of a woman's back, especially the part at the small of her waist where it dips in.

And Paige's dip is beautiful. It's so deep I could drink from it. Maybe I'll do that sometime.

I push the sheet away so I can better see the slope of her back. I'm relieved when I don't find a tattoo in my favorite spot because that ruins the beauty of it for me. I don't think she has any tattoos, and the only piercing I've found besides her ears is the dangling jewel in her navel. I don't mind that one at all.

I can't resist putting my fingertips against her upper back and slowly following her spine downward. Her skin is so soft and smooth. So perfect. And I can't wait to have her from behind.

She stirs a little so I lift my fingertips because I don't want to wake her. I place a butterfly kiss against the skin of her lower back and then leave her to sleep.

I get the newspaper and have my first cup of coffee at the bar in the kitchen. Nothing of much interest in the headlines—mostly last-minute Christmas deals.

Christmas is in two days. I smile when I think of the delivery Paige will get from me while I'm at my parents' house in Sydney. I'm a little sad I won't be with her when she opens it. I'd love to see her face.

I'm on my second cup when Paige sneaks up behind me. She steals my MO when she snakes her arms around my waist and kisses the side of my neck. Her lips are warm and wet against my skin. "Good morning."

I turn my face toward her and kiss the corner of her mouth. "And good morning to you. Want some coffee?"

She inspects my cup. "Hmm… I guess not. I only drink flavored coffee with lots of creamer and sweetener. It ends up being dessert by the time I add everything I like. I'll take some juice if you have any."

"I have orange juice."

She walks around the bar and goes for the cabinet above the dish-washer. "Glasses?"

She almost guesses right. "The one to the right."

"Have you eaten breakfast?"

"No. I wanted to wait for you so we could eat together."

She waltzes over to the fridge and takes inventory. She's wearing the khaki shirt I stripped off and tossed to the floor last night. It hits her high on her thighs and when she bends over to see what's on the bottom shelf of the fridge, I see her black lace panties peeking out just below the hem.

I love having a woman in my life again.

"Mrs. Porcelli stocked the refrigerator well before she left. Want me to cook something?"

I don't want her to think I brought her here to be my cook or house-keeper. "I don't mind eating a bagel or cereal."

"I'm no gourmet chef like your sister." She stands with the door open, searching another minute while she sips her juice. "What about an egg and bacon sandwich?"

"A sanger for brekkie sounds good."

"A sanger for brekkie," she repeats (with her southern accent I find so charming) as she pulls out the bacon and eggs and sets to work. It doesn't take her long to prepare our breakfast and so far, so good. We're finishing up when I hear my phone ring in the living room. I dash to catch it before it stops ringing.

It's my mum. I wouldn't answer except I know she'll keep calling until she gets me. We haven't spoken in a few days, so I'm sure she's calling to finalize plans for Christmas Eve. "Hello, Mum."

"Good morning, Jack Henry. How's everything at Avalon?"

"Things couldn't be better."

"That good, huh?"

I walk into the kitchen and Paige is clearing our breakfast dishes. I walk over to her and whisper, "Don't. I'll get it. You did the cooking."

"Who are you talking to?" Damn. My mum has sonar ears. That's why I never got away with anything as a kid.

"I have a guest."

"A female guest?"

She's going to love this. "Yes, Mum. It's a woman."

"She must have spent the night if she's at your house this time of the morning. I can't believe you have a girlfriend you haven't told me about. Are you bringing her home with you for Christmas?"

"No."

"I want to meet her, son."

Of course she does. "It's not that kind of relationship."

I hear her huff. Really? My mum huffed at me. "And it never will be if you just said that in front of her."

"She understands." It's you who doesn't understand.

"Trust me. She doesn't."

I try to steer her in a different direction. "I think you were calling to touch base with me about your plans for the holidays."

"That's right. Everyone will be here around five, and we'll eat at six."

She doesn't have to tell me this. It's the same every year. "Okay, Mum. I'll see you then."

"Please, consider bringing her. It would make me very happy." Wrong. What she and I are doing wouldn't make you happy at all.

"No."

"You break my heart, but I still love you, son. Be careful driving in."

"I will. Love you too."

When I hang up, I feel like I need to apologize to Paige for talking about her while she's standing right in front of me. "I'm sorry about that."

She shrugs. "There's nothing to be sorry about."

The old girl thinks it's a tragedy to be almost thirty and unmarried without any prospects. She wants to marry me off to a wife who will start pushing out babies before our first anniversary, like my brother's wife did.

Not. Gonna. Happen. Hell will freeze over first.

I help finish the dishes and then we're free. "I'm going to work out. Want to join me?"

She frowns and shrugs. "I didn't bring the right kind of shoes or clothes for working out. Plus, you don't have the right kind of equipment for what I do, so I think I'll take a shower and get ready."

"Okay, but I'm installing a pole in the gym." Or maybe the bedroom. I haven't decided.

She smiles and dismisses my statement with the wave of her hand as she walks toward the bedroom. "Yeah, yeah. Whatever."

She thinks I'm kidding, but she'll see I'm not.

Time passes quickly while I do my workout; I can't stop replaying the last twenty hours in my head. Paige is so different from the others, but in the most spectacular ways.

CHAPTER FIFTEEN
LAURELYN PRESCOTT

THE SHOWER IS HUGE AND THERE'S PLENTY OF ROOM FOR TWO PEOPLE. Somewhere not too far in the back of my mind I hope Lachlan joins me, but I don't expect him to. He'll be working out for a while. No one has a body like that without spending a lot of time in the gym.

The hot water feels glorious—I'm a little sore today. Because of my usual workout regimen, it's hard to put me in many positions that will stress my muscles, so props to Lachlan for achieving that.

When I finish in the shower, I linger a little longer. Just in case. When he doesn't come into the shower with me, I'm a little disappointed, but I don't dwell on it. We have until he leaves for his parents' house tomorrow.

I get ready and dress casually since I think we're staying at the vineyard today. I guess I should've asked, but I didn't, so I choose faded denim shorts and a solid ivory tank. Maybe it's a little over the top, but I finish the ensemble off with my brown cowgirl boots.

I'm braiding my hair when he comes into the bathroom and we both smile when our eyes meet in the mirror. He's shirtless and glistening with sweat. Damn, if I hadn't just showered. "Someone had a productive workout."

He stands with his hands on his hips, a towel thrown over one shoulder. "I did, thanks to you. I couldn't stop thinking about yesterday and last night, so time got away from me."

"You don't look very happy about it."

"That's because I wanted to catch you still in the shower."

"I stayed in a long time because I was hoping you would, but you didn't, so I gave up on you."

He walks toward me and I hold up a hand to stop him. "Nope. Too late now, caveman."

"Okay. Later then." He smiles and drops his sweaty bottoms to the floor before he kicks them toward a hamper and gets into the shower. Steam immediately billows into the space. "I have some vines I need to check today. Do you want to go out with me to see how they're doing?"

"I'd love to. There's not a problem, is there?"

"I hope not, but that's why I'm going out to check."

It feels like a sauna in here and I have to get out. How can he stand the water so hot after a workout? "Okay. I'll wait for you in the living room."

I'm watching some kind of Australian Christmas special when he plops on the couch beside me. He's wearing khaki cargo pants and a fitted navy V-neck T-shirt. I can see a few sparse hairs peeking over the V's point, but I know there's more underneath and think about how I ran my hands over them last night.

Oh, my. He's a fine specimen of a man. Very fine indeed.

He puts his hand on my leg and massages it. "Ready?"

"Whenever you are."

He stops by the refrigerator as we pass through and grabs a couple of bottled waters. "It's going to be a hot one and we could be gone for a while. It's probably not a bad idea to take a cold drink."

He grabs his Indiana Jones hat from the hook as we're on our way out the door. I shake my head because I can't believe the good-looking suit can also be rugged sexiness on a stick. No man should be this desirable.

I follow him to the ATV garage and he gases up before we drive out to what must be the edge of the property. He parks and walks over to a vine, lifting it for inspection. He puts his hand up and motions for me. "Come here, Paige. I want to show you this."

I walk over and he points to a section on the vine. "I came to this vineyard for a very specific reason. The acidity of the soil and this partic-ular type of grape are no longer compatible. The quality of the grapes is deteriorating. That means the quality of the wine is as well, so I'm grafting a different variety onto the existing rootstock. If it doesn't reject the change, there will be a more compatible grape growing on these vines within two years."

The process sounds similar to skin grafting. "Is it working?"

"It's still too early to tell, but it's doing well so far."

He releases the vine and we walk back to the ATV. "I've never really thought about all that goes into making wine. It seems like it's a very complicated and demanding business."

"It can be."

"I see why your boss pays you well. You're very good at what you do. Did you learn all of this at the university where Ben attends?"

"No. I learned from growing up around it and then I went to another university to learn what I needed to know about the business part of the industry, but that's been many moons ago."

"You sound like you think you're so much older than I am."

He studies me like he's searching my eyes for something. "I'm eight years older."

I roll my eyes at him. "It's seven, but whatever. I don't mind. I have daddy issues, remember?"

He leans over and kisses my mouth. "Yes. How can I forget that, my sweet young thing?"

We make several stops throughout the vineyard so Lachlan can inspect more grafts. He seems pleased with everything he sees, so I know he'll be able to leave the vineyard for the holidays without worry.

"What time will you be leaving tomorrow?"

"My mum wants me at the house by five, so I guess I'll drive you back before lunch. What are your plans?"

"Addison has invited me to Zac's house with her and Ben, but I'm not going."

"Your friends are going to leave you by yourself on Christmas? That's shitty."

He has no idea how much I agree. "I'll be okay. I rather be alone than with a house full of strangers."

I don't like the pity in his eyes. It's something I spent my whole child-hood seeing and it makes me more uncomfortable as an adult, so I change the subject and hope he doesn't bring it up again.

We return to the house for lunch and then go back out onto the vine-yard. I don't think Lachlan had the intention of working all day, but he sees how content I am to be outdoors, so we ramble on the ATV until late evening.

When the sun begins to drop from the sky, we go in for an early dinner. We're both pretty quiet while we eat, but we share a lot of smiles and knowing grins because we're anxious for what tonight will bring.

We're cleaning the kitchen together when Lachlan makes his signa-ture move and comes up behind me. Why does he love doing that so much?

He grabs my hips and drags my bottom against him. He grinds against me and I can feel how hard he is. "Go get ready. I'll finish up the kitchen and meet you in the bedroom in five minutes."

He kisses my neck and lets me go. I have to hurry because he isn't giving me long, so I scramble to the bathroom with my bag.

I'm excited for this—for him—as I quickly freshen up before slipping into my naughty little Santa-themed lingerie. I think it's been a little longer than five minutes when I hear him call out from the bedroom. "Time's up, Miss Beckett. I'm waiting."

I call out from inside the bathroom. "Sit on the bed and close your eyes. No peeking. I'll know if you do."

I open the door and see him sitting on the bed, eyes closed. "And just how will you know if I peek?"

"Because I always know when you've been naughty."

I walk out into the room in the red lingerie with white fur trim and candy cane-striped thigh-highs. With hands on my hips, I say, "You can open your eyes now."

He does as I tell him and when he sees me, he breaks into a smile. It's all for me and no one else. "I have a gift for you if you've been a good little boy."

"And what if I've been naughty?"

I stroll toward him. "You'll still get a present."

We reach for each other at the same time and he brings his mouth down hard on mine. It's almost painful, but I rejoice inside because it's the way I want it tonight. Rough and raw.

He quickly spins us around and shoves me backwards onto the bed. He strips his shirt over his head and I enjoy the show from where I'm lying on the bed. "Get on your stomach."

I flip over and hear the sound of his zipper, then that of the opening drawer. Boo. I'm missing that part again.

I feel the bed dip and he crawls over me from behind. Hot skin is all I feel against my back. He's naked. And wanting, obvious from the hardness pressed against my thigh.

I've come to expect him to push my hair from my shoulders, and he does. He puts his lips on the skin of my neck and then slowly moves to my shoulder. He grazes his teeth over it while his hands are all over me at once. I'm squirming beneath him, chills erupting over my entire body. He continues to travel downward until his mouth reaches the band of my panties. He hooks his fingers inside and tugs. I lift my hips up from the bed a little so he can get them down.

When my panties are off and tossed aside, he unfastens my bra. He puts his palm flat against the small of my back and strokes it before his hand drops to my cheeks. I'm afraid because I don't know what he's going to do. I've never done that before, and I don't think I want to.

I'm face down, but I feel his hand creep around to my stomach and then down between my legs until he's stroking me in that delightful place. I temporarily forget my fear because all I feel is longing for more of what he's doing. I must have it. I'll explode with it or without it, but for two completely different reasons.

I feel him prodding me from behind, searching blindly for his way inside me, and I'm back to thinking of his intent. I decide it doesn't matter. He can do anything to me as long as his fingers don't stop what they're doing right now.

He pushes my knees apart with his and then glides into the familiar place. I admit I'm relieved, but I don't have time to think about it for long before he's directing me. "Sit up and lean back against me."

I push myself up and then shift backwards until I'm sitting on him with my knees spread apart. He grips my hips and begins to guide me up and down. This is a new position for me. Shit, I've never felt so full.

He returns his fingers to my pleasureland as he fills me from behind. It's absurd how good he makes me feel.

When he sees he no longer has to guide my movement, he uses his free hand to palm one of my breasts. It's too many sensations to withstand at once. I'm on the ledge, about to fall. Or jump. I'm not sure which, and then I hear his possessive words through gritted teeth and it sends me over the edge. "No one else touches you. Only me. Do you understand?"

The quaking starts in my core and I don't answer him because I can't find my voice. I'm too entangled in the flood of ecstasy to speak. I ride him harder as the waves of pleasure begin because I'll die if I don't. He squeezes my nipple hard and the sensation radiates down between my legs to finish me off. "Tell me you understand."

My hands grip the top of his thighs and I squeeze hard. My answer comes out as a scream. "Yes! I understand!"

I fall forward onto my stomach with exhaustion and he collapses with me on top of my back. His weight pushes me into the mattress and he's breathing heavily against my ear. "I won't share you with anyone."

His words remind me of my initial thoughts about him. Lachlan Henry's world is a dark place I know nothing about. I think it frightens me, but it's too late now. I'm a part of it, no matter what it is.

CHAPTER SIXTEEN
JACK MCLACHLAN

I FEEL IT IN THE WAY SHE'S TREMBLING AND IT HAS NOTHING TO DO WITH HER orgasm. I've been too aggressive with her. Now I need to show her I can be gentle.

I lift myself from Paige's body and kneel between her legs from behind. I kiss the dip in her lower back and taste the salty moisture created during our sexual frenzy. It's another way I love to taste this sweet girl.

I glide my hands from her waist to her shoulders and begin massaging her tense muscles. It takes a few minutes, but I feel her eventually relax under my touch and I contemplate how to justify my possessive outburst.

I could say that I don't know where my irrational demand came from, but that would be a lie. There should've been no room for anything in my head other than how good it felt to be inside her, but something else slipped into my thoughts. Someone else—Ben Donavon. I can't believe I let that little bastard get into my head. He wants what's mine and I'm forced to deliver her to him tomorrow. She might as well be served on a silver platter.

For two days, I'll be in Sydney and she'll be with him in his apartment. They might find themselves alone. That's when shit happens.

I might have gone about it poorly, but I want to be clear with Paige; she is mine while she's in Australia. I won't share her with Ben Donavon or any other dick.

I lean forward to kiss her shoulder and then skim my nose across the nape of her neck. She smells so good—all fruit, sweat, and pheromones. Lots of pheromones. If I keep sniffing her, I could get sidetracked from what I need to do.

I place the side of my face against the center of her back and leave it there while I try to regain some of the footing I may have lost over my less-than-gentle treatment. "I'm sorry if I was too aggressive."

"You were pretty intense." She peers at me over her shoulder. "But I never said I was opposed to intense." I feel her words rumble against my ear pressed to her body. "However, I'm a little confused about what you said."

I roll off her and lie on my side. She does the same and props her head in her hand. She pokes her lips out at me as she mocks me in a husky tone. "You look so serious."

I am. Dead serious. "We may only be together for a few months, but you're mine while you're here. I won't share you with Ben Donavon or any other man."

I see the confusion on her face. "What brought this on?"

Oh, hell. I'm going to sound like such a chick. "You live with him."

She's giving me that duh, really? look that my little sister gives me. Women must be born with that special talent. "And you knew that when we met. You didn't just figure that out."

"I know, but I have to take you back to him tomorrow."

The realization clicks in her head and she understands. "You're not relinquishing custody of me to Ben. You're taking me to the place where I stay with my best friend."

"Which happens to belong to a man who wants you in his bed." I didn't see it before, but it's become clear to me. Now that I've had Paige in my bed, her residency at Ben Donavon's is going to be a problem for me.

She shrugs, as if she couldn't care less. "It doesn't matter if he wants me or not. I don't want him." She gets up and straddles me. "But I do want you."

She is going to use sex to distract me from this conversation. I'll allow it—this time.

⚜

IT'S CHRISTMAS EVE MORNING. WHEN I WAKE, I SEE PAIGE ASLEEP ON HER stomach again. I'm learning things about her. She's a stomach sleeper. She doesn't want to cuddle when it's time to sleep. And she likes her space in the bed. All these things are fine by me.

Instead of getting up to have coffee and read the paper, I stay in bed. I want to be next to her when she wakes because I'm going to have her again before I take her back. I want to be freshly on her skin and inside her when she returns to him.

My American girl isn't a morning person. She likes to sleep in, so I get to lie next to her, studying her form for almost an hour before she wakes. I'm on the verge of going back to sleep when I feel her roll in my direction. My eyes spring open and she's staring at me.

Hmm. The watcher becomes the watched.

She laces her fingers together across my chest and props her chin on top of her hands. "Good morning."

I lift my head and kiss the top of her hair. "Good morning to you, sleepyhead."

"I can't be called the sleepyhead if I'm the one who catches you sleeping."

"I've been waiting an hour for you to wake up, lazy bones."

"And what kept you in bed instead of getting up to have your morning coffee?"

"You."

I'm inside her twice before we leave the vineyard, once in the bed and again in the shower. As I drive her to the apartment, I chastise myself for not being more adventurous and having her throughout the house since all of the staff was gone. It would've been the perfect time. It will be difficult to pull that off once they are back.

I pull up in front of the apartment but keep the Sunset's engine running. I have to get on the road if I'm going to be on time. Mum hates

94

it when anyone is late, and I'm already going to have hell to pay for not bringing my "girlfriend" with me.

I get out of the car and walk her to the apartment entrance. I reach for her hands and give them a gentle squeeze. "I'll call you later tonight. When you hear Bret sing, you'll know it's me."

"That reminds me. You need a personalized ringtone—so you know it's me."

I can't believe she doesn't know she has one. "You have one. You just don't know what it is."

She reaches for her phone to call me, but I stop her. "Oh, no you don't."

"But I want to know what mine is."

"Later." I frame her face with my hands and kiss her hard so she'll be "love drunk" with me on her mind while I'm away.

"Drive carefully."

"I will."

Just like the first time he interrupted us, Ben Donavon appears out of thin air. He clears his throat, interrupting our parting kiss.

He smiles as a look exchanges between us, one that says, "Hey. I'm gonna have this girl."

I give him a smug smile in return that responds, "Hey, guess what. I've already had this girl. And she is incredible."

The little bastard picks up Paige's duffle and stands waiting with it thrown over his shoulder. He knows he's interrupting our last moments together. And he's loving it.

Fuck it. If he thinks he's just ruined this for me, he's wrong. I'm going to kiss the hell out of her regardless. "Excuse us. We were in the middle of something."

I grasp her face and brush my lips across hers, but then I coax her mouth open and she allows me to kiss her like I did when we were alone, as if she has forgotten Ben is there with us.

I trail my mouth over to her ear and my eyes meet Ben's as I whisper, "Remember. I won't share you."

She whispers back, "How could I forget?"

We say a final goodbye and Ben is waiting to take her from me. When she enters the apartment, he turns back to give me a shit-eating grin as he places his hand on her lower back.

Dammit! Not her lower back. That's my spot to touch.

My only choice is to watch. I feel helpless, like a shepherd seeing his favorite lamb disappear into the forest with a dangerous wolf. She thinks he's harmless, but he's not. I know better.

It's juvenile, but I text her before I drive away in an effort to steal her attention away from him.

Miss me while I'm gone

A heartbeat later, I hear the sound of her return text.

Can't miss U til UR gone ;)

I pull away from the curb and wait until I'm out of sight to hit send on the next message.

Gone. Now U can miss me.

I will but no TWD!

She's concerned for my safety. This makes me smile.

K

I use the drive to think about a lot of things, but my thoughts mostly revolve around the beautiful new brunette in my life who doesn't seem to care about the things I can do for her. Knowing how little she cares about the money I could spend, makes me want to buy her the world.

※

My mom greets me at the door, which she never does, and peeks toward my car. She's searching for my "girlfriend."

She sees I'm alone and is pissed off. "You didn't bring her?"

Why does she do this to herself? "No, Mum. I told you I wasn't."

"I hoped you'd change your mind. I want to meet the woman who has caught my son's eye. Is that too much to ask?"

"No, Mum, it's not." I shouldn't, but I give her false hope because it would be the right thing to say if Paige were my real girlfriend. "Maybe I'll bring her next time."

Her eyes sparkle with my proposal. "We have your birthday dinner next month. You can bring her then."

"I'll discuss it with her and we'll see," I lie.

She's satisfied with that answer and finally lets me in the house.

We're sitting at the dining room table when she brings it up again. "I want to hear about your girlfriend."

Everyone around the table stares while they wait on me to answer. I see I'm going to be forced into lying. I'll try to be as vague as possible. "She's American."

I see my mum's face fall. "She doesn't live in Australia?"

"No. She's here on an extended visit with a friend."

"So she won't be returning to the States soon?"

"Not for a while."

That makes my mum smile again. "That's good. What does she do?"

"She's a musician—a very good one. That's how we met... I heard her sing at a club in Wagga Wagga."

I avoid telling them Paige's name, but the illusion feels real for a moment, and I like it. I take pleasure in the happiness I see on their faces, but then the guilt sets in. Everything I tell them about her is the truth wrapped in a blanket of lies.

CHAPTER SEVENTEEN
LAURELYN PRESCOTT

Addison is out with Zac, and I'm uncomfortable because I see a change in Ben as soon as we get inside the apartment. He's next to me every time I turn around, brushing against me any chance he gets, sitting next to me on the couch. He's pursuing me in a much more aggressive manner, and I don't like it.

I lie and say I need to go to the store for tampons to get away from him. He insists on driving me, but I decline by telling him the walk will help with cramps. How asinine. I'm a terrible liar, but I think the talk of tampons and menstrual cramps keeps him from insisting.

I'm walking around in the drugstore a few blocks from the apartment when Bret begins to sing in my purse. I'm standing in front of a mirror in the makeup aisle when I look up and see the goofy grin on my face as I answer. I didn't even realize I was smiling. "Hello, caveman."

"Hey, American girl. How's it going back in Wagga Wagga?"

He may ask how it's going, but what he really means is how is it going with Ben, and there's no way I'm going there. "Everything's good. Are you having fun with the fam?"

"Not really. I'd be having a lot more fun if I were with you." No argument here.

"We'll have plenty of fun when you get back." And what was the plan after the holidays? Would he keep making the drive into town to get me?

"What are you doing to pass the time without me?"

I laugh because it's so ridiculous. "I'm strolling around a drugstore."

"And you'd be doing that because?" He doesn't give me time to answer. "Did that little bastard do something to you?"

I know the worst thing I can do is tell him about Ben's behavior, so I lie. "I was bored and wanted to get out for a while, but it's a bad night to get bored. There's not much open on Christmas Eve."

"It's not safe for you to be out walking the streets alone after dark."

Shit. He sounds mad. "I'm only a few blocks from the apartment."

"I don't care if you're across the street. I want you to take a cab back."

"Really, I'm fine."

"Says the girl right before she gets nabbed by some crazy-ass psycho. I'll be quite upset with you if you are kidnapped and murdered, so please take a cab back. Got it?"

I smile at his concern for my safety, even if he is a little overbearing. "I will if it'll make you feel better."

"Yes, it will make me feel much better. Have you changed your mind about going to your friend's house for Christmas?"

"No, but that doesn't mean I'm without plans. I'm going to watch a marathon of Christmas movies and drink lots of eggnog. I'm an only child so I'm used to entertaining me, myself, and I. It's really not a big deal."

He's quiet and I'm not sure he's buying my story. I hope it's not the pity thing again. I can't stand that. "Not a big deal, huh?"

"No, it's not," I lie. It is a big deal. Who wants to be alone on Christmas?

"If you say so."

"I believe I just did."

"I just wanted to check in for a minute before I got tied up. My brother has solicited my help in putting toys together. Yay."

He sounds annoyed, but I think it would be fun. "Okay. Well, have fun building dollhouses. Merry Christmas, caveman."

"Merry Christmas, American girl."

❦

ADDISON AND BEN HAVE BEEN GONE TO ZAC'S FOR HOURS, SO IT'S JUST ME, Jimmy Stewart, and a half-emptied carton of eggnog. It's possible I mixed it with some mighty fine bourbon and garnished with a dash of cinnamon. Christmas is on now.

I hear Bret singing and I'm surprised because Lachlan didn't mention calling me today. I expected him to be way too busy with his family. "Hey, caveman. This is a pleasant surprise."

"Well, I hope you still think that a couple of minutes from now."

Oh, shit. "Is something wrong?" The words aren't out of my mouth when the door buzzes. "Hang on a second. Someone's buzzing the door."

Weird. Who's here on Christmas Day? I push the intercom button. "Yes?"

"It's me."

It's a man's voice, but this is Ben's apartment. How am I supposed to know who he is? "I'm sorry. Ben isn't home."

"It's me, Lachlan."

Well, shit. Do I talk to the phone or the intercom? "Lachlan! What are you doing here?"

"Do you really want to have this conversation with me standing downstairs?"

"Of course not. Sorry. I'm in apartment 311." I press the button to allow him into the building and stand at the door waiting.

Shit, I look a mess. I'm wearing jogging pants with something stupid written across the ass and an equally stupid T-shirt. I'm not even positive my clothes don't have stains or holes. My hair is piled into a messy bun on top of my head and I'm wearing my glasses. They're trendy, but I'd still rather be wearing my contacts for Lachlan. Too late now.

He comes around the corner from the elevator dressed in dark stonewashed jeans and a white button-up. He's as handsome as I've ever seen him and I want to crawl into a deep, deep hole so he can't see me like this.

I smile because I can't see him and not beam. "What are you doing here?"

"It's Christmas. I didn't want you to be alone. And I wanted to see you."

"What about your family?"

"My mother was rather annoyed with me when I told her you were alone today. She insisted I come and spend the evening with you."

Oh. I feel deflated when I realize this is his mother's insistence.

I shrug and stare at my bare feet. "I'm sorry. I wasn't expecting you so I look like hell."

He reaches out and grabs the hem of my shirt, giving it a little tug. "You're always beautiful. And I love the glasses."

I'm dazed by his simple touch. He has that kind of power over me.

It takes a moment, but I finally come to my senses and invite him in. "I'm sorry. Come in."

He prowls through the door and I feel him on my heels as I shut it. He grabs me from behind. I've come to accept this as his thing, but I like it.

He uses his hips to pin me against the door. His hands are pressed on each side of my head, locking me inside his cage of muscular arms. Because my hair is piled in a messy bun, he has easy access to my whole neck, but I realize I miss the glide of his hand pushing my hair over my shoulder. He leans forward and begins kissing the back of my neck, and I evanesce.

I know what he's doing. He wants the thrill of screwing me in the rival's territory. It means he's won and I'm fine with him taking me as his prize.

He brings his hands to my hips and navigates me to the couch, but we don't sit. He steers me to the arm until it hits me across the top of my thighs. I hear the sound of his zipper behind me and then the tearing of a foil wrapper.

A few seconds later, he pushes my pants and panties to my knees. Shit, I don't remember which panties I'm wearing. I hope they're not some of my old ones.

I feel his hand at my lower back and he pushes me over the arm of the couch. He glides a hand up my spine to my shoulders. I should be mortified at being bent over with my pants to my knees, but I'm not, and the thought dissipates altogether when he slides two fingers inside me. I rock back against his magic hand because I can't hold still. It feels too good.

"You're always so wet and eager." I love the things he says to me when we're like this. I implore him to say something else and he reads my mind. "Tell me what you want."

"You." I manage to whisper, but I'm not as good at this as he is.

He takes his fingers out and I feel his hard tip sliding up and down. "Tell me where you want me."

"Inside me." It comes out a little louder, but still barely more than a whisper.

"When?" He's still teasing me, but uses a little more pressure.

"Now," I manage to say a little louder.

"I'm sorry. I can't hear you, Paige. When did you say you want me?" He's taunting me.

"Right now!" I scream as I push back and force him inside me.

I hear him hiss through his teeth. "Then right now you shall have me."

I feel his hands on my hips and I hear him groan as he sinks deep inside me with more force than I thought possible. I call out from the shock of it. "You like it this way, don't you?"

I can't lie. I love it. "Yes." It's all I can manage with him pounding into me.

He slows his pace a little and I feel one of his hands leave my hip to slide down my spine. "I love having you this way."

I'm like a cat bending to his touch. He holds so much power over me… I wonder if he knows.

I spiral until he takes me to that place, the one where I implode as he drives hard into me one last time. A few moments later, I feel his kiss against my back. "Pack a bag. You're coming home with me. But don't change. I want you just the way you are."

He doesn't have to ask me twice.

CHAPTER EIGHTEEN

JACK MCLACHLAN

PAIGE IS IN HER ROOM PACKING WHEN I HEAR THE LOCK JIGGLE. BEN Donavon comes through the door to find me in his living room, sitting on the arm of his couch—the same one I just bent Paige over—and I stifle my laughter. He's not happy with my presence and is about to question it when Paige comes out of her bedroom.

He sees her bag and reads the situation for what it is. She's choosing to leave with me, not stay here with him. "Going somewhere?"

"Yeah, I'm staying with Lachlan tonight."

He's pissed off and that makes me more eager to get her away from him. "When should I tell Addison you'll be back?"

She looks to me for an answer, but I don't have one. I haven't thought about a plan beyond tonight. "She'll call and let her know."

He's furious because this isn't his plan. His involved coming back to the apartment to have some alone time with Paige. Too bad. The only one-on-one she's getting tonight is in my bed.

I put my arm around her and take her bag. "Ready, baby?"

Paige glances at me and grins. "I think so."

As we walk out the door, I taunt him over my shoulder. "Merry Christmas, Ben."

He doesn't say anything back. Sore loser.

I SEE PAIGE'S GIFT BY THE DOOR WHEN WE PULL UP. I CALLED AND CANCELED the delivery to the apartment and instead had it brought to the vineyard the moment my mum convinced me to spend Christmas with my "girlfriend."

My poor mum. She thinks she sent me here to woo her potential daughter-in-law, not indulge in my latest lewd act.

Paige sees the gift on the porch when we get out of the car. "Check it out. Someone left a Christmas gift for you by the door."

I try not to grin. "Hmm, I wonder who would have done that since all of the staff are still gone for the holidays."

I unlock the door and grab the gift before she has time to investigate the name on the card. We go into the living room and I put it down on the coffee table. "Want to go ahead and take your bag to the bedroom?"

"Sure."

I watch her disappear down the hall, and it makes me smile. She's familiar with all of this—me, my house, the things I want to do to her. She hasn't been shocked or apprehensive about anything so far. The others were uptight and stuffy, but Paige is different. She's so much better.

She comes back into the living room and sits next to me on the couch. I pass her one of the glasses of wine I've poured. "Thank you."

She lifts it to her mouth and then makes a guess at the type. "Merlot?"

"Very good, my young apprentice."

She smiles, pleased with herself. "I have a great master."

"Perhaps." I take the wine from her hand and put our glasses aside. I lift the large gift from the coffee table and hand her the card. "I'm dying to see who this is from. Read the card to me."

She smiles as she takes it. "Merry Christmas to Paige, from Lachlan." Her smile fades when it registers. "You got me a gift?"

"I did."

"When did you have time?"

"When isn't important." I place the box across her lap and I'm surprised by the joy I'm feeling. I've gone from one extreme to the other today. I was discontent when I woke this morning and thought about not being with her when she opened this, but now I'm antsy to see her reaction. "Open it."

"But I don't have a gift for you."

I shrug. "Doesn't matter. Open it already."

She tears the paper slowly. I can tell she's guarded, perhaps thinking of all the things the large box could contain. Of the things running through her mind, I don't think this one she considers.

When she opens the box, she sees the case adorned with one word: Martin. She knows what's inside. I can't decipher what I see on her face. Is she not happy?

My other companions were ecstatic to get gifts. Of course, I usually give them something lavish, like jewelry. Maybe she was hoping for something along those lines. Should I have given her diamond earrings instead?

She swallows hard and pulls the brown case from the box. She places it across her lap and looks at me. She seems sad, and I don't know why. I wish I knew what she was thinking.

She pushes the brass drawbolt latch up with her thumb and opens the top of the case. She stares quietly at the Martin D-45 she admired in the window of the music store before she grazes her fingers over it. I'm no closer to knowing what's going through her mind. It's frustrating and I begin to wonder if I've done something wrong. Perhaps it isn't the right guitar.

I can stand it no longer. "You have to tell me what you're thinking."

She blinks several times and I see the tears in her eyes. Shit. That wasn't what I was going for at all. "I'm thinking it's beautiful but way too expensive and I can't accept it."

"Don't think of how much it cost. I bought it for you because I want you to have it. You're keeping it. Now, take it out and play something for me."

She puts the case on the coffee table and removes the guitar. She slips the strap over her head and hesitates like she's still thinking it over, but then strums it for the first time. And it's over. I know there'll be no more talk of not accepting my gift because she's in love with it.

She begins strumming a song and nothing sounds familiar about it, but I like it. "What song is this?"

"Paperweight." She strums a few more chords and then begins singing. Two lines in and I'm completely lost in her. Her voice is uninhibited and I love everything about her when she sings—her song choice, her voice, her facial expressions, but mostly the feeling I get. She's special and destined for great things when the right person in the music industry discovers her.

When she finishes playing, she looks over at me and smiles. "It's perfect and I love it. It's the best gift I've ever been given. Thank you."

"You're very welcome."

She gets up and puts the guitar in its case before she climbs onto the couch and straddles me. She takes my face in her small, delicate hands. I hadn't noticed how dainty they are until I saw them strumming the Martin. She's watching my eyes. "And thank you for coming back to me."

I'm taken by surprise because her words sound so intimate, like those that would be whispered between two people in love. She's very good at our little game. She makes this feel real.

My first thought is to take her to the bedroom, but then I remember that we are alone and decide I want her right here in the living room. I lift her shirt over her head and unfasten the back of her bra to free her perfect breasts. I suck one of her rosy tips into my mouth and I feel her arch closer as she drops her head back. I roll my tongue around the erect pebble and then scrape my teeth over it.

"Oh, Lachlan," she quietly moans as she grinds her pelvis against mine.

My sweet little American girl isn't much of a talker when we're like this, but I'm going to work on her a little at a time. "Tell me what you want me to do to you, Paige."

"You know what I want you to do."

"I might, but I can't be sure, so I need to hear you say it."

Her face is red because she's embarrassed to tell me, but I'll eventually have her so she isn't afraid to ask me to do anything. I rub my hands over her breasts. "Do you want me to kiss you here?"

"Yes."

"Then say it."

She swallows hard. "Lachlan, I want you to kiss my breasts." It's a soft whisper, but I let it count because this is going to take some conditioning.

I take her other breast in my mouth and suck it hard. I tug lightly on her nipple and it makes a popping sound when the suction breaks.

She's still wearing her bottoms so I lift her from my lap and lie her down on the couch. "Now, what do you want me to do next?"

"Take off my pants and panties."

"Yes, ma'am." I grin at her as I tug on the waistband of her pants and panties. She lifts her hips and I slide them down for a second time today. I take them all the way down and toss them onto the floor. "Next?"

She smiles and I think she is starting to relax with our game. "Take off your clothes while I watch."

"Anything you want. You only have to ask."

I unbutton my shirt and toss it casually over the back of the couch. I take the two foil squares out of my pocket and put them on the coffee table before I unfasten my daks and drop them and my jocks to the floor. "Next?"

She's licking her lips. "I want your mouth on me."

I grin at her vague request. "You have to tell me where."

She points at her piercing through her navel. "Start here. Then, I want you to go down."

"Anything for you." My American girl is getting braver. This is going to be so much fun.

I kiss her jeweled piercing over her belly button because she's asked me to, but I know that's not where she really wants my mouth, so I begin working my way toward the real prize. She relaxes her legs as I go lower, but I stop just before I get to that spot. "Is this low enough?"

"No."

"Tell me when I get to where you want me."

I start again and I hear her direct me. "Go down a little more."

I know when I hit the spot because she arches her back in response. "Yes. Right there. Don't stop."

I lick her center and then use my tongue to circle the stiff nub, but it's when I slide my fingers inside her below my tongue that she begins to come apart. I feel her hand grab my hair as she squeals out. "Don't stop doing that, Lachlan."

When she's finished coming, I feel her relax and she lets go of my hair. At this rate, I could be snatched bald by the end of our time together.

I reach for the condom on the table and tear into it. She sits up on the couch and watches me roll it on. When I finish, I crawl up her body and search her face. "Now, tell me what you want me to do to you."

"I want you to... fuck me." She's hesitant and soft-spoken.

Not good enough. I grab her thighs and pull her against me.

"Say it like you mean it." I'm hard against her slick entrance and she's lifting her hips to rub against me. She wants me to enter her and I will, but not until I hear her say it the way I want.

She grabs me around the neck and pulls me down until we're eye to eye and there's nothing gentle about it. "Fuck. Me. Now. Lachlan."

That's my girl. "Okay, okay. All you had to do was ask," I laugh.

I give her what we both want and sink deeply inside her. She brings her legs up around my hips to coax me on. "Harder, Lachlan."

"You like it rough, don't you?"

She tightens her legs around me. "Yes!"

I drive into her, filling her as deeply as I can when I have no choice but to explode. Her legs are wrapped around me tightly and there's an unfamiliar feeling deep inside her. What was that?

It was neither bad nor good. Just something I'd never felt before.

"Did you feel something different just now?"

"No, but you obviously did by the look on your face."

"Yeah, I did. I felt something twitch. Or pop."

I'm still inside her, so I pull out to investigate and see if we have an issue. The condom is busted to hell and back. "Fuck! The rubber broke."

My first response is to panic, but then I remember that Paige is on the pill. "You've been taking your birth control pills, haven't you?"

Condoms are the one thing I have absolute control over in my sexual relationships. I refuse to depend on anyone else to be responsible. The cost of failure is too great, but now I'm forced to relinquish control to Paige and really need to hear her say she's been doing what she promised she would.

She sits up and grabs my face. "Yes, Lachlan. I take my pill at the same time every day, so relax. I've got us covered."

She has us covered. Her words work to calm me a little. "You're right. I just panicked for a minute. When are you supposed to start your period?" I need to know how long I have to worry about this.

"Probably Tuesday."

"Good. That means we'll only have to wait a few days to know everything is all right for sure." God, just thinking about everything not being okay makes me want to throw up.

CHAPTER NINETEEN
LAURELYN PRESCOTT

Wow, meet flustered Lachlan. I didn't know he existed.

I work harder to convince him everything is all good. "We're fine, Lachlan. Even if I weren't on the pill, I'm not ovulating."

"Says the woman who gets a surprise pregnancy."

I didn't know Lachlan could be anything but cool and collected, but he has shown me a different side of him. Let's just say he doesn't deal well with "oh, shit" moments.

He picks up the unused condom from the coffee table and tears the wrapper so he can inspect it for defects. "We're not using any more out of that box, just in case it's a defective batch."

When he finishes inspecting it, he flops back on the couch and stares at the ceiling. He's thinking—and worrying—although I've told him I'm taking my birth control pills. Is it because he thinks I sleep around with a lot of men? I admit that I haven't given him much reason to think otherwise, but it's the furthest thing from the truth.

"Before you, I had only been with one person and I was tested for everything under the sun after we ended things, so you don't have to worry about catching something from me."

He doesn't look at me. "I'm not worried about you giving me a sexually transmitted disease. The majority of that stuff can be treated."

I see that there won't be any more sex until we get a new box of condoms, so I get off the couch and begin to dress after I toss him his pants and boxer briefs.

When I finish dressing, I kneel between his legs and put my chin on one of his knees. I peer up at him and he caresses the side of my face with his hand. I don't want this night to be ruined by stress and anxiety. "Don't. Worry. We're good."

His worry has taken him somewhere else, and I want him back here with me. "Want me to play something for you?"

"Yes, that would be nice."

I get up from the floor and take my new guitar from its case. I stand in front of him and strum several times. "Any requests from the audience tonight?"

"You pick."

I know the perfect song to take his mind off what just happened. I begin to strum a bluegrass version of "Gin and Juice," but I can tell he isn't catching on. Maybe Australians aren't fans of Snoop Dogg.

I hit the chorus and see the recognition on his face as he begins to laugh. Hmm. Lachlan thinks I'm funny. It feels so strange because Blake never thought anything I did was amusing.

He picks up and begins to sing the chorus with me. When I finish, he claps and I curtsy. "That was fantastic."

"Bluegrass 'Gin and Juice' isn't fantastic; it's shitastic. There's a huge difference between the two."

"That wasn't exactly the kind of performance I was expecting when I bought the guitar for you, but I loved it. Do something else shitastic for me."

I don't have to think about it. I'm going to do "Whatever You Like" by T.I. my way because the song makes me think of us and our bizarro relationship.

He applauds for me when I finish and I curtsy again. "You're amazing."

He thinks that's amazing? "You know I was just playing around, right? That's not the kind of stuff I sing for real."

"Okay, so tell me. What does Paige Beckett sing for real?"

"Music is what feelings sound like out loud. I sing songs that speak from my heart. They tell my story, how I feel."

"Sing one of those. Pick one that tells me your story."

"I don't know."

"You do know. Come on, tell me your story."

I'm going to regret this. I know I will. I decide on "According to You" by Orianthi. I strum until I find the desired chord and begin singing the lyrics that describe how Blake saw me. Stupid. Useless. Difficult. But then the lyrics change to how the other guy –Lachlan– sees me. Beautiful. Incredible. Funny. Irriesisitable.

And that's as far as I make it before I'm choking on my own words. Shit, I knew I'd regret doing this. I'm mortified as I stand in front of Lachlan with my hands over my face so he doesn't see the ugly cry.

He gets off the couch and is by my side, arms around me. A moment later, he lifts the guitar over my head and puts it in its case. "I don't know who he is, but he's wrong. You are beautiful. And incredible. And funny. And irresistible."

There's so much that's happened in my life to make me feel unworthy of ever being beautiful, incredible, funny, or irresistible. But I don't want to think of those things. Not now. And certainly not in front of Lachlan.

He lets go of me and takes my hand. "It's late. Come to bed with me."

I follow him to his bedroom and shuffle through my bag as he pulls the comforter back. "What did you bring to sleep in?"

I take out a satin lavender slip gown and hold it up for him to see. He shakes his head before reaching into his bureau and tossing one of his T-shirts in my direction. "Here. Wear this." Yep. We are officially on coitus hiatus until we can get our hands on a different batch of condoms.

He's seen me naked, but I still turn around to take my clothes off and slip into his shirt. I'm not sure wearing something of his is helping with the coitus hiatus effort because I can't help but notice how good it smells. Just like Lachlan.

We go into the bathroom together to do our bedtime rituals. He's on his side and I'm on the other. I watch him in the mirror as he brushes his teeth. It feels so domestic. He glances over and I'm not sure if it's because he's sneaking a peek at me or if he feels my eyes on him.

112

When we're finished, we climb into bed and he pulls me close. He doesn't ask me to tell him about the pain I'm hiding. He simply holds me until we fall asleep. It's something I've never done. And it's beautiful.

⚜

I WAKE THE NEXT MORNING AND MY HAND REACHES FOR A WARM BODY THAT isn't there. The early bird is out of the nest already, which makes me the sleepyhead again, except for the fact that it's only seven in the morning. That does not qualify as sleeping late in any shape or form.

I don't find Lachlan in the kitchen, so I walk toward the gym. I hear "Whatever You Like" blaring through the speakers before I reach the door. When I walk in, he's running on the treadmill and the back of his T-shirt is soaking wet. He's been in here a while.

His back is to me, but his eyes meet mine in the mirror. "Good morning, sleepyhead."

"Good morning, early bird. Nice song choice."

"I think so too, although I like your version better. You just missed Snoop Dogg."

"Hate that. Been running long?"

"Long enough." He stops the treadmill and reaches for a towel to wipe the sweat from his face. His cheeks are rosy and it makes him look younger, like a child playing in the hot sun.

"I probably need to call Addison to let her know how long I'm staying."

"How long do you want to stay?"

I shrug. "I don't know. How long am I welcome?" Listen to me. I'm like Addison now, not wanting to wear out my welcome.

He wipes his neck and chest—jeez, I'd love to be that towel. "I'm leaving to go out of town Monday morning. Will you stay with me until then?"

I don't have to think about it, but I hesitate for a moment so he doesn't see how elated I am to be with him for the next two days. "Sure. That's doable."

He tosses the towel across the treadmill as he gets off and I know what's he's about to do. I see the mischief in his grin. He knows I'm

113

about to run and catches me before I can take a second step. I'm no match for a conditioned runner.

He pulls me against his hot, sweaty body. I wanted to be his towel. Now, I am. Any other sweaty man would be gross, but Lachlan's not. It's the ultimate turn-on, but I remember we don't have condoms since he tossed the whole box of potentially defective ones out last night.

I pretend to be grossed out as I push away from him. "Caveman, you are in desperate need of a shower."

He rubs his sweaty body all over me. "Now you are too."

Has he forgotten about our lack of protection? "Do you think that's the best idea since you threw out all the condoms last night?"

He's wearing that naughty little grin I've come to love so much. "Don't need 'em for what we're going to do."

CHAPTER TWENTY

JACK MCLACHLAN

It's not even noon when we're driving into town, and we both know exactly the purpose of our expedition. We have condom shopping to do.

"I didn't pack enough clothes to stay until Monday. Do you mind swinging by the apartment so I can pick up some things?"

"No problem." Except I do have a problem with it. I'm sure Ben Donavon will be there.

I park along the curb at the apartment. I'm not sure if I'm invited up, but I'm not at all crazy about her going to his place without me. "Will you come up and officially meet Addison?"

"Sure." Abso-fucking-lutely. It's probably not the best idea to hem me up with that little bastard in the same room, but I don't want her going up there without me.

I follow Paige into the building. She knocks instead of using a key and Addison opens the door. I'm relieved to see it isn't her brother. Her friend wrinkles her brow. "Why are you knocking? You live here, silly."

"It's not my apartment. I'm just bunking here."

Addison gives me a thorough inspection. "Well, you haven't been bunking here much, thanks to this guy." I'm not sure what to make of her comment, but she extends her hand. "Addison Donavon."

"Lachlan Henry."

"So, you're the man who's been keeping my best friend so busy."

Yeah, we've been pretty busy all right. "Guilty as charged."

"She tells me you're in the wine business. My family has a vineyard in California. It can be brutal."

"I'll drink to that."

"I'm going to grab some things while you bond over the woes of winemaking." Paige disappears into the bedroom and leaves me alone with her friend. I'm prepared to share more about my career, but once she's certain Paige is out of hearing distance, she suddenly changes the subject and is very serious.

"Please, don't hurt her."

It's a strained moment and I'm not really sure how to respond. "I'm sorry?"

"I'm asking you to not hurt Laurelyn. She's been through a lot. The last guy she dated did a real number on her."

Her name is Laurelyn?

"She told me about the agreement you have and I'm fine with it. Have a great time together—but don't make her fall in love with you. She's been hurt enough."

Fall in love? Who said anything about falling in love?

Paige might have told her friend some things about our agreement, but not everything. Addison doesn't know that Laurelyn chose to keep her name a secret from me because she's unknowingly busted her on it. Honestly, it stings a little to discover that.

"No worries. Laurelyn and I are on the same page." I say her name, savoring how it sounds rolling off my tongue. Paige was all right, but Laurelyn fits her better because it's different. I've never known anyone by that name.

She comes out of the bedroom with a large bag in hand. "All packed and ready to go."

❧

OUR FIRST STOP AFTER WE LEAVE THE APARTMENT IS THE DRUGSTORE. I GET into the car after my shopping spree and pass her the bag of condoms. "How many did you buy?" She opens the bag to peek

116

inside and smiles in my direction. "Did you buy their entire inventory?"

"Hey, I'm not getting stuck without some backup in case we have another blowout."

She's shaking her head at me. "Are you still worried about that?"

Hell yeah, I'm still worried. Why isn't she? "Yes, and I will be until you start your period. If you don't get it before I leave, I want you to call me as soon as you do."

"Yes, sir." I think she's miffed.

I know I sound irrational. I don't mean to, but a pregnancy under these circumstances would be disastrous. "I'm sorry. I don't mean to rub you the wrong way. I'd much rather rub you the right way."

She smiles and I know I'm forgiven. "I need to talk to you about something."

"Okay." I pull out of the parking lot but don't have a clue where I'm going.

I'm nervous about bringing it up, but I do because I realize it's important to me. "I want to call you Laurelyn."

I stare ahead as I drive, but I still catch a glimpse of Laurelyn whirling her head in my direction. "I see Addison ratted me out. I didn't tell her about the anonymous part of the agreement."

"I'm glad she ratted you out because I want to call you by your real name. Laurelyn suits you better than Paige."

"I don't think you have the right to know my real name if I don't know yours." She's angry. Or maybe defeated. I'm not really sure.

"There are very legitimate reasons for that." She turns her head away from me. "You can't be angry at me about this." I reach for her hand and bring it to my leg. I give it a gentle squeeze. "I was honest with you about everything."

She looks back at me. "Except why. You haven't given me any kind of explanation. I'm sure I could accept not knowing if you'd only give me some kind of reason."

"But, I won't." I'm stern when I say it because I have to be disciplined for myself. She makes me want to break down and tell her everything. It's strange—I've never wanted to do that before. She makes me want to do lots of new things.

117

"It's not fair, but I guess there's no point in pretending to be Paige Beckett when you know I'm not, so I guess you're getting what you want. Again."

She's not happy with me, but I still bring her hand to my lips and kiss it. "Thank you, Laurelyn."

"Well, you're not welcome and you can forget getting my real last name."

She's mad because she feels defeated. I don't want her to feel that way. It makes me want to blurt out that she can call me Jack, but I don't. Because I can't.

Laurelyn. Laurelyn. Laurelyn. It's a delicate, feminine name and I say it in my head over and over, wrapping my brain around it so it will flow off my tongue when I'm ready to say it again. It's very easy to forget I ever called her Paige.

"Can I take you to lunch while we're in town?"

"Sure. What about the fifties diner on the square? Ben says it's great and I've been dying to try it."

Ben. I hate the feeling I get when she says his name. I'm really going to hate taking her back to stay at his place again. It pisses me off that he thinks he has a chance with the woman I've claimed. Maybe he needs a warning so he'll back off.

"I'll take you anywhere you want to go."

The diner is exactly what it sounds like and Laurelyn is all smiles when we enter. "Oh, it's retro, just like a real fifties diner. Can we sit at the bar?"

"Anything you want."

The decor is exactly as you would imagine—a black-and-white checkered floor down to red vinyl-covered barstools with lots of chrome. She reaches for a menu on the counter stuck behind a napkin holder and passes one to me. "I don't know why I'm even looking. I already know what I want—a cheeseburger, fries, and a chocolate shake."

A waitress wearing the classic dress and white apron approaches us. "Do you need a minute to look over the menu?"

I figure a burger is as good as anything else I'll find on the menu. "No. We'll have two cheeseburgers with fries and a couple of chocolate shakes."

"Coming right up."

Laurelyn replaces the menus and scans the surroundings. "I've always thought of the fifties diner theme as an American thing, but I guess it's not."

"No, I guess not."

I hear an old song playing overhead and I decide to try to stump my little musician. "Okay, musical genius. What song is this?"

She doesn't have to listen because she already knows. "'In the Still of the Night' by The Five Satins."

It amazes me how she knows. Always. "How can you possibly have all that information in your head?"

"It's a gift. Oh, wow. A jukebox!" She flies off her stool and stands over the jukebox viewing the song selections. She's so into the music, I don't think she realizes she's keeping time to the music with the shake of her hips. Wow, I love her ass. Especially when she shakes it like that.

She digs into her purse and drops several coins into the box. When she returns, she's grinning. "What?" I ask out of curiosity.

"Nothing. I just like this place," she shrugs. "I'm glad you're the one who brought me here."

"Me too." The alternative pisses me off.

Our lunch arrives and Laurelyn makes no pretenses about enjoying her meal. The girl loves a cheeseburger and a milkshake. I'm not used to it. Mostly because this isn't the type of restaurant I would take any of my companions to, but also because they always order salads and eat like birds.

I like watching her eat while she enjoys the music playing overhead. The next song starts and she points up to the ceiling, cueing me to listen as she bites her bottom lip and moves her shoulders with the beat of the song. She waggles her eyebrows. "This is one of the songs I play. Do you know it?"

Of course. It's a classic. "'These Arms of Mine' by Otis Redding."

As we finish eating, she continues my education on the artist and name of every new song. "Do you think, sleep, breathe music all the time?"

"Pretty much. I don't think I could stop if I wanted to. It's in my blood and I have to have it. When I'm in a writing mode, it's weird how such simple acts can trigger lyrics in my head." She peers over her shoulder. "You see that man and woman over there?"

I hadn't noticed anyone in this diner except her, so I glance at the couple she's talking about. I see a man and woman sitting across from one another in a booth. They're probably in their early twenties and having what appears to be an intense conversation.

"They're breaking up. I see the pain in their eyes and it makes words come into my head. When it hits me, I'll write it on anything until I can get to my guitar. I see potential song lyrics happening all around me."

She's right. This is in her blood. Only someone genetically engineered toward music could come up with the things she does. "And what would a song about us sound like?"

She looks up as she slurps the last drink of her milkshake and shakes her head. "No way. I'm not touching that one with a ten-foot pole."

CHAPTER TWENTY-ONE
LAURELYN PRESCOTT

WE'RE DRIVING BACK TO AVALON WITH THE TOP DOWN AND LACHLAN IS exceptionally sexy behind his sunglasses. I can't resist taking out the phone he gave me and snapping a picture of him. He briefly takes his eyes away from the road as he glances in my direction. I take the opportunity to snap a frontal shot. Oh, my. He is so good-looking.

"No pictures with your personal phone. Ever." His words are rigid and I wonder what the big deal is.

I innocently hold up the phone he gave me. "It's not my personal phone. It's the booty-call device you sent me and I want your picture on here so I can see your handsome face pop up when you call me."

I realize it's the first time I've called it that in front of him. "Booty-call device?"

"Yeah. If we're being honest, that's what it is. You're the only person who knows the number and when you call, it's always to make arrangements to get together. We both know what we're going to do, so that's what it is."

He glances at me again. "Laurelyn, you're not a booty call."

"When I agreed to this relationship, you told me there would be no pretending. Please don't go back on your word now and try to act like this is more than it really is. It's unnecessary."

He pulls the convertible over on the side of the rural road. "I'm not pretending this is anything more than a short-term relationship, but I like being with you even when there's no sex involved. That means you're not a booty call."

I melt into a puddle in the passenger seat when he says he likes being with me. Damn, I like being with him too, even if I know it's only temporary. It's too bad we don't live closer and I only get three months with him.

He reaches over and caresses my cheek with his hand. "You got it, babe?"

I love to hear him call me that. I don't say anything, but nod instead. I'm rewarded when he leans over to gently kiss my lips. "Good. I'm glad we're on the same page."

After he pulls back onto the road, he reaches for my hand and rests it against his thigh. I lean my head back against the seat and let my hair go without trying to keep it wrangled. I savor this time with Lachlan. These moments will eventually come to an end. But not today.

The ride, however, does come to an end when we're back at the vineyard. Lachlan takes my hand and places a kiss against it before we get out of the car. It helps make this arrangement feel more like a relationship. But as sweet as it is, it doesn't change the fact that all of this will be short-lived.

I notice a white truck in the drive and I wonder if one of the vineyard employees has returned early or if Lachlan has company. "Someone's here."

"That's Mike's truck. He's the handyman, so I guess he had a maintenance job. Wait here."

Wait here in the car? That's a little on the weird side, but I do it anyway. A few minutes later I see Lachlan walking out of the house with a man. They shake hands and he gets into his truck to leave.

Lachlan walks over to the car and opens my door for me, but says nothing about the man or why he's at the vineyard the day after Christmas when all of the other employees are still off for the holidays. Of course, it's not my business, so I don't ask.

When we're inside, Lachlan grabs a coldie (his name for beer), and we go into the living room to hang out. "Today is Boxing Day. If we were in Sydney, I'd take you to the harbor to watch the start of the yacht race to Hobart."

"I've never heard of that before," I reply.

It's a big day for hitting the after-Christmas sales. And there's a lot of sporting events planned for today. Australia's National Cricket team had a test match scheduled this morning, which is a big deal around here."

He grabs the remote for what he refers to as the idiot box. "I need to see if we won."

After he sees the results of the game, he turns the television off. "That's enough of that. Will you play something for me?"

I can't resist his request or the urge to play since I haven't touched it today. I play several of Lachlan's requests, but he gets that wrinkle in his brow and I know he's thinking hard about something. "What's on your mind?"

He watches me a second before he says anything. "I was just wondering if, when you're back home and you've become a huge success, if you'll write a number-one hit about us?"

"I really hope not."

"Why not?" He sounds offended. Or disappointed.

I watch my fingers strum the strings so my eyes don't have to meet his. I don't want to see them when I explain. "Because the best songs are written from the heart and the emotions you feel must be one extreme or the other. I'd have to be desperately in love or devastatingly hurt by you."

Lachlan settles back onto the couch and kicks off his shoes, casually propping his feet on the coffee table. "Have you ever experienced either of those things?"

"I've never been desperately in love."

"Does that mean you've been devastatingly hurt?"

I think of Blake and the way I felt when I found out he was married. "I've been hurt and it felt shattering at the time."

"I don't think you can't have one without the other, so the two must coincide."

He sounds like he knows a little something about love and pain. "Is that your opinion because you've experienced both?"

123

He laughs loudly and I look up from my guitar. "Hell, no. I've never been in love, so no one has ever hurt me."

How is it possible that someone as beautiful as Lachlan has never had that experience? "You've never even thought you might be in love?"

"Never. What about you?"

Blake is in my thoughts again, reminding me just how wrong a person can be when it comes to love. "I thought I was in love once, but I was dead wrong."

"I'm guessing he's the one you were telling me about last night?"

I almost forgot about that. "Yeah, that would be him."

"Did you ever dance for him?"

That came out of left field. "No. I never even told him I did it."

Lachlan gets up from the couch. He grabs my wrist, pulling me to his side, and sets my guitar in its case. "Come with me. I want to show you something."

He leads me to the gym and stops outside the door. "This is why Mike was here. He was installing this for you." He opens the door and I see a shiny new pole toward the back wall. I cross the room and touch it before I look at Lachlan and smile.

Damn, he wasn't kidding. He freakin' installed a pole for me. Or for him.

"I want you to dance for me." He opens one of the cabinet doors and takes out a box. "And I want you to wear this while you do it."

I lift the top to find a black one-piece romper inside. The sides of the waist are cut out, leaving only a thin strip to cover me down the middle between the top and bottom. It's hot and not like anything I've worn while dancing. When I take it out of the box, I have another surprise underneath: a pair of red fuck-me pumps. I hold one up—they look like they'll fit me perfectly.

He swallows hard. "Will you do it for me?"

I know in that moment that I'll never be able to tell him no to anything. I want to be the woman to make his fantasies real. "Yes, I'll do it."

He leans forward to kiss me and catches my bottom lip between his. "Now?"

"If it's what you want."

"Oh, it's what I want."

"But I need a minute to get ready."

"Absolutely."

I take the box from his hands and go to his bedroom. I quickly line my eyes with black kohl and make them smoky with gray and black eyeshadow before adding a fresh coat of mascara to make my lashes extra lush. My hair is windblown from riding in the convertible, so I brush it out before I flip my head over and fluff it with the hair dryer. I leave it down because I like it to cascade when I'm upside down on the pole.

I slip into the romper and damn, is it ever skimpy. There's way less of it covering me once I get into it because it's stretched so taunt from my shoulders to my crotch. I put the pumps on and give them a test drive as I walk circles in the bathroom. I wouldn't want to walk too many blocks in these tall-ass things, but they'll be fine for what I'm going to do.

I inspect myself in the mirror. I'm hot as hell and it boosts my confidence to an all-time high. I'm about to make Lachlan's fantasy a reality.

I go to the gym and wonder where he is. I ease the door open and see him sitting in a chair facing the pole. He's waiting for me with all the lights off except the ones over the area where I'll be dancing. I walk up behind him and lean around to whisper in his ear. "Close your eyes."

I connect my phone to the receiver in the cabinet by Bluetooth because I need to use my own music. The deep, dark thumping bass of "Angel" by Massive Attack begins and I put it on repeat because I expect this performance to run long.

I take my place by the pole and inhale deeply before I start my performance. "You can open your eyes now."

When he sees me, he begins to smile. Big time.

I turn my back to him and reach over my head to grasp the pole. I slowly bend my knees and slide my bottom down it and then back up again as I peer over my shoulder at him. I circle with slow agility and hold the post with one hand as I step out and whirl around a few times. It's total amateur stuff until I kick my leg up and over to lock the pole behind my knee and climb the brass staff while swiveling upward.

I do a series of elaborate spins and stunts that took years to master. When I finish the lengthy routine, I'm upside down. I reach for the floor with my palms and spin several times before dismounting. I look at Lachlan when I stand and I'm not sure he has even blinked since I started.

The music is still playing and I walk to where he is sitting. The song playing is one of my favorites to dance to because it's bizarre and almost hypnotic. I love the way it makes me feel, like I want to lose control and do strange things.

"Baby, you've fucked my mind without touching my body."

I turn my back and smile as I lower my bottom to give him a lap dance. He grabs my hips and I swat his hands away. "You know the rules. You can't touch the dancer."

He sits all the way back in the chair and I take a seat on his lap with my legs spread on each side of his thighs. I put my hands into my hair and lift it from my neck. I lean against him with my back to his chest and let it fall into his face. I'm torturing him. I know this, but it's all part of the fantasy.

"You're my private dancer."

I lean forward and spread my legs further apart as I put my hands on his knees. I begin a steady rhythm of stroking my bottom against his groin and I can feel how hard he is beneath me. "Oh, I'm much more than that."

He groans and I know I'm pushing him to his brink. And I love it.

I get up from his lap and then lower myself to straddle him. I take his face in my hands and search his intense blue eyes. They're different, darker. And fixated on me.

I feel him tremble under me and then his fingers slide into the crotch of my romper. But he doesn't touch me. I feel a sudden jerk downward and I realize he has ripped the bottom of my romper and pushed it up over my hips. "Laurelyn, I need to fuck you right now. Don't make me beg."

I reach for his fly, but my hands miss it because he almost bucks me off trying to get his pants shoved out of the way. He's feral and demanding and I know there won't be anything gentle about what's going to happen. I'd be disappointed if there was.

When his pants and boxer briefs are out of the way, he jerks me down onto him as he thrusts up into me. I cry out because it's so much deeper in this position. It feels like he's pounding against my womb and I can't decide if it's pleasure or pain. He continues to thrust upward as he grasps my hips tightly to slam me down against him. There's no doubt I'll have bruises on my hips tomorrow from where his fingers are digging into my skin, but I don't care. I wouldn't have him stop for anything in the world right now.

I feel my explosion building and I don't know how or why, but my mind registers the fact that Lachlan didn't put a condom on. After all that grief over the busted rubber the night before, I can't believe he doesn't wear one tonight.

Dammit. I'm about to ruin the best sex I've ever had.

I lean back to see him and he thrusts deeper than ever. "Lachlan, you didn't put a condom on."

He grabs my hips painfully and thrusts deeply one last time as he groans loudly and then hisses through his teeth. "Ooh, Laurelyn."

Shit. He just came inside me, no doubt at the door of my womb since he's been knocking on it so hard. My immediate instinct is to get off him, but he's holding me so tightly, there's no way I can budge an inch.

When he's finished, I'm still straddling him. We're face to face. I fist a handful of hair and bring our foreheads together. I'm staring him directly in the eyes, about to chastise him for the missing rubber, when he grabs me around the neck to pull me down for a kiss.

When he stops, our foreheads are still touching and we're both gasping for breath. "You are fan-fucking-tastic. I've never seen anything like that. When you told me you pole danced, that is not what I thought you did."

"What did you think I meant?"

"I thought you'd hold on to the pole and spin around, maybe climb it a little if I was lucky, but damn, baby… you're bewitching on that pole."

I kiss him because I'm pleased by his praises, but I'm still going to bring up the absentee condom. "Was it my dancing or the hypnotic music that made you go crazy and forget to put on a condom?"

"I didn't forget. I put it on when you started dancing."

Oh. He slipped that one on without me knowing. "I should have known you wouldn't forget after the huge deal you made about it last night."

"It's a good thing I put it on while you were dancing because there's no way I could have stopped to do it once you straddled me." He's shaking his head like he's in disbelief and pulls me into a tight hug. "I don't want you to dance for anyone but me."

I'm confused by that. Does he mean he doesn't want me to dance for anyone else for the next three months?

As I'm catching my breath, the thought fades and my mind moves on to other things I don't understand. I have to know if he felt the same unexplainable energy I did. "Did you feel different?"

He laughs and it vibrates against my chest. "I swear I've never come so hard in my life."

That's exactly how I felt. "Me, either, but it was strange. I almost felt hypnotized, like I was being controlled by something else more powerful than myself."

"I think we were both being controlled by some mighty strong orgasms."

"And you gave it to me. Thank you."

He kisses my forehead. "Thank you for dancing for me. And for giving me sex so spectacular, I'm not sure it can ever be topped."

I don't say it, but I definitely think it—we've both just experienced something that can never be topped.

CHAPTER TWENTY-TWO

JACK MCLACHLAN

WE'RE FINISHING DINNER AND I HAVEN'T BEEN ABLE TO LOOK AT LAURELYN one second without remembering her on that pole. I've been in a lot of strip clubs, but I've never seen anything like what she did. No stripper on a pole ever made me feel that way.

Putting that aside, there's much more to her than being sexy, and I can't wait to peel back all the layers to see what's underneath. If she'll let me. I worry she might not when I remember how she was about me learning her real name.

I'm glad I found her. And grateful she is willing to give us a chance.

She lifts her eye from her plate and beams. "What?"

I struggle, wondering if I should say anything. She might think I'm being too much like a chickie babe if she knows what I'm thinking, so I keep it simple. "Thank you for saying yes."

"To what?"

"To us."

She smiles and reaches across the table to touch my hand. "Thank you for choosing me. And for running into me at the club. And for moving Ben's wine so you could steal a dance with me."

"The dance that was cut short." By none other than lover boy Ben. He is good at ruining things for me, but he won't ruin this now. I get up from the table and offer Laurelyn my hand. "I would very much like to finish our dance."

I take her in my arms and pull her close as we begin to move back and forth.

"Do you remember the song that was playing?"

I'm not musical like she is, but I could never forget the song. "It was 'Someone Like You' by Van Morrison."

She smiles. "You remember."

We sway to the silence for a while and then Laurelyn takes her head from my chest and asks me to kiss her. So I do. And that's the end of our dance. For now.

⚜

WE'RE LYING IN BED. LAURELYN IS SO BEAUTIFUL, I CAN'T RESIST.

"What are you doing, Lachlan?"

She knows exactly what I'm doing because she did the same thing to me earlier in the day. Except maybe I was wearing more clothes. "I'm getting pictures of you so I can see your beautiful face every time you call me."

"I'm not so sure you're taking pictures of my face. It needs to be something presentable if it's going to pop up when I call."

"Baby, you're very presentable right now. Besides, I'll need some visuals to get me by while I'm out of town next week."

She holds her hands in front of her face. "No way. I'm naked in your bed with sexed-up hair. That's not presentable by anyone's standards."

I grab both of her wrists in one of my hands and hold them hostage over her head. "It is very presentable by my standards and happens to be perfect for me to look at while I'm away from you." I drop down and kiss her mouth. "Relax, baby. No one's going to see these little beauties except me, so smile."

I put the phone on the bed so I have a free hand to tug on the sheet. "We need to drop this down so I can see a little more."

"Lachlan!" She smiles as she pretends to be shocked by what I'm doing.

130

I'm still holding her wrists as I kiss her neck and whisper into her ear. "Come on, Laurelyn. Please, let me."

"What happened to you staying in Wagga Wagga for three months?"

"I'm responsible for other vineyards and I can't neglect them. I'll still be here most of the time, until the middle of March."

I can sense her considering it, so I nuzzle my nose down her neck and plant a kiss to convince her. "Please, baby."

She sighs deeply. "How long will you be gone?"

"I won't have you for at least three days. It's going to be torture."

She rolls her eyes. "You can take a few, but nothing completely nude."

I reach for my phone, but she stops me with her hand. "I at least get to brush my hair first."

"You're the boss."

She gets up and walks naked to the bathroom. "Yeah, I'm not so sure about that."

I'm tempted to snap a shot of her beautiful behind, but I know she'll kill me if I do. I remind myself of what she said. Nothing completely nude.

She comes out of the bathroom a few minutes later with freshly brushed hair, now cascading down her back. She's wearing thigh-highs with lace toppers. Hey, hey… is this what she means by nothing completely nude?

She climbs onto the bed and is on her knees. "How do you want me?"

Hearing that come from her is like a fantasy come true. I hold up my phone to take a picture and she puts her hand over it. "I mean it. No nudies."

"Okay. Lie down first."

She falls to her back, pulls the sheet under her arms to cover her naked breasts, and waits for directions. "Scoop your hair up and let it spill across the pillow." She does and it falls in all the right places. My eyes roam her smooth, creamy skin against my black sheets and she's so beautiful, it's almost painful.

I take a lot of shots of her like that… more than she intended, I'm sure. When I'm finished with her in that pose, she sits up. "What's next?"

She's sitting with her knees pulled up, ankles crossed. I reach for the sheet and begin to pull it away. "You can't see anything. I promise."

She smiles and rolls her eyes. "You're such a liar, but it doesn't matter. I'm inspecting these pictures when you're done and any tits, ass, or vagina shots are getting deleted."

"We'll see."

"Umm, yes, we certainly will."

"Lie down on your stomach."

"That sounds an awfully lot like a command," she complains, but does it anyway. I pull the sheet low on her hips and caress her lower back. "I love this part of your body."

"You love my back? Why?"

"I don't know why. I just know I do." I take picture after picture of her silhouette with her lying on her stomach, her side, and sitting. When I can, I sneak the sheet down a little at a time until she busts me and lifts it higher again.

"Are you done? Surely you've used up all the phone's memory."

"No. I have one more pose I want you to do, but I won't if you're not comfortable with it."

She lifts her brow at me. "That sounds suspicious."

"Can I position you?"

"You can, but that doesn't mean I'll agree to it."

"But you'll try it?"

She rolls her eyes at me again. "Yes, I'll try it."

"Lie on your back." She does as I tell her and waits for my direction, but this one won't be verbal commands. She'll never do it if she hears me say it.

I put my hands on her knees and spread them apart. I gather the sheet between her legs and twist it so that only a thin strip of material covers her. I bunch it up between her breasts and then take one of her hands and lay it over both breasts. She's still covered, so it's not really a nudie, but damn… she is so hot.

Before I take the picture, I ask her. "Can I?"

She swallows and then lifts her head to see what's covered. "Don't move. You'll mess up your hair. Just let me take it and if you don't like it, I'll delete it."

132

She's torn. "I promise everything is covered. No tits, ass, or vagina."

"Okay." She rests her head back on the pillow and I take picture after picture of her. She eventually relaxes and drops her knees further apart and relaxes the arm covering her breasts.

When I'm done, I ask for the hell of it. "Just one nudie?"

"No!"

I can see I've pushed my luck as far as I should, so I put the phone on the bed and drop down to kiss her. "Thank you."

"Don't thank me yet. I may not let you keep any of them."

"I'm not deleting them."

"I have to approve. That's our deal."

I start peeling through them at rapid speed before she gets her hands on the phone. "None of them are nudie, so I get to keep all of them."

She holds out her hand. "Gimme." I pass her the phone like a teenage boy in trouble with his mum over a Playboy. I swear I'll take them all again while she's asleep if she erases the good ones.

I sit. I watch. I wait. She hoots and laughs as she goes through the first several and then I almost hear her brakes skid to a stop. "No way, bro. That one shows my nipples." She goes through a few more and then scrunches her eyebrows and brings the phone closer to her face. "You said you couldn't see anything when I was sitting like that, you liar. You can see my vajayjay in these."

Dammit! She's deleting all the great ones.

She passes the phone back to me and I go through to see what's left. It's not too bad. She only erased a handful. I'm surprised I get to keep all the near nudies with her legs sprawled apart. In fact, it shocks the shit out of me. I wonder if she overlooked those, but I choose to not mention it, just in case.

She picks up the phone I gave her from the bedside table and then lies next to me on the bed. She holds it at arm's length to take our picture together. "Say cheese."

I smile because she asks me to, knowing I shouldn't let her take these kinds of pictures of us in bed together. I only give in because she doesn't know how much money she can make by selling these photographs to the media. She has no idea I'm Jack McLachlan. Even if she knew my name, she still wouldn't know I'm one of Australia's richest and most eligible bachelors. I somehow think it wouldn't matter to her, even if she did know. She's the daughter of a superstar and his fame doesn't seem to phase her at all.

Oh, to hell with it. What's a few pictures going to hurt? I take the phone out of her hand and hold it out to get one of me kissing the side of her face. Then her mouth. Then her neck.

After my mouth reaches her breast, I drop her phone to the bed because our photo shoot is forgotten.

CHAPTER TWENTY-THREE
LAURELYN PRESCOTT

I WAKE BEFORE LACHLAN FOR THE FIRST TIME, BUT IT'S BECAUSE I DON'T FEEL well. I try to go back to sleep for an hour, but I'm unsuccessful. My head is pounding at the base of my skull and I'm nauseated as waves of heat flash throughout my body. I kick off the covers in an unsuccessful attempt to gain a little relief from the uncomfortable sensation.

Please, don't puke.

The urge to vomit becomes more and more pressing. I try to suppress my body's demand, but my stomach betrays me and wins the battle. I dash from the bed to the bathroom and make it to the toilet right before I spew. I try to keep the noise to a minimum, as if subdued heaving is a possibility.

I hear a light tap at the bathroom door. Shit. I didn't lock it in my haste to reach the toilet. "Don't come in here."

The door opens and Lachlan enters in spite of my warning. I reach up and flush the toilet because I'm uncomfortable with him seeing any of my body's previous contents. There are some pretenses I wish to maintain. "Trust me, you don't want to see this."

"I've seen people chunder before." Maybe so, but he's never seen me throw up.

He wets a washcloth with cold water and places it on the back of my neck. He takes my hair into his large hands and secures it with a clip. I don't even want to know how he learned to do that. "Thank you."

"No problem."

I'm embarrassed for him to see me this way. "I'm sorry you're seeing me worship the porcelain god. I know how attractive this must be, but in my defense, I told you to not come in here."

He's rubbing my shoulders to comfort me. "I'll survive seeing you chunder. Think you're finished for now?"

This has been happening to me for a while and I know the routine. Once I vomit, I'm fine. "I'm better now."

Lachlan helps me back to bed. "Do you think you ate something bad?"

"No. This happens to me out of the clear blue sometimes. I get a headache during the night and when I wake up, the pain is so bad, it makes me throw up. It's weird because once I vomit, I'm fine. The pain goes away and so does the nausea."

"Have you told your doctor about this?"

"Yeah. I've had scans and everything seems normal. My doctor diagnosed me with migraines."

He examines my face like he's not so sure. "I think you should lie down and rest."

I walk to the sink so I can brush my teeth and I argue with his reflection in the mirror. "I'm okay, Lachlan. It was a migraine and now it's over. Promise."

He lets me finish brushing my teeth before he objects to what I'm saying. "I have to go out and check the grafts today. I want you to lie down while I'm out."

There's nothing wrong with me, but this is what he wants, so I agree to do it. "I'll lie down while you're gone, but let the record show I'm only doing it to make you happy, not because there's anything wrong with me."

He watches me in the mirror as he kisses my cheek. "Thank you."

It's ridiculous to go to bed when there's nothing wrong with me, but I do it because he asks me to. I hear the shower cut on and consider getting up to step inside with him, but I know that won't go over well.

Why am I so eager to please this man?

When he finishes getting ready, he comes out of the bathroom and sits next to me on the bed. He strokes his fingers over my forehead and pushes my hair away from my face. He takes my phone from the nightstand and puts it on the bed for easy accessibility. "I'll be gone a couple of hours, but I'll have my phone with me if you need anything. Don't hesitate to call." He leans down and kisses my forehead. "Feel better."

I could argue that nothing is wrong with me, but I don't. "Sure thing, boss."

When he's gone, I reach for my phone and scroll through the pictures we took last night. He has the seminudes on his phone. I have the sweet ones where he's kissing my face, my mouth, and my neck. I come across one where he's looking at me like he adores me. He makes it so easy to forget about our agreement, but then I remember that there's a very logical reason for why. He's good at this game because he's played it before. On twelve prior occasions to be exact.

I put the phone down and close my eyes. When I open them again, Lachlan is sitting on the bed next to me. I lift my head to see the clock. Shit, it's almost ten o'clock—I must've dozed off.

He passes a glass of orange juice to me. "Are you feeling better?"

He's so thoughtful. I sit up and take a drink. "Yes. Can I get out of bed now, Dr. Henry?"

"I suppose you may, but I happen to like you in my bed."

"I like it too, but it's no fun in here without you."

He grins and kisses the top of my head. "Let me prepare you some breakfast. Would you care for a bagel with cream cheese or some cream cheese on a bagel?"

"Hmm… I think I'll take the bagel with cream cheese."

"Good choice. Come into the kitchen after you get ready and I'll have it in the toaster waiting for you."

I didn't ask Lachlan what we were doing today, so I shower and then dress in denim shorts, a tank, and flip-flops.

I go into the kitchen and as promised, there's a bagel in the toaster. Lachlan sees me walk into the kitchen and pops it down.

"Now, that's what I call service." I walk over to where he's standing and put my arms around his waist. "Am I dressed okay?"

"For what?"

"For whatever we're doing today?"

He slips his arms around my waist and squeezes me. "I'm going to be busy the next few days. I thought we might hang out here and take it easy. Do you mind?"

"No. Not at all." But I know why he doesn't want to get out and about. He's concerned about what happened to me this morning. I'm fine, but I don't think I'll convince him of that. It's really too bad I'll be forced to lie around with him all day. Not.

CHAPTER TWENTY-FOUR

JACK MCLACHLAN

I SIT ON THE EDGE OF THE BED AND LOOK AT LAURELYN LYING ON HER stomach. I don't want to wake her, but I won't leave without saying goodbye.

I lean over and kiss the bare skin on her back and she stirs. I do it again and she makes a seductive moaning sound. It makes my dick twitch, but I don't have time to satisfy his needs this morning. I have to get on the road.

I kiss her shoulder. "Baby, I'm leaving."

She rolls over and smiles. "Don't go. Stay with me."

"I would if I had a choice, but I'd like to keep my job, so I have to go."

"Give me one minute." She hops up and I hear the water running in the bathroom. I'm sure she's brushing her teeth so she can give me a goodbye kiss I won't forget anytime soon.

She comes out, still naked, and pushes me back against the bed until I'm sitting. She climbs up and straddles me. She must love doing that. I know I do. "At least kiss me before you go."

Her lips touch mine and I know this isn't good for my dick. How am I going to get out of here without rolling her onto her back and burying myself in her?

I keep it short, but not because it's what I want. "Baby, I have to go."

"I know. Call me when you can."

I give her one last peck on the mouth. "I will. Daniel will be here around ten, but stay as long as you like."

I get in my car and start my drive to Lovedale so I can take care of the problems at Marguerite Vineyard. While I'm there, I have other business I need to tend. It's personal, and its name is Audrey Bagshaw.

I use voice command to call the one person I can trust with this issue. "Call Jim Callaghan."

There are several rings before he answers. "Callaghan Investigations."

"Jim, Jack McLachlan here." We politely greet each other, but we both know I'm not calling about his well-being, so I cut the shit. "I have a job for you. I understand it's short notice, but I need you to find someone for me fast."

"Of course, Mr. McLachlan. You know I'm always glad to help you in any way I can."

He means he is always willing to be paid a generous sum, but I don't mind his motive. He gets the fast results I like and always keeps the work he does for me on the down-low. "Perfect. Her name is Audrey Bagshaw and she lives in Lovedale. That's where I'll be for the next three days and I want to see her while I'm in town. There's an extra thousand in it for you if you can have her located for me by tonight."

I fill him in on the information I have and he gives me reassurance that I will be reunited with companion number three within the next twelve hours if he finds her still living in Lovedale.

It's late afternoon when I arrive at Marguerite, and everything appears to be business as usual, but I know this isn't the case at all. There is evil fuckery afoot here.

First, there was the attempt to burn the crops at Chalice and now someone has poisoned a section of Marguerite. The damage at both vineyards has been minimal, but the intent behind the act is what disturbs me. Is someone trying to ruin me or draw me away from Avalon?

My head man, Alfredo, greets me in the drive. He's a plump, round Italian with a talent for the vine that only rivals that of my father.

As we drive out to the area where the crop is stunted and crinkled, Alfredo briefs me on the problems. He stops the ATV in front of an injured vine and walks toward it. He takes the leaves in his hand. "I tell you, it's glyphosate poisoning, Mr. McLachlan."

I don't have to inspect any further because he's correct. I've seen it before. "You're right, Alfredo."

"We don't use glyphosate here. This was brought in and done on purpose."

"Yes, I agree."

"I don't know who would do it, Mr. McLachlan. None of the help has a grievance with you."

He appears nervous, as though I might blame him since he is overseer of the vineyard, but I know he's not responsible. "This wasn't your fault, Alfredo. It's sabotage, but I don't think it's by anyone at Marguerite. There's another party involved and I intend on finding out who it is and what they hope to accomplish."

He drives me around so we can inspect the damaged vines. It's a much larger area than I expected and I wonder if there's damage we don't see yet. By no means is it a ruined crop, but this is a serious attempt at ruining my livelihood. With this second sabotage, I'll be forced to put the other vineyards on alert. I'll need additional staff to watch and patrol all of them until harvest time. The extra staff through March will be a huge expense. The responsible party might not have accomplished what they set out to do, but they achieved plenty by targeting my pockets.

When I finish inspecting the fields, Alfredo takes me back to the house. It feels lonely. I don't have Daniel or Mrs. Porcelli with me this trip since I'm only staying a few days, but that's not who I'm missing. I've already become accustomed to having Laurelyn with me.

I couldn't ask her to come since I'm planning a visit with Audrey. Despite the terms regarding our relationship, I wouldn't expect her to respond well to being left at the house alone while I'm with a previous companion.

I haven't been to the Marguerite vineyard in months, so the house has been vacant and I find the kitchen empty. I don't see a point in a trip to the market since I don't have Mrs. Porcelli here to cook, so I'm reduced to eating out alone, which I despise.

Lovedale restaurants aren't formal, but I decide to change for dinner. All I find in the closet are trousers and dress shirts. No jeans or T-shirts. That's the problem with not having a permanent home. I never know what I need where.

I go to my favorite restaurant in Lovedale and I'm escorted toward the back of the restaurant. I'm seated at one of the tables I've shared with Audrey many times during our month-long relationship over three years ago. I'm scanning the wine selection when my phone rings. It's Jim. Perfect. I hope he has good news for me.

"Jack McLachlan."

"Mr. McLachlan, I'm calling you with some good news. It appears that Miss Bagshaw is still living in Lovedale. I have her current address and phone number. Would you like me to email those to you?"

"Email the address but call off her number to me now."

"55-7031-3210."

"Great work. You'll have your money, along with the extra thousand, in your account tonight."

"Thank you, Mr. McLachlan. As always, it's been a pleasure doing business with you."

Yes, it's been a five-thousand-dollar pleasure.

I immediately dial Audrey's number and it goes to voicemail. I was Drake Connelly to her three years ago, but she discovered my true identity so there's no reason in pretending to be anyone but myself. "Audrey, it's Jack McLachlan. I need to see you as soon as possible. Please, call me at this number."

I order a merlot and the lasagna and I'm finishing when my phone rings. I see Audrey's number and I'm happy she has returned my call so soon. Maybe she'll agree to meet me tonight. "Hello, Audrey."

"Hello, Jack. Long time, no see. How have you been?"

"I'm very good. And you?"

"I've been better, but I think you know that already."

"I want to see you."

"Oh, so now you want to see me. Am I supposed to come running because the great and all-mighty Jack McLachlan has changed his mind?"

I tell her huskily, "Don't be that way, Audrey."

She hesitates but we both already know she'll agree. "Okay. Where do you want to meet?"

"The usual place. I'll text you the room number."

"How long?"

I'm not far from the hotel, but I want to finish dinner. I'm not that anxious to see her. "An hour."

After I end the call, I flag my server. "I'll need another merlot." And then probably another for what I'm about to do.

Three glasses of wine later, I check into the Hotel Armand and text Audrey with the room number. I'm there less than ten minutes when I hear her knock on the door.

I open the door and she's wearing a black trench coat with extremely high heels. She has traded her long, fiery hair for a medium-length cut with blunt bangs. I hate it.

"Hello, Jack."

"Hello, Audrey." I open the door wider. "Please, come in."

"Thank you."

She grazes her finger across my chest as she walks through the door.

"Please, have a seat." I walk over to the wet bar. "Would you care for a drink? A bourbon, perhaps? Seems like I recall that being your favorite."

"You remember well."

I pour her drink and then take it to her where she is sitting on the bed. She holds it up to me. "A toast?"

"What should we toast to?"

"To reunions."

I sit next to her and tip the edge of my glass to hers. "To reunions."

We sip the bourbon and then she gets up and places her glass on the table. She unties the waist of her coat and opens it to reveal her naked body underneath. She walks over and stands between my knees. "I've missed you so much, Jack."

She leans forward to kiss me and I stop her by placing a finger over her lips. "I didn't ask you here for that."

She tries to climb onto the bed to straddle me and I catch her by her waist. "I can change your mind, Jack. You know I can."

"No. I'm afraid you can't."

She drops to her knees in front of me and reaches for my belt buckle. "You know what I can do for you and you love it. I know you remember how much you love being in my mouth."

I try to push her hand away, but her grip is like steel. "No, Audrey. There's someone else."

She immediately stops, but her grip doesn't loosen. She's angry. I see it in her eyes. "There will never be anyone else for you but me. I'm the only one who knows you, Jack." She puts emphasis on my name as she says it.

"You might know who I am, but you'll never be the one for me."

"This new woman doesn't know your name. She's just another no one to you. You don't owe her monogamy." Again, she's fumbling with my belt. "I'm right, aren't I? She's no one special. Just another one of your fake relationships."

I've had more than enough of this and there's only one way to make her stop this nonsense. "Quit, Audrey." I lean forward until we're eye to eye. She thinks I'm going to kiss her, but she's dead wrong. "I know you started the fire at Chalice. I also know you poisoned Marguerite and I'm here to give you the courtesy of a warning. Don't fuck with me, Audrey."

She sits back on her heels. "Jack…"

"I don't want to hear it. I came here to let you know I'm on to you. Now I've done that, so put your coat back on and get the fuck out of my sight. I never want to see you again."

She grabs her coat from the floor and cinches the belt. "You're going to regret what you've done to me."

"I already do."

◌◌◌

AFTER I LEAVE THE HOTEL AND I'M CLOSED UP IN MY CAR WITH HER SCENT, the only thing I can smell is that damn sweet, floral fragrance. It's on my skin and clothes and I despise it. I can't believe I ever thought it was pleasant, let alone appealing. It's nauseating and I want it gone. Now.

As soon as I'm back at the vineyard, I forgo calling Laurelyn and head straight to the shower. I have to wash away the last bit of physical contact I hope to ever have with that crazy bitch.

I hear Laurelyn's ringtone, "Crash Into Me", as I stand in the shower scrubbing my skin, but she'll have to wait until I erase the last evidence of Audrey's touch from my body.

I listen to Laurelyn's voicemail as soon as I'm out, not even waiting until I'm dressed. "Hey, caveman. I just wanted to tell you something before I went to bed. Call me back when you get a chance."

I walk toward the bedroom wearing only a towel and call her immediately. I don't want to wait another minute to hear her voice. "Hello."

"Hey, baby."

The tone in her voice elevates. "Hey, you. I'm glad you called. Normally, I'm not all that excited about this and needing to share it with anyone, but you wanted to know, so I'm calling to tell you I got my period."

Hmm. I'd forgotten about it, so I guess I wasn't as worried as I thought. "That's good to know."

"I thought you'd like that. Have you been very busy today?"

What's kept me busy while I've been here disgusts me. "I've been busier than I wanted to be, but I've still thought of you."

"That's a sweet thing to say. Everything okay at the vineyard?"

I fully expect it to be now that I've told Audrey I'm onto her little game. "There are some definite issues at Marguerite, but I think I'll have them under control soon."

"So, they just needed the big man to come along and take care of things. Show them how it's done, right?"

Yes, the big man is on campus. She has no idea how big the big man really is. "You've got it, babe."

"Will you still be staying until New Year's Day?"

I don't want to, but it's necessary. I wish I could be back to celebrate with Laurelyn. "I'm afraid I have to. Will you be making plans with Addison for New Year's Eve?"

"She's going to The Blues Club with Zac and they've invited me to go. It's open mic night again."

I'm certain that means Ben Donavon is going too and will probably consider Laurelyn his date, but I don't ask because I don't want the confirmation.

"You'll have a great time. I wish I could be there to hear you sing."

"I'll dedicate one to you."

"Well, that's hardly fair. I won't be there to hear it."

"Yes, that's very unfortunate."

I miss her. "What are you wearing?"

"Do you want the truth, or shall I describe some terribly sexy lingerie so you can fantasize?"

I can't help it. I want to know what she's wearing while Ben Donavon is sleeping only a few feet from her. I need to know what he'll see if they run into each other on the way to the bathroom. "The truth."

"I'm wearing an incredibly unsexy T-shirt and boxer shorts."

I've seen her definition of unsexy and I couldn't agree less. One of her sexiest moments was when she was wearing jogging pants and had her hair piled in a messy bun on top of her head. "Baby, you couldn't be unsexy if you tried."

"Lachlan. You're wrong, but I thank you anyway."

"You've felt all right today? No more headaches or vomiting?"

"I've felt really good today."

She scared the shit out of me. "I was worried yesterday."

"I'm sorry I worried you, but really... I'm fine."

Is she really okay? "You'd tell me if you weren't?"

"Yes."

"It's late and I should probably let you get to sleep. It's not a bad idea for me to catch up on my slumber since someone has been keeping me up late at night."

"Well, you might find it easier to get a little sleep if you weren't insti-gating late-night activities."

"You don't like my instigating?"

"I didn't say that."

"So, you like it?"

"Very much, Mr. Henry. I like your late-night instigations. And your morning ones. And your midday ones. Hell, I like all of your instigating."

"I'll remember that next time I see you."

"Yes, be sure you do. Now, get some sleep, Mr. Henry. You have a lot of instigating to do when you return."

"Yes, ma'am, I do."

CHAPTER TWENTY-FIVE
LAURELYN PRESCOTT

I'M APPLYING MY MAKEUP TO GO OUT FOR NEW YEAR'S EVE AND I'M TOTALLY bummed. I thought bringing in the new year in Australia would be some kind of spectacular experience, but it won't be because Lachlan isn't here to celebrate with me. And he won't be here to kiss me at midnight.

I'm smoking up my eyes with black liner while Addison is in the shower talking nonstop about Zac. I really want to tell her to shut up. I know I'm being completely selfish, but if I can't be with Lachlan, I don't want to hear about all the things she's going to do to rock Zac's world tonight.

Enough is enough. "I'm going to the bedroom to get dressed."

"Okay. I'll be out in a minute."

"Take your time." I'm wrapped in a towel as I peek out the door to be sure Ben isn't around before I streak to the bedroom. After I see that the coast is clear, I make a break for it. I'm not four steps down the hall when I run right smack into him. Literally.

I look up as I grasp my towel tightly. Being so close to him while wearing so little feels wrong. Really wrong. "Excuse me."

He doesn't make a move or say a word as his eyes roam my body. I dart around him and run for the bedroom door, slamming it behind me. Shit. That was more than just a little unpleasant.

I stand in front of the closet searching through what has now become community property. There's no mine or yours. I pull out a black strapless with a wide red waist sash and hold it up to myself as I look in the mirror. It's Addison's so of course it's going to be short on me, but I like it. It's sexy as hell. I don't know why I care. I have no one to impress.

I'm standing in front of the mirror with the dress when Addison comes into the bedroom. "Nice choice."

"You weren't going to wear it, were you?"

"No, I'm wearing the electric blue one."

I put on the dress and Addison zips it for me. It's tight but it squeezes me in all the right places. It's a sexy dress and I'm hot in it, but instead of being proud of the way I look, I'm disappointed Lachlan isn't here to see me. Maybe I'll text pictures of myself to show him what he's missing.

When we're finished getting ready, we go into the living room where Zac and Ben are ready and waiting. Zac is up and at Addison's side immediately, telling her how beautiful she is. Ben is staring at me and I begin to feel really uncomfortable. Even more so than I did when we met in the hallway. Somehow I feel more naked than I did when I was wearing only a towel.

I wish things weren't like this between Ben and me. I wish we could talk and laugh like friends instead of constantly being swallowed up by all of this uneasiness.

The four of us leave the apartment building and catch a cab to the club so everyone can drink. I'm sure to take the seat in the front so I'm not stuck sitting with Ben in the back. Maybe it's childish, but I don't care. He doesn't need the least bit of encouragement.

Ben holds the door for me as we walk into the club. As I walk past him, he leans close to me. "You're exceptionally beautiful tonight, Laurelyn."

It's sweet the way he says it. I don't know. Maybe I would've been interested in him if there had been no Lachlan. But there is a Lachlan. And he's the only one I want. "Thank you, Ben. You're very handsome tonight. Every girl in the place is going to swoon over you."

"Except the one I want."

Shit. Why'd he have to call out the pink elephant in the room?

I say nothing and walk to the table Zac and Addison have chosen close to the stage. Of course, they're sitting together so that means Ben and I must sit together.

Since it's New Year's Eve, I'm guessing there's going to be some real entertainment. Open mic has already started and there's a woman doing an Adele song on the karaoke machine. She's mimicking every note like Adele—I imagine she's been singing in the mirror all week to get ready for her big performance.

"There's a sign-up sheet if you want to sing. You might want to go ahead and put your name down. I'm sure the list is long since it's a big night."

I grab Addison by the hand and pull her from her chair. "Come on. You didn't sing last time and you were the one chanting the loudest for me to get up on stage."

Ben is right—the list is very long. Addison and I sign up, but I'll be surprised if we're called before midnight. I'll probably be too drunk to remember how to sing.

Our waitress places a Sauvignon Blanc in front of me. I ordered it because it's one of the wines I've come to enjoy since meeting Lachlan. I take a drink and I'm surprised how a glass of wine can make me feel closer to him, even when he's seven hours away.

One after another, people take the stage. Some are decent while many are a disaster, but it's all for fun and I think everyone in the club claps louder for the ones who suck. It's called a pity clap.

About fifteen minutes before midnight, Addison is called to the stage, which means I'm next. She's pretty drunk and I'm just hoping for her sake that she doesn't screw this up.

She takes the guitar from its stand and sits on the stool before she puts the strap over her neck. She strums several times and I get a glimpse of how I must've looked on stage, minus the drunk part.

She begins to sing "You Were Meant for Me" by Jewel, and I'm not sure if it's because she's trying to send a not-so-subtle message to Zac or because it's a song she felt certain she could pull off drunk. Regardless, Zac doesn't take his eyes off her and I'm envious.

She finishes and the crowd claps wildly. As they should. She gave a great performance.

I'm called to the stage next and I take my place at the piano this time.

There's no damn way I'd sing this song if Lachlan were here, but he's not and it's my own little private joke with myself.

I lean into the mic and address the crowd because I can't help it. I'm an entertainer. It's in my blood. It's what I do.

"Everybody ready to bring in the New Year?" The crowd responds loudly, letting me know they're having a right nice time. "I toyed with this song on a piano the other day and decided I'd do my own rendition. I sort of liked the way it sounded." I play a few notes as I speak to the crowd. "Hell, I loved the way it sounded, but I'm going to let you guys tell me what you think. This is 'Private Dancer' by the lovely Tina Turner."

Chills come over me as I lean toward the mic and begin to sing about men very similar to the one I met in this bar not so long ago. I close my eyes because I don't want to see the crowd. I want to think of the private dance I did for Lachlan.

I forget I'm in front of a crowd and become lost in the lyrics. When I'm finished singing, I return from the place I've been. I come off stage and they announce that the countdown is only three minutes away.

Geez, I hope Ben doesn't try to lay one on me. What would I do about that?

I prop my chin in my hand and wish for the millionth time I were with Lachlan when my phone vibrates on the table and lights up with a new text message. I smile when I see it's from Lachlan. He's probably wishing me a Happy New Year.

Yes. I'd like 2 CU do the shimmy again.

He heard me sing 'Private Dancer?' That means he's here. My head pops up and I begin my search in the sea of faces. When I don't find him in the crowd, I text him. I'm afraid I won't find him in time for the countdown.

Where RU?

A moment later I feel his hands around my waist and his mouth against my ear. "Right here."

I spin around and look at him in disbelief. "I thought you wouldn't be back until tomorrow?"

"I busted my ass to get everything done and left Lovedale this afternoon so we could be together for the countdown. I didn't want anyone else kissing you at midnight."

I know how that translates. He doesn't want Ben to kiss me, but what Lachlan doesn't realize is that there would've been no New Year's kiss for me if it didn't come from him.

"Five. Four. Three. Two. One!"

He takes my face in his hands and kisses me hard as "Auld Lang Syne" plays loudly. When he lets me go, he pulls back so he can see my eyes.

"Come home with me."

CHAPTER TWENTY-SIX
JACK MCLACHLAN

WE DRIVE TO THE APARTMENT AND I SIT IN THE CAR WHILE LAURELYN GOES inside to pack a bag. While I'm waiting for her to return, a cab stops at the curb and Ben gets out. He stumbles as he makes his way to the building. He appears drunk. I want to go up to the apartment as I watch him, but I don't because Laurelyn should be on her way down any second. And I'm sure I won't get along with drunk Ben any better than I do with sober Ben.

She doesn't come down but I wait a little longer and then something doesn't feel right. To hell with this. I want to know what's taking her so long, so I get out and stalk toward the building. I press the buzzer and get no answer, so I press it again and then hear Laurelyn's voice.

"I'm almost finished. Be right down." I hear Ben shout something in the background, but I can't make out what it is.

"Buzz me in, Laurelyn. Now."

I hear the latch on the door release and I don't wait for the elevator. I take the stairs two at a time until I reach the third-floor apartment. I pound on the door and as soon as Laurelyn opens it, I can see she's been crying. I glance at him and then back to her. "What did he do to you?"

"Nothing." She won't look at me and it's because something happened. And it's something that's going to piss me off.

"Tell me what the hell he did to you, Laurelyn!"

She picks up her bag. "Can we just go, please?"

I don't feel like going. He did something to her and I'm going to find out what. I step inside the apartment toward Ben. "What the hell did you do?"

Laurelyn steps in front of me, between Ben and me. She can see where this is going. She puts her hands on my chest and shakes her head while she pleads, "Please don't, Lachlan. He's my best friend's brother. I don't want this to become a problem between me and Addison."

I reach for her bag on the floor as I glare at Ben. I'm going to find out what you did.

We leave the apartment and I say nothing until we're in my car and I can't stand it any longer. I have to know. "Tell me, Laurelyn."

Her head is lowered and she's staring at her hands in her lap. "I don't want to talk about it."

"I'm not moving this car until you tell me what he did."

It's dark, but the spill from the streetlights shines on her face and I see that she's crying. "I really just want to get out of here."

She's not going to tell me anything while we're here. She knows I'll go up there and beat the shit out of him if he hurt her. I start the car and pull away. When we're on the highway, I reach for her hand and bring it to my lips.

She sighs deeply. "He came into my room and saw me packing. He knew I was going to stay with you, so he asked me not to leave. When I told him I was going with you, he grabbed me and started kissing me. I pushed him away and he told me I was nothing more than a whore to you."

There's only one word to describe the feeling raging inside me: fury.

I'm glad she didn't tell me while we were there because I would have flown into a blind rage. I wasn't entirely sure I wasn't going to turn around and go back to kick his ass. "You're not staying with him anymore."

"Lachlan, don't be ridiculous. I have to."

"No, you don't. I'll get you your own apartment."

She's shaking her head. "No, Lachlan. I can't let you do that."

"Then the only other option is for you to stay with me at the vineyard because you're not going back to stay with him." I'm watching the road, but that doesn't keep me from feeling her watch me in the dark. "Packing every few days is getting old anyway, right? And you never have all the things you need."

"Won't you have to go out of town sometimes? Where will I stay when you're gone?"

"You can stay at the vineyard without me. Mrs. Porcelli would probably like the company and Daniel can drive you if you need to go anywhere. I don't know. Maybe you'll come with me on some of my trips."

Is she considering it? "Baby, I don't want you there with him anymore," I add.

"Addison will be upset with me if I move out."

"I think she'd be more upset if something happened between you and her brother and it ruined your friendship," I counter. "Besides, she stays with Zac most nights, doesn't she?"

"That's true," she agrees.

"Tell me you will."

She hesitates before answering. "Okay, I will."

I bring her hand to my lips again and kiss it. "We'll go back for your things in a day or two after I cool down. There's no way I can be near that little fucker right now without killing him."

Okay. It's a done deal; Laurelyn is moving in with me for the next ten weeks. This isn't something I've done before. Hell, I'd never allowed any of my companions to visit one of my houses or vineyards. I couldn't chance the connection afterwards, but it doesn't matter if Laurelyn makes the connection. She will be nine thousand miles away once we're over so it doesn't matter.

She's being unusually quiet and I'm worried about the things spinning through her head. I hope she isn't putting any merit into Ben telling her I think of her as my whore.

I give her hand a little squeeze where it rests on my thigh. "Ben is wrong. You're not a whore to me."

"How am I not? Didn't I agree to a sexual relationship with a man I didn't know in exchange for the time of my life? That's as good as being paid for sex."

"Laurelyn, we are two consenting adults. We have great sex, but I don't pay you for it. We have a great time together because we're friends. We enjoy spending time together and it has absolutely nothing to do with sex. Got it?"

"Yeah."

She doesn't sound convinced but the doubt Ben placed in her mind is fresh. She'll need time to forget about his cruel words. For now, I choose to say nothing else about it and instead change the topic. "Yanks have New Year's traditions, right?"

"Yes. There's a southern tradition of eating black-eyed peas and ham hocks on New Year's Day. It's supposed to bring you luck throughout the year."

"Should I have Mrs. Porcelli cook that for you today?"

She's laughing now. "No, I don't eat ham hock, whatever that is, so that won't be necessary."

At some point in the drive, she becomes quiet and I think she has Ben's accusation on her mind again until I realize her hand has relaxed. She's fallen asleep. I pull into the garage and park, but take a moment to watch her sleeping. As I brush her hair from her face, she reminds me of a sleeping angel and I can't understand how that bastard could hurt her by saying such horrible things.

I brush my fingers against her cheek. "Laurelyn, we're home." She stirs a little and I think about how that came out all wrong. "We're at the vineyard."

She doesn't wake so I get out and go around to her side of the car. I scoop her out to carry her to bed. I take a few steps toward the door and she tries to focus on me with exhausted eyes. "What are you doing?"

"I'm carrying you to bed."

"I haven't been carried to bed since I was three."

"Now you can say you haven't been carried to bed since you were twenty-two."

I place her on what I have come to think of as her side of the bed. She seems to have gone back to sleep already. I note the cocktail dress she's wearing and I'm certain she doesn't want to sleep in it, so I pull a T-shirt out of my drawer for her.

I slip off one of her shoes and she inhales heavily as I remove the second one. "Thank you, Lachlan."

I place her shoes on the floor next to the footboard. "I don't mind."

Her eyes are closed as she says, "No, I don't mean for carrying me to bed. I mean for everything. You treat me like I'm somebody instead of a nobody."

She's showing me a new side of herself. It's childlike and damaged. I know in my gut that this moment has nothing to do with anything Ben said. She carries an old scar and it causes her deep pain.

I brush my fingers down her cheek. "You're such a special person. You should always be treated like somebody."

She reaches for my hand and holds it against her face, but doesn't say anything. I want to tell her how her heart belongs to someone she's yet to meet and she'll be loved and adored by one bloody lucky man someday. She'll have his babies just like she told me she wanted to do and he'll love her in a way like she's never known.

But I can't tell her these things. And I don't know why.

CHAPTER TWENTY-SEVEN
LAURELYN PRESCOTT

I open my eyes and I'm alone. Waking in Lachlan's bed without him has become a routine morning for me since I haven't been spending many nights at Ben's. And then it hits me. I remember what happened with my host and why I won't be staying with him anymore.

I dread telling Addison because I don't know what I'm going to say. I find my purse and overnight bag in the chair in the corner of the room and I take my phone out to call her. I might as well get it over with.

I see a missed text from Addison at three in the morning.

RU w/ L?

There's really no reason in worrying about what to say. I'll just tell her what happened and that I can't stay there anymore. It's that simple.

She answers on the first ring. "Call back when I'm not hungover and ready to hurl."

She must have drunk a lot more after I left. "Rough night?"

"No. Rough morning. You don't sound too bad."

"I'm not." I stopped drinking after Lachlan came to the club.

"You disappeared on us last night. I guess you went home with lover boy."

It's just like her to not remember. "I told you I was leaving with him. Your drunk ass just doesn't remember it."

"Oh."

Here goes nothing. "I need to talk you about something that happened last night."

"Is everything okay?"

It definitely isn't okay. "No, it's not. Are you at Ben's or Zac's?"

"Zac's."

Good. At least she finally had the guts to stay all night. "Ben and I had an incident last night. He came into our room while I was packing a bag to take to Lachlan's. He asked me to stay with him instead of leaving. I told him no and he tried to kiss me. When I pushed him away, he called me a whore."

"Oh, Laurelyn. Ben was really drunk last night. I'm sure he regrets the whole thing this morning."

She's his sister, but I didn't expect her to take his side so completely. "He may, but I can't live with someone who calls me a whore. We're coming for my things and I'm going to stay with Lachlan."

"You mean until this blows over."

"No, he's asked me to stay with him until we go home, and I've decided I'm going to. I'll make arrangements to come to the apartment for my things in a couple of days."

"But you don't know him."

"Addison, I know him as well as you know Zac. There's no difference." That wasn't entirely true, but I felt like I knew most of the important things, even if it didn't include his name.

"Fair point well made, I guess." Good. I didn't feel like arguing with her over this.

"Lachlan works long days, so call me next week when Zac is busy and we'll get together. Maybe we'll go shopping."

"Okay."

I hang up and think of how differently our stay in Australia is from what I imagined. Addison and I haven't been apart for more than a day in four years, and now our time together is barely existent. I could tell she didn't care much for me staying with Lachlan, but she'd get over it. She was spending as much time as she could with Zac and that meant I was going to be stuck alone with Ben, so I didn't feel a bit guilty about leaving to be with Lachlan.

I'm still wearing Lachlan's T-shirt, which barely covers my panties, when I leave the bedroom in search of him. I go into the kitchen first and find the open refrigerator door. I slip over to him with the agility of a lioness and wait for him to close it so I can surprise him, but when the door swings shut, it's me who gets the shock.

I'm standing face to face with a woman, not Lachlan.

She smiles at me while diverting her eyes away from my bare legs. "Miss Beckett?"

I reach for the bottom of the T-shirt and pull it lower on my legs, as if it's somehow going to cover my bareness. "Yes."

I tug harder on the shirt and realize I'm stretching it to the point of almost ripping. "I'm Mrs. Porcelli. It's very nice to meet you. May I cook you something for brekkie? Do you like omelets?"

Oh, shit, I'm mortified. I completely forgot that Mrs. Porcelli would be here today. Now, here I stand to greet her wearing my panties and Lachlan's T-shirt, which I'm sure she recognizes since she does his laundry.

"Umm, yes. Thank you. If you'll excuse me, I'll be back in just a moment."

"Of course, dear."

I pull the shirt over my panties as I streak toward the bedroom. Once inside, I shut the door and lean against it. I put my finger gun to my head and pull the trigger. "I can't believe I did that."

I'm bent over rummaging through my bag when I'm startled by hands creeping around my waist and warm breath on the back of my neck. I let out a panicked screech and spin around to give Lachlan a slap across his chest. "Don't sneak up like that. You scared the shit out of me."

He thinks it's hilarious. "Sorry. I promise that scaring you wasn't what I was going for. I had something much more like this on my mind."

He brings his lips to mine and I forget my disgruntlement with him. I feel one of his hands slide inside my panties over my bottom. "Oh, no you don't, Mr. Henry."

"Why not?"

"I just met Mrs. Porcelli, while wearing this, I might add, and now she's cooking breakfast for me. It'll be rude, not to mention awkward, if I don't go back out there to eat what she's cooking for me."

He slides his other hand inside my shirt until he reaches my breast and flicks his thumb over my nipple until it's hard. He lowers his mouth to my ear. "She'll never know, babe. I'll be quick."

"Yeah, but I'll know and then she'll see it all over my face."

"No, she won't. You're making too much of it." He moves his hand from the back of my panties to the front.

"She's already going to know that I'm the latest one."

"The latest what?"

"Companion or whatever she calls us." Maybe whore.

"No, she won't."

He's confusing me and it has nothing to do with his hand in my panties turning my brain to mush. "How could she not?"

"She doesn't know about the others. She's going to think you're my girlfriend."

How can she not know about the others if she goes everywhere with him? "I don't understand."

"The others never came to the vineyards, so you're the first one she's seen."

Well, this is a revelation. "Where did you take the others?"

"Hotels."

I'm surprised by this news. And puzzled. Why am I allowed into his private world when none of the others have been?

I don't have much time to absorb what he's told me because I feel his hands on my hips pushing my panties down. "I'll be a minuteman. Promise."

I give into him like I always do and step out of my panties before letting him guide me toward the unmade bed. I fall back and he reaches into the nightstand drawer. I hear those familiar sounds before he grabs my ankles to yank me to the edge of the bed where he's standing. "Put your legs around me."

I do as he says and then he's inside me. "This is going to be quick, but only because it's the way you want it."

He wasn't kidding. He's slamming into me fast and hard. He grasps my thighs tightly to keep from propelling me to the other side of the bed. In one quick motion, I bring my legs from his waist to his shoulders and it does him in. He thrusts deeply one last time and I hear him call my name. "Oh, Laurelyn."

I love the way he says my name when he comes.

My ankles are still hooked over his shoulders and he's smiling down at me. He kisses the inside of my leg before he helps me to stand. "I'm going out to check the grafts while you have brekkie. I'll be gone a couple of hours and then we'll have the rest of the day to do anything you want."

I'm guessing his vacation from work will be over tomorrow, so I want to take advantage of our last free day together. "Can we hang out by the pool and swim?"

"Anything you want, baby."

He grabs my panties from the floor and holds them out for me. He kisses the inside of my thigh as I step into them. My hands are on his shoulders for balance as he pulls them up my legs and I can't resist commenting on it. "You put my panties back on almost as much as you take them off."

He pats my bottom when they're in place. "I guess I do. Now, get dressed and go enjoy your brekkie. I'll see you in a couple of hours."

I'll have to shower after breakfast, so I pull my hair into a ponytail and quickly slip into shorts and a T-shirt of my own. The aroma coming from the kitchen is heavenly and I enter just as Mrs. Porcelli is plating a scrumptious-looking omelet. "Smells delicious."

"Thank you. May I pour you some coffee?"

"I'm not much of a coffee drinker. I'll have juice, but I can get it. You've already done so much."

"I'm happy to get it for you, dear." I don't argue and take my seat at the bar where my omelet awaits. She places a tall glass of orange juice in front of me and I feel uneasy about allowing her to serve me.

"Thank you."

I begin to eat while she cleans the mess from preparing my breakfast.

This makes me feel even guiltier. "I can do that when I'm finished eating."

"Miss Beckett, relax and enjoy your omelet."

Miss Beckett isn't my name. "Okay, but will you please call me Laurelyn?"

"Okay, Laurelyn."

"How long have you worked for…?" Oh, shit. I don't know his name. At least not the one Mrs. Porcelli would use.

"I call him Mr. McLachlan, dear. He's my employer and although I'm old enough to be his mother, I wouldn't feel right calling him by his first name."

McLachlan. I laugh to myself because it appears as though we had the same idea when we chose our aliases. I have to wonder. Is this a slip-up in his carefully orchestrated plan or is he relaxing his unbending relationship rules?

Surely, he considered this possibility. He must've known Mrs. Porcelli would say his name in front of me at some point since I'm staying here full-time.

I decide I won't mention the discovery of my newfound information about Mr. McLachlan. Learning his last name changes nothing for us. I won't try to find him once I leave Australia. There's no reason to worry him, so let him continue to believe he still holds this secret from me.

CHAPTER TWENTY-EIGHT
JACK MCLACHLAN

Spending the day with Laurelyn stretched out on a lounge chair by the pool is a perfect way to spend New Year's Day. The view is mighty fine with her barely there black bikini, but I worry her skin isn't prepared for the harsh Australian sun.

"You should put on sunscreen so you don't sunbake too much."

She rises on her elbows and peers over her sunnies at me. "I thought I might get a little sun before I put it on."

"I'm afraid it'll sneak up on you."

"I guess you would know better than I do."

She sits up and grabs the bottle of SPF 70 from the table and begins to massage it into her skin. "This is a new one for me. I've never been swimming on New Year's Day."

"I guess lots of things seem backwards to you."

I can't see her eyes through her sunnies, but she smiles and I wonder what she's thinking. "Yeah, a few things." She holds the bottle out in my direction. "Would you do my back for me?"

I cover her in a generous application. When I finish, I return to thumbing through the summer issue of the Winery and Vineyard Journal. I find the article I wrote on vine grafting and I'm in the middle of it when Laurelyn asks, "Whatcha reading?"

"Nothing in particular."

"So, you're working even when you're not working."

I'm sure it appears that way to her. "I guess so."

I place the magazine on the table and she reaches for it. "Maybe I should read this so I can understand more about what you do."

"Winemaking interests you?"

"Not really, but you interest me."

She thumbs through the magazine and I see her stop on my article. I panic as I pray she doesn't recognize me in the photograph. "I'm getting into the pool. Why don't you join me? You can read all the exciting articles on winemaking later."

"Vine grafting." She glances at me. "Is this the same process you're doing here at Avalon?"

I get up to take the journal and place it on the table. "It is, and you can read all about the thrilling adventures in grafting later. It's hot. Come into the pool with me to cool off."

She has no idea how close she is to figuring me out, so I tug on her hands. "Come on."

She shakes her head and gets up from the lounger. "You always get your way, don't you?"

Laurelyn follows me into the pool. She takes her hair out of the bun and tosses the elastic band to the sidewalk before she dips her head backwards. She lifts her head out of the pool and pushes the water away from her face.

She's a magnet and I'm metal. I can't resist the pull between us so I move closer and put my hands around her waist. She puts her arms around my shoulders and wraps her legs around me, but not in a sexual way. She's being playful.

"So, Mrs. Porcelli and Daniel travel with you when you're stationed at different vineyards?"

Stationed. That's a good word to describe the way I travel with work. "They come with me anytime I stay more than a week, and I try to give them several days to be home with their families before we leave again."

"What do you think Mrs. Porcelli thinks of you never bringing a woman home?"

I laugh as I picture Laurelyn prancing into the kitchen in nothing but her panties and my T-shirt. "She probably thought I was gay until you showed up in the kitchen barely wearing enough to cover this." I glide my hands over the bottom of her bikini.

"It's not funny, Lachlan." She pretends to be mad but can't quite pull it off—not with the underlying grin trying to break through.

"I'm very sorry you were embarrassed, but I did tell you she would be here today."

"I know, but it slipped my mind because it's only been the two of us in the house since my first night with you."

I like the full-time privacy when we're the only ones here. Perhaps I should give Daniel and Mrs. Porcelli some additional vacation during our stay at Avalon.

I haven't explained my employees' routines to Laurelyn. "None of the staff is in the house before eight or after five unless asked to be."

"Oh. They don't sleep in the house?"

"No, they have their own quarters in the guest house. They need their privacy as well."

I see the relief on her face. "Of course they do."

Mrs. Porcelli comes out of the house carrying a serving tray with two plates. "I thought you might be hungry, so I brought some sangers and fruit."

"Thank you, Mrs. Porcelli. We'll have lunch at the patio table." She leaves the food and returns inside the house. "Are you hungry?"

Laurelyn winks at me. "I had a late breakfast, but I could eat again."

"You always have brekkie late, sleepyhead." She retaliates by splashing water in my face. I lift my hand and make a production of wiping the water from my eyes. Laurelyn lets go of me and begins backing away because she knows what's coming. "Oh, you asked for this. There's no backing out now."

I catch her by the arm and pull her to me. I lock my arms around hers, holding them by her side as I prepare to dunk her.

"Please, don't," she screams and I hear hysteria in her voice.

I release my grip so I'm able to turn her around. I'm shocked by the pure terror I see in her eyes. "What's wrong, Laurelyn?"

She drops her face. "Nothing." She pushes away, so I let her go. She gets out of the pool and wraps a towel around her body before sitting at the table where lunch is waiting.

I get out to join her, but I'm not sure if I'm welcome. Her eyes continue to avoid mine and it's because something isn't right with her. "Lunch looks good."

"Uh-huh." That's all I get.

I begin to eat while she ignores the food on her plate. "Mrs. P. will think you don't like her food if you don't eat something." This isn't my happy, carefree Laurelyn in front of me. This one is guarded and withdrawn. I want the other one back. "I didn't mean to upset you."

She has a distant look on her face and I wonder where her mind has taken her. It certainly isn't here with me. "My mom was an addict when I was a kid. She was addicted to prescription drugs—painkillers, sedatives, whatever she could get her hands on. When I was eight, I found her passed out and submerged in the bathtub. I tried to pull her out, but she was too heavy. Every time I'd get her face above the water, she'd take a breath and then slip from my grasp. She pulled me into the tub under her and I was drowning. I still remember what it felt like to be held under that water knowing I was about to die."

"How did you not drown?"

"I had pulled the plug in the drain as soon as I found her. It took a while, but the water drained low enough for me to breathe."

"What happened to your mum?"

"Almost killing both of us was her wake-up call. She got clean and has been for almost fifteen years." I would hope so if her addiction almost killed her and her eight-year-old daughter.

She's watching my face. "I've never told anyone that."

How could she not tell anyone? "What do you mean?"

"It's been our secret all of these years. You're the only person who knows."

"Both of you almost died. That's not the kind of thing you keep secret."

She pulls the towel tighter around her shoulders. "I learned to keep secrets at a very early age, Lachlan. I would've been taken away from her if I had told."

"Maybe you should have been taken from her."

"We survived and she went to rehab that night. I stayed with my grandparents while she got clean and I was there for her when she came home."

She was only a child. Her mother should've been the one there for her, not the other way around. No one protected her and she was robbed of her childhood. She says she learned to keep secrets at a very early age, so I have to wonder what else she's hiding.

CHAPTER TWENTY-NINE
LAURELYN PRESCOTT

I SEE THE LOOK IN LACHLAN'S EYES AND I KNOW WHAT HE'S THINKING—MY mother is sorry and lowdown. And there have been times when she has been; she isn't perfect. If I'm honest, she has been a shitty mother, but she's the only parent I have. At least she's been there—that's more than I can say for the sperm donor.

Maybe I should regret telling him this secret I've kept for fifteen years, but I don't. I feel a burden lift from my heart and soul. Only one word describes what I'm experiencing: peace.

Lachlan's squatting in front of me, his hands on my knees. I slide to the edge of my seat and he wraps his arms around me. It's in this moment that I realize something—I can tell Lachlan anything. There is no pretense of perfection between us. I don't need him to believe I have it all together when I don't. "That felt so damn good."

"What did?"

I'm almost giddy by my epiphany. "Telling you what happened with my mom and finally admitting what a shitty job she did as a parent before she got clean. I had no idea how great it would feel to finally tell someone."

"I think that's why therapy is so highly recommended."

There he goes with the medical advice again. "Yes, Dr. Henry. I believe you could be right on this account."

"I'm always right on every account."

We go back into the pool after we finish eating and I can tell that Lachlan is nervous. I assure him I'm fine, but he won't venture past the steps, and we sit staggered in the water with me between his legs. The dam holding all my secrets is breached and I tell him things I thought I would take to my grave.

Lachlan listens and says little. I'm not sure if it's because he doesn't know how to respond or if he's too disturbed by what he's hearing. It doesn't matter because reaction isn't what I need. Listening is, and it's one of the things he does very well.

By the time I finish telling Lachlan my childhood tales, the water has shriveled us like little old people. I hold my hand up to examine it. "I think this is a sign that it's past time to get out."

"I think you're right."

Once we're dried off, I wrap my towel around my waist. As I'm tucking it, I see Lachlan studying me. "What?"

He drops his head to peer over his sunglasses at me. "I hope you haven't caught too much sun today. You're a wee bit red."

I look at my shoulder and pull the strap of my bikini to the side. I hear Lachlan suck air through his teeth. "Damn, Laurelyn. I'm afraid that's going to sting tonight."

Lachlan is not the least bit pink, so I move the top of my bikini down for an inspection. It doesn't hurt or appear burned to me, but I won't be able to tell anything until we're out of the sun.

We stop in the kitchen to drop off our lunch plates and Mrs. Porcelli's eyes grow large when she sees me. "Oh, Laurelyn dear. There's an aloe vera aftersun lotion in the medicine cabinet when you're ready for it. There's lidocaine in it and it should help with the pain."

Oh, shit. What have I done?

We go into the bathroom together and I slip off my towel. Things aren't so bad when I remove my bikini top. Sure, there's a distinct contrast between my freshly sun-kissed skin and the white lines of my swimsuit, but it's not terrible.

He's standing behind me surveying the damage. "I'm so sorry. I should've noticed when you started burning."

"Don't worry. I don't stay pink for long." He looks doubtful as he assesses my shoulders. "Really, Lachlan. You'll see. This will be on its way to turning brown by morning."

"In the meantime, why don't you take a cool shower? That should help, and I'll rub you down with lotion when you're out."

A rubdown by Lachlan? Being sunburned is sounding better and better. "That sounds perfect."

He's right. The cool shower feels really nice. I notice my shoulders are a little tender to the water pelting down on them, but it's nothing too uncomfortable.

When I'm finished showering, I pat my skin dry and step out to find Lachlan waiting for me with a bottle of aloe vera lotion. He holds it up and gives it a shake as he grins. "Do you want me to do it in here with you standing, or would you rather I do it with you lying on the bed?"

Hmm, that sounds dirty. "I don't know. Both options sound appealing."

"I vote for the bed."

"Then, the bed it is."

"Here. Mrs. Porcelli sent these for you." He holds out two pills in the palm of his hand. "It's only ibuprofen to help with the discomfort."

"But it doesn't hurt."

"It will, so please take the medicine. I don't want you to be in pain."

I take the pills and the glass of water he offers. I'm terrible at swallowing pills since I've made a habit of avoiding them. These aren't big, so I manage to get them down, but not without some unattractive sputtering. When I'm done, I pass the glass back to him. "Happy now, Dr. Henry?"

"Very."

I twist my towel around my hair before I crawl up onto the bed to lie on my stomach for my post-sun care. I rest my arms over my head and I feel the bed dip when Lachlan crawls up. "This may be a little cool, but it'll feel good."

He squirts it directly on my back and I arch. "Shit, that's cold!" I squeal.

"It's not really. It just feels that way because your skin is feverish."

He rubs the cool lotion into my skin and it's very soothing. My entire body goes lax as I enjoy what feels more like a massage than a post-sunburn lotion application.

I'm so relaxed, I'm almost asleep when I hear "Jolene" playing on my phone. My eyes pop open and I feel Lachlan leave my back. "I'll get it for you."

He passes my phone to me. "Hey, Mom."

"Laurie, I've been calling you for hours. Have you not checked your phone?"

She sounds panicked, which panics me, and my first thought is that something has happened to Nanna or Pops. I sit up in the middle of the bed, preparing myself to hear the worst. "What's happened, Mom?"

"I can't believe you haven't heard. It's been all over the news."

Okay, nothing has happened to my grandparents so I shift to my aggravation mode. "Mom, what's going on?"

"Jared Beckett was killed in a skiing accident today."

I should've known this would somehow involve the sperm donor. "And this is emergency news for me because?"

"Because he's your brother, Laurie."

"Whom I've never met."

"He's your father's son."

"Again, whom I've never met." Am I the only one hearing the common denominator here?

"You need to come home."

Good grief. "This isn't a reason for me to come home."

"You need to pay your condolences, Laurie." Oh, hell. This is about getting me in with the sperm donor. What does she think is going to happen? He's going to suddenly want me in his life now that he's lost his only child?

I realize I'm stark naked and talking to my mom about the death of my sperm donor's son when Lachlan holds out one of his T-shirts for me. I mouth thank you to him and slip the shirt over my head while my mom chatters nonsense about the need of being with family in times like this.

"We share DNA, but I'm no part of their family. They wouldn't know me if we passed on the street."

"Your father is going to want to know you."

I stopped fantasizing about him wanting to know me a long time ago, but she never has. I'm almost twenty-three years old and she's still holding out for something—I don't know what. Maybe she thinks he'll want to meet his daughter and it'll lead him back to her.

"I'm sorry, Mom. I'm not coming home for this."

"I think you're making a mistake."

"If I am, then I'll be the one who has to live with it." I'd always been the one to live with both of our mistakes anyway, so I was used to it.

She isn't happy with me when I end our call and it leaves me feeling unsettled, although I know I'm making a logical decision. Between the two of us, someone has to be rational and I can't depend on it to be her. She isn't well known for making the best choices when it comes to my father.

"I assume there's trouble at home."

Yes, but only what my mom is making for me. "My father's son was killed in a snow-skiing accident."

"I'm sorry."

"He's a half-brother I've never met and my mom is acting like I should be in mourning. Hell, when she said his name, it took a minute for me to realize whom she was talking about. He's a stranger to me. I'm sorry for his family's loss, but I don't feel anything more. Is that wrong?"

"No, Laurelyn. You're not wrong for the way you feel. Please, don't let your mum make you feel guilty."

I'm certain he thinks she is a terrible mother after everything he's learned about her today. "You must think even worse of my mom now."

"She doesn't make the top-ten list of my favorites today. You, however, make the number-one position." He pulls me close to kiss the top of my head. I love the way he makes my worries disappear.

How can this be? This man, almost a stranger, brings me comfort and makes it easy for me to bare my soul to him. As I ask myself how it's possible, I know the answer. I don't have to guard my heart with Lachlan. I'm safe with him. And it's nice.

CHAPTER THIRTY

JACK MCLACHLAN

L<small>AURELYN DOESN'T KNOW IT'S MY BIRTHDAY OR THAT THE ONLY WISH</small> I <small>HAVE</small> is to stay home with her. But I can't. I have to go to my parents' house for my annual birthday dinner with the whole family. What a ripper day this will be.

She's been living with me for two weeks and I'm surprised by the way I feel as I drive away, leaving her at the house. I want to go back for her. I consider whipping the Sunset around, but I remind myself of the rules I have in place and why meeting my family is one that can't be broken.

I haven't seen my family in almost three weeks, not since my mother sent me back to Avalon to be with Laurelyn on Christmas Day. Thank you, Mum. It was the best gift you could have given me.

My mum has made a point to speak to me weekly about my relationship with my "girlfriend" and I'm not looking forward to showing up without her again. Margaret McLachlan is going to be very put out with me over Laurelyn's absence. I shouldn't have told her I'd bring her to my birthday dinner, but I didn't have a reasonable excuse to give her when we discussed it.

I walk through the door and Mum flies into the foyer. She's smiling and her eyes are wide with anticipation, but then I see them fill with disappointment when she notes the emptiness beside me. I feel like a shitty son. "Where is she?"

"I'm sorry, Mum. Laurelyn wasn't feeling well. We think she has the stomach flu. She told me to tell you how sorry she is that she couldn't make it."

She gives me a look of disapproval and I know I've done all wrong. "And you left her alone while she's sick?"

Shit. I didn't think of that. "I'm paying Mrs. Porcelli to take care of her."

Now, she's really giving me her disapproval. "What kind of message does that send if you leave her when she's sick, Jack Henry?"

I feel like a cur, although I'm guilty of nothing. Almost. "I didn't think of that."

"You boys never do, but it's not from lack of me trying." Mum stalks out of the foyer into the kitchen. She's pissed off and I want her to know her lessons weren't in vain. She'd be proud of how considerate I am with Laurelyn, but I can't tell her, so I'm forced to endure her disapproval instead.

I go into the living room where my dad and brother are, hoping to find neutral ground among them. I have no doubt Mum is in the kitchen telling Chloe and Emma what I did. Soon I'll have the whole adult female household against me. I'll be lucky if my nieces, Celia and Mila, aren't included in the pact.

Evan is sitting in the floor with his kids and laughs at me when I plop on the couch. "I heard Mum fussing at you all the way in here. What did you do?"

"Fussing? That's your vocabulary now?"

My brother points to his three-year-old. "Delicate ears, Jack, and little mouths repeat interesting words. You'll understand what I mean one day."

Yeah, when hell freezes over. "Mum is mad because I left Laurelyn while she's sick."

My dad is shaking his head. This is my mistake, but he's the one who'll have to hear about it when I'm gone. "I'm sorry, Dad."

He sighs. "Jack, you don't know how much she's been looking forward to meeting this woman you're dating. It's all I've heard since

Christmas and now all I'm going to hear is her carrying on about you screwing it up."

"Dad, I can't do anything about it now."

"You can fix this by telling your mum you'll bring her for a visit."

I can't lie to my mum again. "You know how things pick up this time of year. I might not be able to get away from the vineyard."

"Don't forget how well I know the business, son. You're in charge and you have very capable staff. You can get away for a couple of days to bring that woman here to meet your mum."

Dammit! "Fine. I'll tell her."

We hear a slamming cabinet in the living room. "Tell her now, Jack."

Fuck! I don't want my family interfering in my personal life. I get off the couch and walk into the enemy's territory. Two new pairs of rebuking eyes, those of my sister and sister-in-law, cast upon me in support of my mum's grievance. My sister flashes her signature hand gesture in the shape of an "L" in my direction as she mouths loser.

"Mum, I'm sorry. Will you forgive me if I bring Laurelyn for a visit? Maybe sometime next month, depending on how things are going at Avalon?"

She stops her physical abuse of the poor potatoes. "I will, but do try to bring her sooner if you can."

"Of course I will, Mum."

She's smiling because she's hoodwinked and I'm a lying sack of shit. My false promise is a temporary fix for this situation. I'll soon have to dupe my mum again, and I'm not looking forward to it.

The conversation at dinner is pleasant, much more so than it would have been had I not made nice with Mum, so I'm glad about that much. My dad is especially interested in hearing about the progress I'm making with my grafts. No one else gives a shit, but they assuage Dad by pretending to listen.

After dinner, I'm sitting in the living room watching Mila hold the coffee table for support and then she bravely removes her hand. She's trying to decide if she wants to take a step and I think I'm about to witness her valiant attempt to walk. "Bro, I think your kid is about to take her first step."

Evan's standing in the doorway and his head is buried in his phone, as usual. "Did you hear me, Evan? Mila looks like she's about to walk."

He lifts his head for a quick peek at his daughter and is unimpressed. "She teases us like that all the time—acts likes she's going to do it, then grabs back onto whatever's in front of her."

I don't know. She seems pretty serious to me, but I see Evan isn't interested. I wonder if I should call Emma to watch. I'm sure she'll want to see her daughter's first steps.

"What exactly have you been doing at Avalon, Jack?" Evan asks.

At dinner, I talked for ten minutes about the grafting and he didn't listen to a damn thing I said. Now he asks me what I'm doing. What a dick. "I'm not explaining all of it again. You should've listened at dinner if you were interested."

"No, bro. That's not what I mean." He's holding my phone and it clicks in my mind what he's talking about. He's going through my pictures of Laurelyn—the nearly naked ones.

I dive off the couch and reach to take my phone from him, but he snatches it from my grasp. "Why the hell are you looking at the pictures on my phone?"

He's leaning away from me so I can't reach it, but he continues to scan Laurelyn's pictures. "We have the same phone. I thought it was mine when I picked it up. I wanted to show Mum some pictures of the girls. Good thing I didn't call her over to take a gander at these."

"Give me my phone. Now!" I hiss through gritted teeth.

He twists the phone to see a picture from a different angle. "Damn, Jack, are you screwing her in this picture?"

"No!" I don't know. Maybe. Depends on which picture he's talking about.

I jerk it out of his hand and he has this look in his eyes. I think it's admiration, but I can't be sure. "You lucky bastard. Emma would never let me take pictures like that of her. Not even before she had the kids. And there's no way she'd let me take a picture of her getting screwed. How did you talk her into letting you do that?"

I'm pissed off at my brother for invading my privacy—and Laurelyn's—but I roll with it rather than start a fight. It wouldn't go over well to beat his ass in front of his wife and kids. "Just lucky, I guess."

I don't want to talk about Laurelyn this way with him. She's my secret—one I don't want to share—and my family is showing way too much interest in her.

"Are you serious about this girl?"

Has my brother lost his mind? I give him my "are you fucking kidding me?" face while I laugh. "I've known her a month. What do you think?"

The little shit is laughing at me. "I think you don't like it that I saw nudie pictures of your girl."

That part I can't deny. It makes me sick that he saw what was supposed to be for my eyes only. "She's not naked."

"Bullshit."

Emma comes into the living room and sees the glares passing between us. "What are you two fighting about?"

"Baby, my big brother was just showing me some pictures of his American girlfriend. Go ahead, Jack. Show Emma your girlfriend."

The fucking traitor wants to sell me out? I'll fix his ass so he doesn't get any naughty all month. I thumb through the pics until I find one portraying us as the doting couple and hold it up for Emma. "Evan told me she's a hot piece of ass and he'd do her. I can't believe he'd say that about my girlfriend."

Evan: score zero. Jack: score thirty. As in the number of days my little bro was going to be cock blocked. Hah! Take that you little fucker!

Emma stares him down. "Em, I didn't say that."

"Jack's thirty years old. Am I supposed to just believe he made that up because he has nothing better to do?"

"Yes, he does shit like that to get me in trouble. He doesn't have a wife so he finds it entertaining to mess with mine."

Her eyes shoot daggers in his direction. "I'm not discussing this with you now, Evan."

That's right, little bro. While you're not screwing your wife, you can spend the next month with your hand around your dick thinking about how to not fuck with me.

Emma reaches for my phone to take a better look at Laurelyn. "Jack, she's beautiful. May I show Margaret?"

It's probably safer for me to hold onto the phone so I can ensure there are no more peep shows. "I'll show her when she's finished in the kitchen."

Emma isn't going to let me get away without showing Mum pictures of Laurelyn, so I check the camera roll to see where the sexy ones start. The first twelve are all clear, but I'll only show her the first ten to be safe.

Mum comes into the living room when she's finished in the kitchen and Emma doesn't let it slide. "Margaret, Jack has some pictures of his girlfriend on his phone."

My mum is ecstatic. "Wait, I need my eyes." She scurries to the kitchen and returns wearing reading glasses. She takes the phone from my hand and holds it where she can see it better. "Oh, Jack Henry. She's a lovely girl. She'd have beautiful babies."

Oh, hell. Here we go.

She thumbs to the second picture and it's Laurelyn holding her Martin guitar. The third is her playing my piano at Avalon. "And she's a musician. She'd teach your children to play instruments and sing."

I can hear the wedding bells in my mum's head.

The next several pictures are random candids Laurelyn doesn't know I took. Some smiling, some solemn, but always beautiful.

CHAPTER THIRTY-ONE
LAURELYN PRESCOTT

Mrs. Porcelli kept me company after Lachlan left. She stayed and joined me for dinner, per my request, but now she is gone to her quarters for the evening and I'm alone in the house at night for the first time.

I'm not scared. I'm bored. And lonely. I want Lachlan here with me.

I call Addison, but don't get an answer, so I leave a voicemail. "Hey, Addie. I thought we might get together for lunch tomorrow. Give me a call if you're up for it."

I turn on the television, but can't find anything I want to watch. I decide Lachlan's absence might be the perfect time to use my pole for a workout. I haven't used it for exercise once since it's been installed. Every time I try, he puts on some sexy music and my workout becomes a show for his pleasure.

I put my hair into a bun because I'm going to get hot and sweaty. I change into the two-piece set I bought for practice. It isn't sexy like the ones Lachlan buys for me. It's a practical black racer-back top with matching sport shorts, the same type of outfit I would wear if I were going to class.

I go into the gym and turn on the receiver. I put "Lift Me Up" by Christina Aguilera on repeat. I've been thinking about choreographing a slow, graceful routine to that song for months and this is the first opportunity I've had to be alone with a pole.

When I finish stretching, I start by doing the Phoenix pose. I've practiced it in my head time and time again. I think I stick it perfectly, but it sucks not having an instructor to tell me if I'm doing it right. All I can do is watch in the mirror and judge it based on memory.

I do several spins and transitions I've mastered to get warmed up before I try a new invert—the Rainbow Marchenko. It's difficulty level is a 5, and I have no business trying it without an instructor, but this could be my only chance to go for it without Lachlan around to see me drop on my head if I don't stick it. Hopefully, Mrs. Porcelli won't find me with a broken neck in the morning.

I manage to do it without killing myself and now I have a feel for it. I know I can do it more gracefully, but my heart rate needs to return to normal before I give it another go. I lower myself to the floor to catch my breath.

I'm standing with my hands on my hips when I see motion in the mirror through my peripheral vision. I spin around to see if my eyes are playing tricks on me, which is a real possibility, but they're not. There's a woman standing in the middle of the gym floor and she's staring at me.

I don't know why, but I sense that she's been there for a while watching me. There's no initial shock on her face, at least not like what's on mine right now. Who is this woman, and why is she here?

I tell myself she could be Lachlan's sister, or Mrs. Porcelli's daughter, but I know it's wishful thinking. My gut tells me I've met a pit bull in a dark alley, ready for a fight.

I reach for the remote to turn off the music and she speaks before I have the chance. "That's a beautiful song. It goes well with the slow spins, but not that upside-down thing you were doing." She uses her fingers as she speaks.

"The Rainbow Marchenko. It's an invert."

"I wouldn't know because I'm not a stripper."

I admit she had me for a brief moment with her friendly opening statement, but the stripper comment is her attempt to put me in my place. This is no sister or friend to Lachlan. This is a former girlfriend or companion, and she's pissed about me being here.

She's tall and slender in an elegant taupe dress with matching heels. Her natural red hair is cut in a medium-length bob with bangs that are too blunt, just like the way she walked in here and called me a stripper.

I want to tell her Lachlan isn't here, but I don't know what to call him, so I go for generic. "He's not here."

She's laughing. "Honey, you don't even know his name, do you?"

I don't answer.

"And I know he's not here because I left him at his parents' house. I wanted to see you when he wasn't around so we could get a few things straight."

Now, I'm confused. I know he's at his parents'. How does she know and why does she say she left him there? "I'm sorry, but I'm at a bit of a disadvantage here. You seem to know me, but I don't know you."

She slinks over to the chair Lachlan uses when he watches me dance. She sits and crosses her legs as though she plans to stay a while. "How rude of me to not introduce myself. I'm Audrey, his wife."

No. This is not happening again.

"You didn't know, did you?"

I feel sick. I'm devastated. He could have had any number of women who didn't mind if he had a wife—except me. I agreed to all of his crazy-ass rules and the only thing I asked of him was to not lie about being married.

"What's your name?"

"Laurelyn."

"Laurelyn," she repeats. "What a pretty name. I've never heard it before." She's smiling at me in a friendly way. It's confusing. "I'm not angry with you. I can read your face and tell that you didn't know he was married, but you can understand why I must ask you to stop seeing my husband, can't you?"

"I do, but you don't have to ask. I'll gladly leave on my own accord."

"Thank you, Laurelyn. I want you to leave tonight and never see him again. I know my husband's… tastes. I trust you don't know his real name and he doesn't know yours."

There's no point in telling her I know his last name. "That's right."

"And you won't call him on the phone he gave you? You'll leave and never come back?"

She even knows about the phone? "I can't leave tonight because I have nowhere to go, but I'll be gone first thing in the morning, before he comes back."

"Thank you for being so understanding, Laurelyn. I love my husband very much and he has a problem, but I'm willing to work through it for our children."

Children? That's when I can't look at her anymore. "If you'll excuse me, I have some packing to do."

⚜

I GO INTO THE EXTRA BEDROOM TO GET MY LUGGAGE. I TOSS THE SUITCASES onto Lachlan's bed and go into the closet to strip my clothes from the hangers. I hurl them in without any kind of structure. I know all of my things are never going to fit in there like this, but I don't care. I'll leave what I can't jam in.

Somehow, I make everything fit. I pull my luggage into the kitchen and park it by the door for my departure first thing in the morning. I remember I'll need a ride. I call Daniel, the only other contact programmed into the phone given to me by Lachlan.

"Hi, Daniel. It's Laurelyn. I need you to drive me to town in the morning. Can you be ready at seven?"

"Certainly, Miss Beckett. I'll see you in the morning."

Miss Beckett. I feel a frown form on my face and I sigh. "Thank you, Daniel."

I survey the pile of luggage and wonder where I'll go in the morning. I have no idea. I'm short on money so a hotel for longer than one night is out of the question. I can't ask to come back to Ben's after the way I left, so I guess I have no choice. I'm forced to go home. Jolie will be happy.

I decide to shower tonight so there's no delay in getting away from this place first thing in the morning. Under water that's as hot as I can stand, I need this torment to be washed away. I'm unsuccessful at ridding myself of the pain, and the water eventually runs cold, much like the feeling I have deep inside.

I'm lying in bed, but nowhere near sleep, when Lachlan calls for the fourth time. I finally silence the ringer because I don't want to hear Bret

183

sing anymore. It's too bad I'll never hear him sing again without thinking of Lachlan Henry.

CHAPTER THIRTY-TWO

JACK MCLACHLAN

I CAN'T STAY AWAY FROM LAURELYN UNTIL TOMORROW AFTERNOON. I LEAVE my parents' house early to come home to be with her, but not without hearing a shitload of trash talk from my brother about being pussy-whipped. I may be, but I'm not complaining.

I come through the garage door and stumble over a pile of luggage. I turn on the light and recognize the bags as Laurelyn's. What the hell is going on here? First, she wouldn't answer my calls and now her luggage is by the door?

I walk to the bedroom, not sure of what I'm going to find. Please don't be gone, Laurelyn. I hold my breath as I stop in the doorway. It's pitch black, so I turn on the bathroom light and see her asleep in my bed. I release the breath I was holding.

It's three in the morning and I only want to strip down and climb into bed with her, but I don't because I know something isn't right. I sit on the bed next to her and brush her soft cheek with the back of my fingers. "Laurelyn."

She stirs, but doesn't wake, so I say her name again. "Laurelyn, baby."

She opens her eyes and bolts up in the bed, taking the sheet with her. "What are you doing here?"

This isn't the welcome home I'd imagined. "I live here."

"You told me you wouldn't be home until this afternoon."

"I left early because I wanted to be with you. I've sort of developed a habit of doing that." She doesn't say anything. "What's going on? Why are your bags by the door?"

"Because I'm leaving."

I feel my heart jump into my throat. "Why?"

"Your wife thought it would be the appropriate thing for me to do and I tend to agree with her."

What the hell is she talking about? "I don't have a wife."

"Audrey paid me a visit, and she says differently. She's stunning, Lachlan. And I should know because she stunned me."

That psycho has traced me to Avalon. She's getting smarter. And braver. Attempting to destroy two of my vineyards was ballsy, but now she has walked into my house and fucked with my personal life through Laurelyn. "I'm not married to that woman."

"I don't believe you."

"I swear I've never been married." She doesn't say it again, but I see she doesn't believe me. I run my hands through my hair. How am I going to prove this to her?

There's only one way. I reach for my phone in my pocket. "You can ask my mum. She'll tell you."

It's three o'clock in the morning, but I bring up my contacts and press the one labeled "Mum." I put it on speaker and it rings a few times before she answers the phone.

"Hello?"

"Mum, this is going to sound crazy, but am I married?"

"What are you talking about, son?" My mum has no idea she's the only one who can save me with Laurelyn right now.

"Have I ever been married?"

"No. What's this all about?"

"Laurelyn and I had a bit of a misunderstanding. She just needs to hear that I'm not married."

"He's not married, dear, but I'd sure like for him to be. How are you feeling?"

Oh, hell. I mute the phone. "Tell her you feel much better. I'll explain later."

I unmute the phone and hold out for Laurelyn to answer my mum. "I'm feeling much better, ma'am. Thank you for asking."

"I'm sorry to wake you, Mum. Go back to sleep and we'll talk later."

After I end the call, I put the phone down on the nightstand. "She wanted to know why you didn't come with me, so I told her you had the stomach flu."

"Oh."

"Tell me what happened with Audrey."

"I was in the gym working out. I stopped to take a break and I thought I saw something in the mirror. When I looked, I saw this redheaded woman in the middle of the floor watching me. I'm pretty sure she'd been standing there for a while, but I can't be certain because I didn't hear her come in."

"What did she tell you?"

"That she was your wife and she loved you. She wanted to work things out because of the children."

"Children?" Wow. She is desperate.

"She asked me to stop seeing you and leave without any contact ever again."

Huh. "You were going to leave me without saying goodbye?"

"Only because I believed you were married with children. You know how I feel about that."

"And you know I understand how bad it would hurt you if I were married. Why would you doubt me?"

"Because I don't know you."

Wow, that hurt. "But you're wrong. Maybe you don't know my real name, but you know me like no one else does."

"Who is she?"

Psycho bitch. "Number three."

"A previous companion?"

"Yes, of the deranged sort. Crazy stuff has gone down with that woman. She found out my real identity after our relationship ended and she's been stalking me for three years. Because I travel so often, it's hard for her to keep up with my whereabouts. When she can't find me, she causes mischief at the vineyards to draw me out."

"What has she done?"

"Countless things, but the most recent include the fire at Chalice and the crop poisoning at Marguerite."

"I didn't know about a poisoning."

"She's the reason I had to leave Avalon after Christmas. She hasn't been able to find me since I came to Wagga Wagga. I think I evaded her after the fire at Chalice and that's why she poisoned Marguerite—to bring me onto her turf at Lovedale."

"That's where she's from?"

"It is, but I didn't give her the opportunity to find me. I had a private investigator locate her first so I'd have the upper hand. I contacted her and told her to meet me in our old spot. She thought she was coming because I wanted to rekindle our relationship. I confronted her about the fire and the poisoning, but of course, she denied doing either."

"Did you sleep with her?"

"Hell no, but not because she didn't try. I turned her down and told her there was someone else. She didn't take it well, so we didn't part on good terms. Convincing you to leave me was her way of proving she could fuck with my personal life."

"She almost succeeded. I would've left last night if I'd had a place to go. I was going to the airport this morning to make arrangements to fly home."

I kick off my shoes and crawl into bed next to Laurelyn. I need to feel her against me to prove she isn't gone. I don't tell her how glad I am she's still here or about the fear I had when I thought she was leaving me. Maybe she already knows. If she does, she doesn't mention it. She lets me pull her close, and I'm content with simply holding her in my arms after almost losing her.

CHAPTER THIRTY-THREE
LAURELYN PRESCOTT

I'M ALMOST GLAD AUDREY CAME. LACHLAN IS FORCED TO GIVE ME INSIGHT he would've never volunteered. I now understand why he's so secretive about his life, and I can't really say I blame him if that's the kind of bat-shit crazy he's had to deal with.

We don't talk after I tell him about how I was going to leave. He holds onto me like he's afraid I might get up and sneak away in the night. He was scared when he thought I was leaving him. I heard it in his voice and saw it in his eyes.

I somehow make it to sleep with him wrapped around me, and he's still holding on when my phone vibrates on the nightstand at seven o'clock. I'm sure it's Daniel calling to see if I'm ready to leave.

Lachlan rolls away from me and grabs it before I'm able to make a move. "Daniel, Miss. Beckett won't be needing you to drive her this morning after all."

After he ends the call, he rolls back to me. "You'd be leaving me right now if I hadn't come home early."

He's right, yet I don't want to admit it, so I say nothing. He pulls me close again, the same way he held me all night. "We have two more months together. Please, don't plan to leave again unless it's a mutual decision."

189

"Okay."

"Promise me, Laurelyn. I don't want to worry about coming in and finding you gone one day."

"I promise." He relaxes with my assurance and I know this is the end of it. He'll never bring it up again because he believes me.

"What would you like to do today?" he asks.

"I wasn't expecting you to be here, so I asked Addison to meet me for lunch before the whole Audrey thing happened."

"That's fine. I seem to have fallen down on my office work since you've been around, Miss Beckett. My books could stand a little catching up."

"Mr. Henry, you're blaming your lack of productivity on me?"

"Only my lack of concentration," he explains. "It always seems to be on you these days."

"Then it's probably a good idea for me to get out of your hair today."

"Let's call it a girls' day out. You and your friend can shop or whatever it is you do when you're together."

I shrug because I don't really have any extra money to spend. My budget is super tight after my lingerie spending spree before Christmas. "I don't really need anything."

He gets out of bed and takes his wallet from his pants. He places several hundreds on the nightstand under my phone. Wow, that really makes me feel like a hooker.

"When you buy for yourself, you're buying for me because I like you in nice things." He leans down and kisses my mouth. "I'm taking you somewhere next week, so buy some new things for our trip."

"Where are you taking me?"

"New Zealand. It's a business trip, but we'll have plenty of time to play while we're there, so buy some sundresses and a few new swimsuits. I'd like to request skimpy bikinis."

No freakin' way. Addison will be so jealous. "You're taking me to New Zealand?"

"Yes. I have some business at one of the vineyards and my boss has a house on a private beach. He's letting us stay there a couple of nights."

"Lachlan. I don't even know what to say." And I don't. I'd never get to do anything like this on my own. I wouldn't have been able to come to Australia if Addison's parents hadn't bought my airline ticket.

"There's only one word I want to hear."

"Yes?"

"That's the one."

I hold my arms out and he lets me hop on him with my legs around his waist as I squeal. "We're going to New Zealand," I squeal in excitement.

৩৫৩

I CALL ADDISON WHEN I'M ALMOST TO THE APARTMENT. I DON'T PLAN ON going up because I don't want to run into Ben. "Hey, I'm a block away. Are you ready to come down?"

"I need five or ten more minutes." Of course she does. She's never ready on time. Won't I ever learn to tell her to be ready thirty minutes earlier?

"I'll wait in the car."

"No way. Come up, please."

I know I shouldn't, but I agree against my better judgment. "Okay. Buzz me in, but please hurry."

Daniel stops in front of the apartment. "Addison isn't ready so I'm going up. I shouldn't be long."

I reach for the handle, but it doesn't work. Child safety locks, I guess. They're probably activated because Daniel knows I don't give a rat's ass about having a door opened for me. I'm not helpless. I can open my own door, but that's not the way Lachlan wants it.

Daniel appears displeased with me as he lets me out the car. I think he doesn't approve of me going up to the apartment because he knows his employer won't like it. "I won't be long, Daniel."

"I can't tell you what to do, but you know he won't like this." Daniel knows about my run-in with Ben, maybe not the specifics, but Lachlan has told him something.

"I'll hurry."

"Take your phone and call me if you have any problems. Anything at all."

191

Great. I have Lachlan and Daniel wanting to kick Ben's ass. "I'll take it, but don't worry. I'll be fine."

"I'll worry until I see you come out of that building safe and sound." What did Lachlan tell him?

"I'll be ten minutes max," I promise.

"Make it five." He sounds irritated.

I knock on the door and Ben answers. He gives me a crooked grin, but he's embarrassed. He should be. "Hi, Laurelyn. Please, come in."

I walk into the apartment and I can't remember a more uncomfortable moment in my life. I stand there trying to think of polite conversation, but I can't come up with anything I want to say to the man who called me a whore after he tried to kiss me.

"I'm gonna walk back and check on Addison."

He touches my arm as I walk by and I go stiff. "Can I please have just a minute?"

I pull my arm from him. I don't want to do this, but I feel like I have to because he's my best friend's brother. "I'll give you one minute."

"I'm not saying it's any kind of excuse for what I did, but I was really drunk New Year's Eve. I never would've acted that way otherwise. I just wanted to tell you that I'm sorry."

"Apology accepted." That's all he's getting from me.

I walk to the bedroom I once shared with my best friend and she's sitting on the bed, ready to go. She jolts when she sees me in the doorway. I knew this was a total set-up. "Don't be mad, Laurie. He wanted to see you so he could apologize and I knew this was the only way."

"You lied to me." As I accuse her, I think of all the half-truths I've told her about Lachlan and decide it might be a good idea if I'm not too quick to call the kettle black. "But it's okay. I understand why you did it."

"I had to, Laurie. He's been so sick with himself since it happened."

"Well, it's over now. I told him I accepted his apology."

"Thank you, Laurie."

❧❧❧

ADDISON AND I HAVEN'T SEEN EACH OTHER SINCE I MOVED OUT, SO WE HAVE a lot of catching up to do. We decide it's best to do it over cheeseburgers and shakes at the fifties diner on the square.

"So, how's it going with the suit?"

That name is all wrong for him now. I've rarely seen him in a suit since those first few days. He's all sexy, rugged wear these days, but I choose to not debate it with her. "He works a lot of hours, but things are good now."

"What does 'now' mean?"

Do I really want to discuss Audrey with her? Yes, I think I do. She's my best friend. I need to get this out and tell someone about it. "One of his bat-shit crazy exes came to see me last night while he was out of town."

Addison sits up straighter, ready to hear the juicy details. She loves a good catfight. "What happened? Did you have to whip her ass?"

"She walked in the house like she owned the place and told me she was his wife and mother of his children."

I suspect she's seeing the same red flag I saw. Where there's smoke, there's fire. Right? "And is she?"

"No, but of course I believed her. You know how I am when it comes to men. I don't trust them."

"Laurie, how do you know she's not telling the truth?"

I'm playing with the napkin in my lap, tearing off small pieces and rolling them into little balls. "I packed my stuff and had it by the door so I could get out of there first thing this morning. He came home early and then the shit got real when he saw I was leaving. Addison, he called his mother and woke her at three o'clock this morning so she would vouch that he isn't married."

"That's good, right?"

"The part about being single is good, but what happened afterwards was unexpected." I'm not sure this uncomplicated relationship thing is going to stay that way.

"Chillax, Laurie. Sex is sex. Roll with it and have fun. Stop trying to make it complex."

I'm not trying to make sex with Lachlan complicated. "We didn't have sex."

She narrows her eyes at me. "Did he tell you he loved you or some bullshit like that?"

"No, we didn't talk."

"If you didn't talk and you didn't have sex, what did you do?"

"He just held me all night."

"Psst. That sounds boring as hell."

"But it wasn't. I liked it."

"You need counseling." Addison can be such a dude sometimes.

"You're my best friend. You're supposed to counsel me when I lose my way."

"Honey, you lost me on this deal back when you said you didn't have sex." She shrugs her shoulders. "I got nothing for you."

"He's taking me to New Zealand next week."

She punches me in the shoulder. "Shut the hell up. No way."

"Yeah, he is." I reach into my purse and hold up the money he gave me. "We're staying at a house on a private beach and he wants me to buy new clothes and swimsuits for the trip."

Addison's eyes widen. "Shit! How much money is that?"

"I don't know. I didn't count it."

She reaches over and takes it from my hand to thumb through it. "The suit gave you a grand to buy bikinis and flip-flops."

I remind myself of what Lachlan said. When I buy for myself, I'm buying for him because he wants me in nice things. "I feel guilty taking his money, but I can't afford to buy the things he wants me to have for the trip."

She waves the money in front of me. "He promised to show you the time of your life. This is one of things he was talking about. You have two months left with him. Have fun while you can."

She's right. I'm making too much of this. We discussed what he wanted from this relationship in the beginning, and he told me he wanted to pamper me and make us feel genuine. This is him following through with his part of the bargain, so I should keep mine too. If he wants us to feel real, I can give him real—every day and twice on Sunday.

CHAPTER THIRTY-FOUR
JACK MCLACHLAN

AFTER TAKEOFF IN OUR SMALL PRIVATE PLANE TO AUCKLAND, NEW Zealand, I check my watch to see if we're on schedule. I notice the date—February 1st—and I'm struck by the memory of a conversation Laurelyn and I had on our second date. She told me she would turn twenty-three on Groundhog's Day. That's tomorrow. I can't believe I didn't remember until just now.

She hasn't mentioned it. I think she would tell me if I asked her, but I decide I want to surprise her with something special. I just don't know what it will be.

Our flight lands and I usually have a driver waiting, but not today. Instead, I rent a convertible for the twenty-minute drive to the house so Laurelyn and I can have this experience alone and at our own pace.

After pulling off the road several times for Laurelyn to admire the coastline, we arrive at the house in Auckland. She hasn't traveled much outside her small world at home and her eyes are wide with elation. I love seeing her like this. Her expression makes me want to show her the world.

"It's amazing."

"Wait until you see the beachfront."

I carry our bags from the car into the house. I give her the tour, purposely making the bedroom our last stop. I'm proud of this room, even if I can't take credit for how lovely it is since the house was furnished when I purchased it last year. The previous owner did a fantastic job making this bedroom romantic.

Laurelyn walks over and runs her fingers down the sheer fabric draped over the canopy. "I can't think of a word to describe this room. Romantic isn't enough to do it justice."

"I know."

"You've stayed here before?"

"Many times." I feel the question she doesn't ask and I answer it. "But always alone. You're the only one I've brought here." I want her to know she's the first and only.

She sits on the bed and falls back across the mattress. "Your boss has great taste."

I look at the beautiful woman sprawled across my bed. "I agree."

"What are we going to do first?"

Now is the only time I have to go into town for Laurelyn's gift before tomorrow. "I have to go out to the vineyard for a quick visit. I should only be gone a couple of hours." She frowns at my news. "This is still a business trip for me, but don't worry. We'll have plenty of time for fun."

"I'm ready to hit the beach."

"You can go while I'm gone, but I don't want you to go into the water while you're alone."

She pokes her bottom lip out. "Boo."

"I know you're a big girl, but it's still the ocean. Sometimes unexpected things happen and I'd feel better about you not going in by yourself."

"I get it."

She sits up and I kiss her. "I'll be back before you know it. Don't forget to wear sunscreen. I don't need you burned for what we're going to be doing while we're here."

⚅⚅

I DON'T FIND LAURELYN'S GIFT RIGHT AWAY, SO I'M GONE LONGER THAN I anticipate. When I return to the house, I leave her gift in the car's glove box. I want her to think I'm clueless about her birthday since she hasn't mentioned it.

I walk around to the beach and see Laurelyn's towel on the lounger where she was lying, but no sign of her. I call her name several times without a response. Where is she?

Deciding she is probably inside, I open the front door and shout her name several times without a reply.

Would she have gone into the water after I asked her not to? I know the answer. Yes, she would. The moment I answer my own question, I dash toward the beach and shout her name. I hear panic in my voice and feel it in my chest as I search the water. I don't see a sign of her anywhere.

I hear my name in the distance and I turn to see her walking along the beach's edge. She's wearing a bright red bikini. How did I miss that? I'm flooded with instant relief and that's when I notice my hands trembling. She lifts her hand to wave and I lift my shaky one to return the greeting. I sit on the lounger to wait on her because my knees are threatening to buckle beneath me.

I'm calmed, or at least appear to be, by the time she reaches me. I hold my arms out for her to come sit across my lap. I pull her close and bury my face in her hair.

"Wow, someone really missed me while he was gone. Is everything okay?"

"It is now." I forgo telling her about my near breakdown when I couldn't find her.

"Good." She reaches for the buttons on my shirt and begins unfastening them. "You, sir, are overdressed. Go change into your trunks and swim with me."

"Yes, ma'am."

When I come out of the house, she's already shoulder deep in the clear blue water so I don't get to feast my eyes on her in the skimpy red bikini. "You just couldn't wait, could you?"

"Nope. It's been calling to me for hours and now I'm not alone, so I didn't break your rule."

I toss my towel next to hers and walk out to meet her in the ocean.

She swims over and puts her arms around my shoulders. "I've never been anywhere so beautiful. Thank you for bringing me."

"It's my pleasure."

"I'm pretty sure it's going to bring you some."

"Oh, is it?"

"The eight ball says chances are good." She kisses my mouth and rests her forehead against mine. "Do you come here often?"

"I try to make rounds on Aurelia at least once a month during the summer."

"Why do you always come alone?"

"I've never been with anyone I wanted to bring. Until you."

"Oh." That's all she says and doesn't press it further.

When we're tired of swimming, we come out of the water to relax on the loungers. She's stretched out with one of her long legs bent.

"I want to take you into town for dinner."

"Okay."

"Maybe dancing afterwards?"

"Sure, that sounds like fun."

❧

AFTER DINNER AT A ROMANTIC CAFÉ, I TAKE LAURELYN TO A DANCE CLUB I noticed when buying her birthday present. Lights flash around us in the dark and it's packed shoulder to shoulder. It's not really the relaxed dancing I had in mind, but she seems happy about being here.

She grabs my arms and we move toward the dance floor. The music is loud and there's a fast song playing. Laurelyn moves to it like it's something she's done a million times.

"Go out dancing much?"

"Yeah. Addison and I hit the dance scene in Nashville a lot."

She turns her back to me and grabs my hands. She places them on her hips and backs up until her whole body is rubbing against mine as she dances. She knows what she's doing to me. She can feel the evidence grinding against her ass.

We're packed on the dance floor and everyone is in his or her own little world. No one is paying attention to us, so I slide my hand from her hip to between her legs. She leans her head against my chest. "You are so bad."

"I can't help myself when you're rubbing on me like that."

"Sorry. Want to get a drink?"

"Yeah, I need one. A big one."

We get a couple of glasses of wine from the bar and migrate to the corner so we can hear each other over the pounding bass. "Have you been here before?"

"No. I saw this place today and thought it might be fun. Do you want to leave?"

She shakes her head. "No. I'm having fun."

I feel someone bump into me from behind and I spill my wine down the front of my shirt. "Shit."

I turn to look at the jerk behind me and he sees the damage he's caused. "Man, I'm sorry. Please, let me buy you another drink and pay for your dry cleaning."

I'm afraid dry cleaning isn't going to save this. "That won't be necessary."

He offers his hand. "I'm Chris and this is my wife, Trisha."

I'm not really interested in introductions, but I choose to be friendly instead of telling these people to get lost so I can be alone with my girl. "I'm Lachlan and this is Laurelyn."

I'm shaking his hand but he's looking at Laurelyn. And for longer than I like. "Is the missus your wife or girlfriend?"

"Girlfriend." Laurelyn gazes at me and we both grin.

The music is loud, so the wife leans closer. "Have you been together long?"

"Six weeks," I answer. That means we're half-over. I wonder if she's thinking the same thing.

Trish is screaming over the music. "Wow. Things are still in that new, fun, exciting stage for you." Exciting is an understatement. I should tell them what kind of relationship we have just to freak their married asses out so they'll go away.

We laugh at our shared secret. I put my arm around her and pull her close. "There's very little about us or our relationship that's boring."

Laurelyn holds her glass of wine out for me. "Will you hold this for a moment while I step to the restroom?"

Trisha takes the last gulp and then slides her empty glass toward the bartender. "I need to go too."

Perfect. I'm left with my new best friend, Chris. "Your girlfriend is a Yank?"

I take a drink from Laurelyn's glass since I'm wearing my wine. "Yes."

"She's very beautiful. I couldn't help but notice her when you were dancing. I'd really like to fuck her."

What? The music is loud and I decide I misunderstood what he said, so I tilt my head toward him. "What was that?"

He steps closer and puts his hand on my shoulder. "My wife is really turned on by you. She wants to give you head while you watch me fuck your girlfriend. I mean, if you're into watching. Our only rule is no kissing. We save that for each other."

Swingers.

I know I do some weird shit when it comes to women, but this tops the fucking cake. I look like an altar boy next to this joker. I'm so stunned I don't answer. I don't know how to.

Laurelyn and Swinger Trisha come back from the bathroom and rejoin the circle. Laurelyn takes her drink from my hand and I watch her face, wondering if the wifey propositioned her while in the bathroom. Her demeanor seems unchanged, so I assume Trisha left her husband in charge of closing this deal.

She loops her arm through her husband's. "So, did you ask him, honey?"

"We're in the middle of discussing it." He grins at me. "So, what do you think? Are you guys up for it?"

I think Laurelyn is trying to read my face, but can't. "Are we up for what?"

I pass my empty wine glass to Laurelyn. "Will you hold this for me, baby?"

I guess it can be called a sucker punch since he has no idea it's coming, but I make a fist and slam Swinger Chris in the jaw, sending him face down onto the dance floor. I want him to get up so I can beat the shit out of him, but he's smarter than that and stays down. "Get up."

Laurelyn stands there in shock staring at me because she has no idea what this freak wants to do to her. "Lachlan! What are you doing?"

I point to Chris on the floor. "You want to know what I think? Is that a clear-enough answer for you?"

Security is stalking in my direction to throw me out, so I put both hands up. "No need. We're out of here."

I take Laurelyn by the arm and pull her toward the door. "What's going on?"

"Not now," I growl at her.

She follows me outside and comes to a halt. "Why did you hit him?"

I keep walking toward the car. I'm afraid I'll go back inside and kill him if I don't get out of there.

We get into the car and I grip the steering wheel. That's when I realize how damn bad my hand hurts.

"Lachlan, you're scaring me."

"No more than I'm scaring myself." I just lost my shit over some guy telling me he wanted to fuck her. He made me see red. I wanted to choke the life out of him for what he said.

She's staring at me. "I highly doubt that."

I can't talk to her about this right now. I'm too furious. I start the car and drive to the house in silence. I'm pissed off. She's scared and confused. Not a great combination.

Neither of us says anything when we get to the house. She walks inside and goes straight to the bedroom. I go to the kitchen and search the freezer. I don't find frozen peas, so I wrap ice in a dish towel and put it around my swollen hand. It hurts like hell, but I don't regret hitting that asshole. I'd do it again in a heartbeat.

I calm down after I stand in the kitchen for a while. I decide I owe her an explanation, so I go into the bedroom to find her. She's wearing her nightgown and standing in front of the sink washing her face. She watches me in the mirror as I come up to stand behind her.

I put the dishcloth-wrapped ice on the counter before I place my hands on her upper arms and kiss one of her bare shoulders. She reaches up to touch my injured hand. "You're bleeding. You need to clean this so it doesn't get infected."

She takes my hand. "Is there any antiseptic here? Or maybe some triple antibiotic ointment?"

I'm rarely here, so I don't make a habit of keeping stuff like that around. "I doubt it."

She brings it closer for a better inspection. "You should at least wash it with soap and water."

She cuts on the water and soaps a lather onto her fingers. She washes my knuckles until the dried blood is gone and then blots it dry. "I'm afraid you're going to owe your boss some new towels."

"He'll get over it."

She's still holding my hand when she looks up at me. "Tell me what happened."

I focus on her eyes as I remember his words, "I'd really like to fuck her." The thought of anyone else having her makes me crazy.

I reach out to hold her face. I lean forward and kiss her, not knowing if she will let me or not, but she does. When I finish, I take her hand and pull her into the bedroom toward the bed. I sit on the edge and pull her hips toward me so she's standing between my legs. Her fingers play in my tousled hair.

"I want to know."

I take a deep breath and blow it out slowly. "That guy, Chris, told me he wanted something of mine—something I wasn't willing to share."

"I don't understand."

"You. He wanted you."

"Me? But he's married."

It makes me sick that I can't say it without picturing it in my head. "He asked me to watch him fuck you while his wife gave me head."

Her eyes are wide. "Oh?" I see it on her face when it clicks. "Ohh. Swingers?"

"Exactly."

"You pounded his face in because he wanted to have sex with me?"

"I damn sure did and I'd do it..." She cuts off my words with her mouth as she slams it against mine. Her hands are at my chest working to unfasten the buttons of my wined-stained shirt. Unsatisfied with such slow progress, she reaches for the bottom and pulls it over my head while it's still buttoned.

She unfastens my belt buckle and then the button on my pants, this time more successful with the process. She slides my zipper down and puts her hand inside my jocks. Her hand encompasses me as she glides it up and down. Damn, this girl knows how to give a hand job.

She kisses me hard while her hand pumps me. I'm close to coming, but she doesn't let me. "Where are the condoms?"

"Outer pocket, big suitcase."

She kisses my mouth. "Don't go anywhere."

Hell, there's no chance of that. I stand and kick off my daks and jocks while she's digging for the rubbers.

She slinks toward me flipping a foil package between two fingers. She uses her palms to push me down on the bed. "I'm putting it on this time."

"No argument here, baby."

She opens the packet and I'm such a guy. I lift my head because I want to watch her put it on me. It's hot watching her hands touch me like that. When she finishes, she shimmies her panties down her legs and steps out of them. She climbs one knee at a time onto the bed and straddles me. My hands are splayed over her hips as she watches my face. "So, you don't want Swinger Chris to have me?"

Ugh, I need that image out of my head. "No fucking way."

My tip is at her wet entrance, but she doesn't slide down on it. She's rocking her hips back and forth, teasing me. "Can anyone else have me, or is Swinger Chris the only one who can't?"

"No one else can have you, Laurelyn. I'm the only one."

She smiles. "Then show me."

CHAPTER THIRTY-FIVE
LAURELYN PRESCOTT

LACHLAN COMES UP FROM THE BED AND FLIPS ME ONTO MY BACK. HE'S kneeling between my legs and hooks them around his arms so he can push them back. He's not gentle about it. He drives into me without mercy, but that's the way I want this. His mouth is against my ear.

"You're mine. Do you understand?"

"Yes!" I scream partly because it's my answer, but mostly because what he's doing feels so good.

"I want you to say it."

We're sideways on the bed and each thrust shoves me farther across the mattress until my head is hanging off the edge. "I'm... yours... and... no... one... else's."

He releases one of my legs and his hand slides down so his fingers can stroke me above our point of fusion. "No one else touches you here like this."

I'm panting as I lift my hips against him and his fingers. "Only you, Lachlan."

He hits my sweet spot perfectly and I feel myself contract around him, detonating his orgasm. I feel like screaming at the top of my lungs, so I do because no one's around to hear me. "Ah, ah!"

"Ah, Laurelyn." There's my name, just like always when he comes.

He rolls off me and collapses onto the bed. My head is still dangling off the side so I scoot back onto the mattress. I'm on my back and I stare up at the beautiful sheer panels draped over the canopy above us with one thought—this bed was meant for making love, but that isn't what we just did. It never is.

❄

THE BEDROOM FILLS WITH BRIGHT SUNLIGHT DESPITE THE CURTAINS. I SMELL breakfast—definitely bacon—maybe pancakes. I'm hungry, but I'm sleepier, so I pull the sheet up over my head. It was a late night.

I get a few more minutes' sleep before I feel Lachlan reach under the sheet to tickle my nose. I wiggle it to relieve the need to scratch, but give in and reach under the covers and rake my nails across it. "I thought you got to sleep in on vacation."

"This isn't vacation for me. It's work and I have to leave soon, but I wanted to have brekkie with you for your birthday."

How does he know? I lift the covers to see him. He's grinning because he's so proud of himself. "How did you know it's my birthday?"

"You told me on our second date."

"I don't remember that."

"Well, you did, and I remembered, so get up for your birthday breakfast."

I can't believe he remembered. He has such an eye for detail. Did he tell me when his birthday is? If he did, I forgot.

I walk into the kitchen and there is a huge breakfast buffet across the counter. There's no way we could eat all of it. "Did you do all of this?"

"Would you think less of it if I didn't?"

"No."

"I had it catered from one of the local restaurants."

"It smells delicious."

He passes a plate to me. "Birthday girl goes first."

While I'm plating my food, he pours me a glass of juice. He puts it on the dining room table and then joins me with a mile-high stack of pancakes. "Hungry much?"

"I had a famishing night, but I always eat this much in the morning.

You'd know that if you were ever awake to join me for breakfast." He's never going to stop teasing me about being a late sleeper.

"How's the hand today?"

He holds it up to make a fist and then releases it. "It hurts, but I can move it, so it's not broken."

"No one's ever done anything like that for me."

"Anytime, babe."

When I finish, I slide my plate away because I'm stuffed. "That was wonderful. Thank you. It was a thoughtful gift to wake up to."

"The food isn't your gift." He reaches into his pocket and pulls out a black velvet jewelry box. He puts it on the table and slides it to me. "But this is."

I'm not fool enough to think, or hope, this little box contains a ring. I know it doesn't because that would be ridiculous, but it definitely contains a piece of jewelry.

I reach for it and flip the top open. Inside is a star-shaped pendant covered in what I assume are diamonds. "I chose it because you're going to become a huge superstar after you get home."

It's the best birthday present ever. And the worst.

It's the best because it's so encouraging and thoughtful. It's the worst because it means that when he's telling me I'm his, he leaves off the part about it only being for the next six weeks.

"You don't like it?"

I force a smile. "It's perfect and I love it. Thank you."

I take it out of the box and pass it to him. "Will you?" I turn and lift my hair so he can put it on me. After he closes the clasp, he kisses the back of my neck.

"I wish I could stay with you all day."

I turn around and touch the pendant with my fingertip. "Me too."

He smiles as he admires his gift around my neck. "I'll try to get back early."

"Early or late, either way, I'll be here."

"I still don't want you to go into the water without me."

"Ugh! There's a country song called 'Don't Go Near the Water.' Now it's going to be stuck in my head all day and I hate that freakin' song. Thanks a lot, slick."

He kisses the top of my head. "Don't know it, but you can thank me every time you catch yourself singing it."

He's wearing a suit today. Damn, he's hot in it—scorching hot. He's standing over me and I grab the lapels of his jacket to pull him down for a kiss. The peck he gave me on top of my head wasn't near enough to do me all day. When I let him go, I tell him, "That's your incentive to work fast so you can leave early and come back to me."

⁂

I SPEND THE DAY READING ON THE BEACH, NOT SWIMMING IN THE WATER, although it's hot as hell. It's midafternoon and I decide to take a break from the sweltering heat, so I go into the house for a snack and some air conditioning.

I'm sitting at the dining room table having some leftover fruit from my birthday breakfast when my personal phone rings. It's my mom, no doubt calling to wish me a happy birthday.

"Hey, Mom."

"Happy birthday, baby girl."

"Thank you."

"Are you having a good one?"

"The best." And it is. I'm staying at a house on a private beach in New Zealand with a beautiful man I can't get enough of. Nothing beats this.

"Well, I've got some news that's going to make it even better."

Her idea of good news and my idea aren't always the same. "What is it?"

"It's your dad. He came to see me, baby. He wants to meet you."

This is a perfect example of when our ideas of good news are on two different spectrums. "Why?"

"Because you're his daughter."

I would've given anything to hear those words when I was a child. All I wanted was for my rich and famous father to rescue me from her when I was surviving off tap water and moldy bread because she was too strung out to go to the grocery store. I prayed he'd come and save me, but he didn't. "He hasn't wanted me as his daughter for twenty-three years, and he doesn't get to change his mind now because the only child he claimed is dead."

"It's not like that, Laurie."

"It is like that, Mom. I've been his dirty little secret all these years. At least have the balls to be honest about it." I don't know the exact moment the tears start, but I can't stop them once they begin. The more I try to hold them in, the harder they come. "He's pretended I didn't exist my whole life and the only reason he wants me now is because he has no other children left."

I'm shocked to feel warm arms around me as Lachlan takes the phone from my hand. When did he get back? "I'm sorry. Laurelyn will have to call you back later."

He hangs up on my mother and silences the ringer before he tosses the phone to the couch. He wraps his arms around me and I melt into him. He doesn't ask what she's said to upset me, but I think he has a good idea if he heard any part of our conversation.

This is another one of those moments like the morning I almost left him. He holds me and his embrace speaks without saying a word.

CHAPTER THIRTY-SIX

JACK MCLACHLAN

I'M PISSED OFF BECAUSE LAURELYN'S MOTHER WOULD CALL AND UPSET HER this way, especially on her birthday. This isn't improving my opinion of her at all. She's a selfish, immature woman.

I don't understand her thought process behind her decision to tell Laurelyn this news about her father on her birthday. She knew it would upset her. Even I know that. I want to be a total caveman and slam the thing against the wall so Laurelyn's mother can never call her on it again, but I can't.

Maybe I don't understand because it's a mother/daughter thing, but something feels off to me about their relationship.

I rub circles on her back. "Do you want to talk about it?"

I feel her head oscillating from side to side, telling me no. I kiss the top of her head and pull her to the couch. I'm still in my suit so I take off my jacket and toss it across the chair. I sit on the couch and pat the cushion between my legs. "Come sit with me."

She sits and leans against my chest. She's wearing a black string bikini I've never seen and she smells like coconut and sweat from being in the sun. I'm twitching in my pants because she's so close. I can't help it. Whoa, settle down, boy... now's not the right time.

Laurelyn can be difficult to read at times, but she's hurting and I

209

want to give her the support she deserves. She damn sure doesn't get it from anyone else in her life. I think simply holding her is what she wants, so that's what I do. I'm content to sit here with her for as long as she needs me.

We sit together like that for at least a half hour before she stops crying and says anything. She lifts her face to see me over her shoulder. "You came back early."

"Of course I did. I want to be with the birthday girl on her special day."

She reaches for my hand and laces her fingers through it. "I don't think you know how good you are at this."

"What am I good at?"

"Whatever this is we're doing."

I no longer have any idea what we we're doing. I only know I like it. "I think you're pretty good at this too. Whatever it is."

She lifts the hand I used on Swinger Chris and inspects it. "Your hand looks a lot better. The swelling is down."

"It's fine. It barely hurts anymore." She brings it to her lips. "Your kiss will make it all better in no time."

She puts her finger on the leg of my daks and draws an imaginary infinity symbol. I remember another time when she did it. It was after our second date when I explained everything to her about what I wanted. She does it when she's nervous.

"He wants to meet me."

He. I heard enough of the conversation to know she's talking about her father, the sperm donor. That's how I've come to think of him after hearing her call him that so many times. "How do you feel about that?"

"I think I've already met him."

"Why do you think that?"

"I have a memory from my childhood. It's very vague, but I'm sure I remember meeting him when I was little. My mom dressed me in a navy sailor dress. It had this huge collar on it and she pulled my hair up in pigtails. I was adorable," she laughs. "She took me to a place where ducks paddled around in this fountain. They fascinated me, but she wouldn't let me stay to watch them. She took me to him. I know it was the sperm donor, even if I don't remember his face. As far as I know, I never saw him again—except on television and in the music department at Wal-Mart."

"You're not curious about him?"

"There have been times in my life when I was and I'd have given anything to see him, but it ain't today. And it won't be tomorrow."

⬥

IT'S LATE EVENING AND LAURELYN IS IN THE BATHROOM GETTING READY TO go out for dinner. I'm sitting on the couch and hear the buzzing vibration of her phone, but it stops before I'm able to pick it up. I look at the screen and see a missed call from Blake Phillips. Who the hell is he?

He could be anyone. A relative. A friend. A boyfriend. I want to know, but I don't dare ask because I'm afraid to know the answer.

Laurelyn comes into the living room and I slide her phone into my pocket. I don't want her to know I saw the call from this man; tonight isn't the right time to have this conversation.

She's caught a lot of sun while we've been here and her skin is golden against her cream sundress. I'm happy to see her wearing her birthday gift, and I reach out to touch it where it rests against her neck. "This is perfect on you."

She smiles as she reaches up to touch it. "It's beautiful and I love it. Thank you again."

"You're more beautiful. And you're welcome."

I take her to an Italian restaurant where I've eaten before when in town on business. The food is great and it's the last place I'd expect to be accosted by a set of sexual deviants. At least I hope. My fist isn't ready to be used again quite so soon. I told Laurelyn it was fine, but I lied. It still hurts like hell.

"You're unusually quiet. What's going on in that head of yours, Mr. Henry?"

I'm thinking of things better left alone. I know she's only been with one other man. Is it Blake Phillips? Not knowing is taunting me. Is he the one who hurt her? I can't get him off my mind, so I decide there are other ways of asking about him without asking.

211

"I was thinking about how a beautiful woman like you must date a lot."

She smiles and the candlelight illuminates her high cheekbones. "I do. I've had a date with an extremely handsome man almost every day for the past six weeks."

She's deflecting from the real question. "No, I mean before you came here."

She shrugs as she looks down at her plate. "Not so much."

"What about a serious relationship?"

Her head oscillates from side to side. "Not really."

I don't think she's lying to me, but I find it hard to believe someone so desirable has never been in a relationship. "You've never had a boyfriend?"

She's fidgeting in her seat. I'm making her uncomfortable, so there's plenty she isn't telling me. "I had something one time, but boyfriend doesn't feel like the right word for what he was to me."

"Was it serious?" Was it Blake Phillips?

She's pushing her food around and I think I've upset her. Dammit. "I thought it was at the time, but we had a difference of opinion."

"Oh." Does that mean he left her? Does she still want him?

"What's with all the questions?"

"Nothing. Just making conversation." She's being vague, which causes me to be suspicious. My gut tells me there's much more to this story. She isn't a woman who has had a single one-sided serious relationship, but I choose to drop it for now, leaving it open as a topic I may want to revisit. Looks like we both have secrets.

۞

She's sitting at the dining room table with her eyes closed when I bring in a cake with twenty-three flaming candles. "You can open your eyes."

"Wow. That's a lot of fire."

"Wait until you're thirty," I laugh. "There's even more."

Her brow wrinkles. "You told me you were twenty-nine."

"I was when we met."

"When did you turn thirty?"

"A couple of weeks ago—on the thirteenth."

"You didn't tell me," she whispers and she looks hurt. I see her thumbing through her filed memories from two weeks ago. "It was when you went to your parents' house, wasn't it?"

"Yes."

"When I almost left you?"

"Yes."

"You should've told me."

"You mean the same way you told me today was your birthday?"

She laughs. "Right. I don't guess I can be too upset with you since I did the exact same thing. I would've given you a gift if I'd known."

I sit in the chair beside her and take her hands. "But, you did. Staying with me was the best gift you could've given me."

I don't think she knows what to say to that, so I make it easy for her. "Make a wish and blow out your candles before we catch the house on fire."

She smiles and draws a deep breath before she leans forward to extinguish the twenty-three tiny flames.

I want all of her wishes to come true. Not just this one.

CHAPTER THIRTY-SEVEN
LAURELYN PRESCOTT

AFTER LACHLAN FINISHES HIS WORK AT THE AUCKLAND VINEYARD, WE return to Avalon and fall back into our routines. He works every day while I keep busy at the house, waiting for him to come home.

Wow. We have routines. How domestic is that? And I called Avalon home? That's a minuscule detail that doesn't evade my attention.

Harvest time for the vineyards is approaching, so Lachlan is working a lot more since our return from New Zealand. I spend time with Addison when she's not wrapped up with Zac, but I'm still left with a lot of time to keep myself busy, so I do the only thing I can: I throw myself into writing music.

I have a career to return to in four weeks. At least, I hope I still have a career. Blake still owns half the rights to my songs from the record we were producing, and he can shove them up his ass. I'm writing new songs. It's the wrecked affair with him I worry about. I pray word of it doesn't get out and ruin everything I've worked so hard to achieve.

Wow. I only have four weeks left with Lachlan.

Our precious time together feels like a candle with wicks burning at both ends. Once the flame meets in the middle, we're over. I'll never see him again, or hear his laugh or touch his skin. I'll never share a bed with him again. Am I prepared for it when that time comes? I don't think I am, but it doesn't matter if I'm not. It's coming, and I'd better figure out how to get ready.

I'm thankful to have the Martin and the baby grand at my disposal because Lachlan's long hours give me a lot of time to compose. Being here inspires me. Hell, I should at least be honest about it. It's Lachlan who inspires me. I know the stuff I'm writing is gold, but the inspiration behind the music is bittersweet, and I fear I've come to that place I didn't want to be—writing hits because I'm terribly in love.

I'm tinkering with a melody on the baby grand when Mrs. Porcelli comes into the living room. "Dinner is ready and on the stove, Laurelyn, so I'm leaving."

"Thank you, Mrs. Porcelli. Have a nice evening."

I play the chorus again, trying to decide if it's right. "It's a lovely song, Laurelyn."

"You've been listening?"

She nods. "I hope you don't mind."

"Not at all. I doubt you've had much choice but to listen. You think it's good?"

"I think it's great."

"Thank you. I hope you're not the only one who thinks so."

"I also think he feels the same about you." I look up from the piano at her. "The song is about Mr. McLachlan, isn't it?"

"Is it that obvious?"

"I'm afraid so, dear. Have you played it for him?"

"Oh, no. I could never do that." And I especially couldn't if the song is that transparent.

"I think you should reconsider. He'd love it."

"I'll think about it," I lie.

"Good. I'll be choofing off now. Have a good evening."

I work on my newest song until Lachlan comes home. Home. There's that word again. I see him standing in the doorway watching me, and I stop singing the moment his eyes meet mine. How long as he been standing there?

"It's beautiful. Don't stop on my account."

"I've been at it all day, so I'm ready to call it quits for the night." I get up from the bench. "Dinner's ready. Would you like to eat now?"

"Only if you're joining me."

I walk to the doorway to kiss him. "I've joined you every night for two months. I'm not stopping now."

I fill our plates with salmon and rice pilaf while Lachlan chooses a vintage, and then we meet at the informal dining table. He pulls my chair out for me and pours my wine. It's one of the many routines we've developed after living together for eight weeks.

"Do you remember me telling you I wanted to take you to Sydney a while back?"

"Yes, and you have tickets for the opera."

"That's right. Madama Butterfly. It's this weekend and I still want you to come with me."

"I'm in, but I have to warn you—I'm no fan of opera. I don't understand it."

"Honestly, I'm not a huge fan myself, but these tickets are a gift from one of my customers in Sydney. They're balcony seats and I'm afraid he has the tickets for the other seats and will know if I don't show."

"You're so considerate."

"I'm not being considerate. I'm being business-minded. I don't want to insult him and lose his account."

"Well, then, you're being considerate in your business-mindedness."

He laughs at me. "Business-mindedness. Say that fast ten times."

"No, it was hard enough to say it once."

"The trip won't be a total bust. We'll do the opera on Friday night and then I have other plans for us."

"Like what?"

"I'm not telling you. You'll have to wait and find out on Saturday, Miss Beckett."

❧

I'M WEARING A FITTED BLACK COCKTAIL DRESS AND A STOLE WITH A PAIR OF tall heels. Devil shoes. That's what I call them because they're going to hurt like hell if I walk much in them. But damn, they make me look

216

great, and that's what I want—to be beautiful for Lachlan, even if it's painful. I can stand the hurt.

I'm in front of the mirror fastening my diamond pendant around my neck when Lachlan comes into the bathroom. "You're missing something."

I inspect myself and take inventory. I don't know what he's referring to, but I take the opportunity to mess with him. "How did you know I wasn't wearing panties?"

His eyes widen and so does his smile as he reaches for the hem of my dress to assess the situation. "You're not? Well, that happens to be very convenient."

I swat his hand. "There'll be none of that until later. What am I missing?"

He pulls a black velvet box from the inner pocket of his jacket. "This."

I look at the box sitting on his opened palm. "You spoil me, Lachlan."

"And you love it. Admit it."

I roll my eyes at him. It's not that I don't love being spoiled by Lachlan. I do, but it makes me uncomfortable when he gives me expensive gifts. Anything housed in a jewelry box is going to cost big bucks.

It clicks as he pops its top and I see a pair of diamond solitaire earrings—big ones. I reach out and touch them. "They're beautiful."

"They are, but you're more beautiful."

He always tells me that. I wonder if he said that to the others.

"What's wrong?"

"Nothing's wrong." I hold out my palm, grinning. "Give me my new earrings so I can put them on."

He takes them from the box and places them in my hand one at a time. I tilt my head to the side so my hair falls out of the way while I put the first solitaire in. Damn, it's even bigger in my ear. I wonder how many carats these are? No doubt a lot.

After I put the second one in, I hold my head upright and Lachlan tucks my hair behind my ears for inspection. "Even if minor, diamonds always have some imperfections, but you make these perfect."

"Thank you for the earrings and the compliment."

"My pleasure. Are you ready to go?"

"I am."

We arrive at the Sydney Opera House and Lachlan has made arrangements to park in the concourse section near the entrance since there is no valet. My feet thank him. Otherwise, we'd be doing some trekking from the public parking area.

We're walking toward the entrance when a man with a huge camera steps in front of us and begins to snap pictures. The flash of light is almost blinding as I feel Lachlan's hand at the small of my back, urging me to move along.

When we are in the building, I look at Lachlan and he doesn't seem fazed by the bizarre incident at all. "That was strange. What do you think that was all about?"

"I'm sure it was a photographer assigned to cover opening night."

"The newspaper should teach their staff to be courteous when photographing patrons. That was rude. And ridiculous. He acted like he had to snap as many pictures as possible before you punched him out—like a paparazzi going after a celebrity."

"We should probably find our seats so I can speak with Mr. Brees, if he's here."

In our private balcony section, we're on the second of two rows. Lachlan leans over once we're seated and whispers, "That's not Mr. Brees sitting in front of us. You want to leave?"

Is he serious? "No. We're here. We're dressed up. Let's act like we know something about opera."

"Oh, I know all about opera. I'm just not a fan. My mother loves it, so I grew up hearing it. Madama Butterfly is her favorite, so I know it inside and out. We can blow this off and go do something else if you want."

"No. I want to stay, especially since I didn't know I was with an opera expert. You can explain it to me."

He laughs. "Awesome. That's just what I wanted to do."

The curtain goes up, and after just a few moments, I'm lost. "I have no idea what's going on."

"Okay. It's 1904 and the man, Pinkerton, is a US Naval officer. He's about to marry a fifteen-year-old Japanese girl they call Butterfly, but he knows he's going to divorce her when he finds a proper American wife."

"Well, that's pretty shitty."

"Don't blame me. I didn't write it. Anyway, Butterfly loves

Pinkerton so much, she converts from her Japanese religion to Christianity. Her uncle finds out she converted and comes to the house where they are being wed. He shows his ass, curses Butterfly, and renounces her. The end of this act is them preparing for their wedding night."

"So this is like bow-chicka-wow-wow, only opera style?"

He starts laughing and earns several shushes from the row of people in front of us. He leans closer and I feel a warm rush of breath against my ear as he whispers. "No, Madama Butterfly isn't bow-chicka-wow-wow by any means, but I'll sure show you some when we get back to the hotel."

His promise sends a flood of need between my legs and I become restless in my seat. Lachlan watches me and smiles. "Everything okay over there?"

"I'm good."

"Are you really not wearing panties?"

"Maybe. Maybe not." There was no way I was ruining this great dress with a panty line.

He's trying to read my face, but he can't tell. He pulls the stole from around my shoulders and spreads it across my lap. "I think your legs are cold."

No, sir, I'm anything but cold right now.

"My hand is cold too. I need you to warm it up," he whispers as he slides it under the fabric across my thighs.

No way. He is not about to do that here… oh, oh, yes, he is.

I feel his fingers spidering between my legs, scaling up my thighs to where I ache for his touch. "Hmm, someone isn't wearing panties. Shameless."

I shift back in my seat and he strokes his fingers up and down, spreading the moisture from my center. "I love how you are always so wet."

Lucky for me, it's dark inside the theatre, but I still glance around to make sure no one is watching us. With what he's doing, I'm not sure I'd care if they were.

His fingers are frustrating, but amazing. I want to buck hard and ride his hand until I come into a million shards, but I can't without drawing attention. It's slow torture. "I'm going to give you more, but you have to behave yourself. Can you do that for me?"

I can't answer so I nod to show my compliance and then I feel his fingers start to slide. In. Out. In. Out. I almost lose it, right then and there, but I hold it together by biting my bottom lip. His fingers speed and I feel it building. It's coming. And so am I as Butterfly prepares for her wedding night.

CHAPTER THIRTY-EIGHT

JACK MCLACHLAN

I'VE NEVER ENJOYED OPERA SO MUCH IN MY LIFE.

Laurelyn and I leave the theatre a few moments before the curtain closes. She doesn't want to face the couple sitting in front of us on the balcony. She's pretty certain they heard her muffled squeal and knew exactly what was going on. I'm pretty sure she's right.

We walk across the parking lot hand in hand and another photographer steps in front of us to take more pictures. Laurelyn puts her hand up. "I'm sorry, but there are plenty of other people for you to photograph. Find someone else."

The photographer lowers his camera to look at Laurelyn. I think she amuses him. "It's okay. I already have what I need."

She really has no idea who I am.

When we're in my car, I take my phone from my pocket to turn it back on and see almost a dozen missed calls from Mum, Evan, and Chloe. "Something's going on because my family has been blowing up my phone for the past two hours."

I call Mum first and don't get an answer, so I try Evan next. He doesn't even say hello when he answers. "Jack, it's Dad. He's been taken to the hospital. We don't know anything for sure yet, but he could be having a heart attack."

"What happened?"

"Mum said they were at home and he started complaining of chest pain. She tried to get him to go to the hospital, but you know Dad. He wanted to see if it would pass, but it got worse so she called an ambulance. They took him back about thirty minutes ago and said they'd give us an update when they know more. Where are you?"

"I'm in Sydney."

"Good. We're at St. Vincent's. How long will it take you to get here?"

"Not long."

"Okay. I'll come down and meet you in the lobby."

I end my call with my brother and I'm numb. This is my indestructible dad he's talking about. He just retired so he could finally spend time with Mum. They were going to travel the world together.

"What's happened?"

"It's my dad. He's been taken to the hospital. My brother says he might be having a heart attack."

Laurelyn reaches for my hand. "Oh, I'm sorry, Lachlan. Will it take you long to get to him?"

"No. He's at St. Vincent's here in Sydney. It isn't far."

She grabs my hand and kisses it. "You need to go. Now. I'll take a taxi back to the hotel."

She pulls the handle on the door to get out and that's when I realize I don't want her to go. I need her, so I touch my hand to her arm. "Don't leave. I want you to be with me."

"You'll have your family."

I swallow before I say the words that will change this relationship forever. "You're the one I need."

"But that would mean meeting your family."

It does, and I'm okay with that if it means she's by my side. "I don't care. I need you to be with me."

She smiles and cradles my face with her hands. "Of course. I'll come if it's what you want, but this is going to change everything."

"I know, but it's what I want."

I RACE TOWARD THE HOSPITAL AND WE'RE THERE IN FIVE MINUTES. WE ENTER the lobby and I see Evan waiting for us by the elevators. "Any news?"

He takes a look at Laurelyn. I know he's putting it all together and remembering the photographs, but now isn't the time to tell him to stop picturing her naked. "I walked down right after I talked to you, so I don't know."

"Do they know if it's a bad one?"

"No. It could be something else, but the tests they're doing now will tell us how extensive the damage is if it's a heart attack. When he comes out, he might have to be in the intensive care unit."

Shit, that doesn't sound good.

Laurelyn squeezes my hand. "I know intensive care sounds scary, but I think being monitored there after a heart attack would be standard care, regardless of the severity."

This is why I need her here. She's my anchor. She calms me.

"This is my brother, Evan." Who better not be picturing you naked right now.

"Laurelyn, it's nice to meet you. I've heard some great things about you from my brother." Evan keeps it tame, but I'm positive he would jack with me if he were meeting her under other circumstances.

We follow him onto the elevator and then he ushers us to where the rest of the family is waiting. My mum is out of her seat the second she sees us and has me in her arms. "I thought we'd never get you, Jack Henry."

"I'm sorry. My phone was off because Laurelyn and I were at the Opera House."

My mum lets me go and gives her full attention to the girl by my side. This is it. This is where it's all going to change. She's going to know my name. "Laurelyn, this is my mother, Margaret McLachlan."

I don't know if it's the circumstances with my dad or the end of her wait to meet the woman she perceives as my girlfriend, but my mother pulls Laurelyn into a tight embrace. I almost think she's going to cry, but she keeps it together. "I wasn't sure I would ever get to meet you. Jack Henry has promised me more than once he would bring you to the house, but something always comes up. I was beginning to wonder if you existed, but I see now that you do, and you're even more beautiful than the pictures he showed me."

And there it is. She knows I'm Jack Henry McLachlan and from the look on her face, it doesn't mean jack shit to her. I want to burst out laughing. All of this secrecy about who I am has been for nothing.

"Thank you. It's very nice to meet you, Mrs. McLachlan. Jack Henry has told me wonderful things about you."

Oh, hell! Laurelyn doesn't know that my mum is the only person on earth who calls me Jack Henry. I see Mum's face and know the shit just got real. "You call him Jack Henry?"

Laurelyn is unaware of this blunder. "Yes, ma'am."

My mum takes Laurelyn's face in her hands and leans forward to whisper something in her ear. God, help me. She's so determined to marry me off, there's no telling what she told her. She may have proposed marriage for me.

Mum recovers from meeting the woman she thinks is her potential daughter-in-law and we join the rest of the family in the waiting room. I introduce Laurelyn to Chloe, and then Emma and the girls. It's an awkward introduction for her to meet my family for the first time under these circumstances, but she handles it well.

We're all antsy because it's been almost two hours since my dad went back, but his doctor finally comes out with an update. "Are you Henry McLachlan's family?"

My mum is the one to answer. "Yes. I'm his wife."

"Mr. McLachlan is doing well. It wasn't a heart attack as we suspected, but he had two very significant blockages. One was ninety percent blocked, the other about ninety-five. That's where the pain was coming from. We've stented both of them and I expect him to make a full recovery. We'll watch him overnight and he should be able to go home tomorrow."

My mum holds her head with her hand, her face flooded with relief. "Thank you so much. When can we see him?"

"He should be coming out of recovery any minute. He's going to a step-down cardiac unit instead of the intensive care. His nurse will come for you when he's settled into a room."

I see Evan huddled with his wife and children while Mum and Chloe are hugging, and I know bringing Laurelyn with me was the right decision, even if my dad's condition ended up being less than life-threatening.

She hugs me and our foreheads touch. "Your dad is going to be fine." She smiles as she adds, "Jack Henry."

I whisper so my family can't hear. "It's weird hearing it come out of your mouth."

"It feels weird to say it." And that's the end of our name conversation. This isn't the time or place to discuss it.

We don't wait long until the nurse comes for us. "I can take five of you, but children aren't allowed."

Emma's holding Mila and looks up at Evan. "He's your dad. You go and I'll stay with them."

Laurelyn peers up at me. "I don't know your father. Emma should go." She turns to my sister-in-law. "I can stay with the girls, if you don't mind leaving them with me."

I see the relief on Emma's face. "Thank you."

"You're welcome." Laurelyn takes a slumbering Mila from Emma and carries her over to where Celia is sleeping in a chair. "Don't worry. We'll be just fine."

We enter Henry McLachlan's hospital room in a cluster. None of us say it, but it's frightening to see this strong man so frail and weak. He's pale against the white hospital sheets—almost white on white.

He hears us enter and opens his eyes. He looks groggy. I'm sure it's the anesthetic wearing off.

He looks at my mum first. That's the way it's always been between them. She's always his number one.

And that's what my mum wants me to have. My very own number one.

She sits in the chair at his bedside while we observe as spectators. My dad reaches for her hand and she places it inside his. "I should have listened to you, Margaret."

"I've been saying that for years, Henry."

The dismal mood in the room is lifted by my mum's humor. She speaks her mind. I get that from her, but she also has a gift for easing the discomfort and tension of those around her.

"Henry, I might ought to thank you for trying to die because you'll never guess who Jack Henry brought to the hospital with him."

"Well, love, judging by the happiness on your face, it can only be the woman he's been dating."

"Yes, and she's lovely. Just beautiful. And she calls him Jack Henry."

The whole family stares at me because they missed that conversation between Laurelyn and Mum. "What? It's not a big deal."

As always, my sister is the first to argue. "You're full of it. That's a huge deal."

I needed to change the subject, and fast. "We're not here about Laurelyn and me. We're here for Dad."

Visiting hours end and my dad's nurse assures us his condition is good. She convinces us it would be best for everyone, including my mum, to go home for the night. The waiting room doesn't make for a good night's rest.

I'm the first one in the waiting room with Mum not far behind. Laurelyn has Celia tucked under her arm like a mother hen and baby Mila draped over her shoulder, sucking her thumb as she looks around.

Her soft voice carries across the waiting room and I hear her singing Brahms' lullaby. "'Close your eyes... Now and rest... May these hours be blessed.'"

My mum stands beside me listening to Laurelyn sing to my brother's ankle-biters. "Jack Henry, she's a special one."

She doesn't have to tell me things I already know. "That she is," I sigh.

She bumps her shoulder into mine. "And you've been a little shit for not bringing her to meet me."

I'm amused, but not surprised by Margaret McLachlan's choice of words. She's the only mother I know who will tell her thirty-year-old son he is a little shit. If the circumstances were as she believes, she'd be right. Because I can't tell her differently, I have no defense, so I don't argue. "I guess I have been."

"Where are you staying?"

Where is she going with this? "The Marx."

She sighs. "Go get your things. I want you and Laurelyn to stay at the house."

Now I see. She's so transparent. "The Marx is much closer to the hospital."

She takes that tone with me. That motherly do as I say tone. "We've just had a very close call with your father. The family should be together."

Maybe she does want the family together, but that isn't what this is about. "You want Laurelyn at your house so you can have access to her."

"You haven't dated anyone in years. Is it wrong for me to want to spend time with her?"

It's unnecessary for her to get to know Laurelyn—she's leaving in a month. "There's nothing wrong as long as you don't have far-fetched ideas about us. She's only here for four more weeks."

"That's not written in stone, is it?"

Geez, this woman is bound and determined. "No, but it's written on her airline ticket."

She huffs. "I swear, McLachlan men don't have a romantic or creative bone in their bodies."

I hate that my mum has the wrong impression. "It's not what you think it is between us. Laurelyn and I knew we'd only have three months together when we started seeing each other. We agreed to date for fun, not for love."

"But the heart wants what the heart wants."

"And yours wants another daughter-in-law and mother for more grandchildren."

"My heart wants you to be happy, and I believe that girl is the one to do it. You have four weeks to convince her to stay." She lifts her brows at me. "I suggest you get on that right away, son."

❧

WE'RE DRIVING TO MY PARENTS' HOUSE AFTER WE GET OUR THINGS FROM THE hotel and I remember my mum whispering something to Laurelyn. "What did my mum tell you at the hospital?"

"Oh, do you mean after the incident where I freaked her out by calling you Jack Henry?" She reaches over and frogs my bicep with her knuckle. Damn, it sort of hurt. "Thanks for the heads-up, by the way. Not."

"Forgive me. I was a little preoccupied with the uncertainty of my dad's survival. What did she say?"

"What she told me is our little secret, not for you to know."

Great. My mum and the woman I'm having an affair with are sharing secrets behind my back. That's not awkward at all.

Now, I'm more curious than ever. "Tell me. I want to know."

"No. She would have told you if she wanted you to know."

"She thinks we're in love. Or at least have the potential to be." I throw the words out like bait on a hook to see if I can get a nibble.

"You think so?" Dammit. I can't tell by her tone if she's asking my opinion or if she's being facetious.

She isn't budging, but I have my ways. I might not get what I want out of her by asking, but I have other methods of making this little bird sing.

CHAPTER THIRTY-NINE
LAURELYN PRESCOTT

Margaret McLachlan's words echo in my head as we drive toward her house. "The only way he'd let you call him Jack Henry was if he was in love with you."

It's a nice theory if he'd asked me to call him that, but he hadn't.

He's dying to know the secret I share with his mother. He's going to try to persuade me to tell him later. He thinks he's smooth, but I've learned his ways during our time together. It'll be fun letting him try, but he won't succeed. My lips are sealed.

Lachlan navigates up a long drive leading to a huge house on top of a hill. Maybe a mountain. I'm not sure because it isn't nearly as impressive as the mansion sitting on it. "Is this where you grew up?"

"Yes."

"It's beautiful." It beat the hell out of the tiny apartments and rental houses I bounced through during my early years.

Lachlan takes our bags from the car and carries them inside. There's no his or mine. Our things are packed together in his expensive luggage so at least I don't have to be embarrassed by my worn, mismatched set.

We enter through the foyer and I can't help but stare at the beautiful spiraling staircase leading to the upper floor.

I hear his mother call out, but I can't see her. "Jack Henry?"

"Yes, Mum. We're here. I'm going to put our things away and we'll be down in a minute."

I follow him up the stairs and he takes me into his large bedroom. I'm a little surprised to see a four-poster bed. It's very romantic and doesn't fit what I'd expect to see in a man's room. I walk over and run my hand down one of the thick pillars. We need this bed at Avalon. I could definitely do some interesting things with it.

We go downstairs to the living room to join Lachlan's family and I remind myself the whole way that he's not Lachlan. He's Jack Henry. "Jack Henry."

He turns at the sound of his name. His real name. The name only his mother calls him. "What is it?"

This is going to take some getting used to. "Nothing. I'm saying your name so I can get used to it. I'm afraid of slipping up."

"Don't worry. If you have a slip of the tongue, we'll tell them Lachlan is your pet name for me. Not caveman."

"I guess that will work. It is part of your last name. Is that why you chose it?"

"I picked it because I wanted to hear you say some semblance of who I really am."

"Do you always do that?"

"No, just with you."

Damn. The conversation ends as we enter the living room. I'd really like to know his rationale behind the things he does. I'm hopeful that this conversation is only postponed until a later time.

⚜

AFTER SPENDING THE EVENING WITH THE MCLACHLAN FAMILY, I'M IN THE bathroom getting ready for bed. I thought meeting them would help me understand why Jack Henry is the way he is, but it only makes things feel more out of sorts. They're all so normal. And loving. Theirs isn't the kind of family I would expect for a man who propositions women for meaningless sexual relationships.

I search through my sleepwear, if that's what we're calling it, and choose the least desirable thing I packed, but who am I kidding? This is the same man I've been living with for the past two months. He isn't going to perceive a short, black satin nightgown as anything but a prelude to sex.

I stop in the doorway of the bathroom before entering his bedroom. "Are you sure it's okay for us to sleep together in your parents' house? It doesn't feel right."

He's lying shirtless in bed with his hands folded behind his head. I sigh with pure pleasure as I behold the sight of him. "Trust me. Mum would have it no other way."

I come to the bed but stop to run my hand down the large post. I love this bed.

"Are you going to give me a private dance on one of these poles tonight?"

Even after all this time together, his forwardness is shocking—he wants to get frisky in his childhood home with his family across the hall? "No way, not in your parents' house. It would be disrespectful."

He gets out of bed and catches me before I climb in. He reaches around me from behind and puts my hands around the bedpost. He locks his hands on top of mine to hold them in place so I can't move. His breath is warm on the back of my neck and chills erupt all over my body. He doesn't play fair. "You're telling me no?"

"I would be mortified if your family heard us."

His mouth is on my earlobe and he sucks it into his mouth before nipping it with his teeth. "I don't care. Let them hear us."

"No." It comes out more like a weak plea than the stern command I intended.

He groans against my ear. "I don't like it when you tell me no."

He's whining but it's adorable. "I know you don't hear it often, but 'no' can be a very good answer for you to hear from time to time."

"Tell me one time when it's good."

"Okay." I look at him over my shoulder, "Ask me if I'm pregnant."

His body becomes rigid before he backs away from me. He releases my hands and I turn around to look at him. "Ask me."

"Are you pregnant?" It comes out as a whisper.

I lift a brow at him. "Do you want my answer to be yes or no?"

I smile, waiting for him to catch on to the point I'm making, but he stares blankly at me. "Are you?"

I smile as I answer. "No. See? Perfect example of when 'no' is exactly what you need to hear."

He runs his hands through his dark hair and fists it. "Don't ever fuck with me like that, Laurelyn!" he yells. "Never!"

I flinch, startled by the loud outburst I'm certain his family must have heard. Shit, he's mad—like, really mad. "I'm sorry. I thought you knew I was only making a point."

I'm afraid I've screwed up big time. I feel the pooling in my eyes and I look toward the ceiling, pleading with my sockets to drink the tears. I hold my breath and cup my hands over my mouth to hold back the sob in my chest.

In my confusion over what has just happened, I go for the wrong door in an attempt to get away from him. "That's the closet."

Shit if I care. I walk into the small pitch-black room where Jack Henry's clothes hang and close the door behind me. I'm sure there's a light switch in here somewhere, but I don't try to find it. I'm too numb.

Several minutes pass and I hear a few light taps on the door, but I don't say anything. I need to absorb all these emotions swirling around in my head right now. I try to put a name to the shock I'm feeling, but there's not a single word that will fit. I'm hurt and belittled because he yelled at me and maybe even a little frightened by the fury in his voice.

I'm sure his family heard the commotion and it mortifies me to think of facing them. The worst part is the shame I feel. How can I be sleeping with a man who would become so furious by a possible pregnancy?

You know what? Fuck him.

I hear the light raps again. "I sort of know you're in there unless there's a hidden passage to a dungeon I don't know about." He's trying to be humorous, but nothing in the world could be funny to me right now.

He opens the door and comes inside to stand with me in the dark. I feel him reach for me, but I step away. I can't bear the touch that once set me on fire because in this moment, it only makes me feel cheap.

"No." And there it is again. The word that started all of this. Now I hate it and don't want to hear it, either.

I'm mad as hell, but I can't control the sob in my chest. "I don't want to do this anymore."

"Baby, please, don't say that. I need to explain."

I'm overcome by the what-if. What if I got pregnant? He'd hate me. "No. Every time we have sex, we risk making a baby together even if we use birth control. Unplanned pregnancies happen to real people every day. Look at me—I'm the result of one and see how shitty that ended up for everyone involved."

"That's not true, Laurelyn."

"It is and I can't do this anymore. I won't risk making a baby with someone who would react the way you did just now. I couldn't bear to ever see you look at me like that again."

I feel him reaching for me in the dark and I try to push him away. His arms entwine me and he squeezes, almost too tight. "I'm so sorry, Laurelyn. I thought you were playing a trick on me about a baby because you thought it was funny. I should've known that wasn't what you were doing. I'm so sorry." I feel his hands move to my face. "I would never be angry because you were pregnant."

This conversation is too much for me. I don't want to talk about how a baby would make him feel because then I might be forced to think about how it would make me feel. "Can we agree that this was a misunderstanding and talk about something else?" I ask.

He hugs me in the darkness and kisses my head. "I think that's a great idea, but can we leave the closet?"

I laugh. "You know I thought I was going into the bathroom, right?"

"I know."

We leave the closet and climb into bed. I scoot close so I can put my head on his chest. I'm reeling from tonight's events. I told him I wanted to end things with him and now, two seconds later, I'm curled around him like a kitten desperate for his touch. Yeah, I really showed him who's boss.

Was I really going to walk away from him? I think I was, but there's no use in speculating. He didn't let me go.

This game has changed. The rules are no longer the same, but I don't have the manual. He does, and I need guidance on where to go from here.

233

He caresses my arm. "What are you thinking about?"

I decide to go for it because I need to know where his head is. "I'm wondering where we go from here."

His fingertips continue to glide up and down my arm as he answers. "Tonight changed everything for us, didn't it?"

The word change seems like such an understatement for what has happened between us. "Yeah, just a little."

"If I'm being honest with you, I don't really know where we go from here. I don't know how to do this new us."

He has lines and I don't dare cross them. "What do you need from me to make this work?"

"I think the new us needs to start with a first kiss." He's playful, not panicked, about this new place we are venturing. This feels like my Lachlan Henry, only better.

He sits up, rolling me to my back. His mouth comes down on mine and he pushes his tongue inside. Every motion is deliberate. He's slow and gentle. This is a new kind of kiss for the couple we are becoming.

When he stops kissing me, I search his face and see a deep wrinkle across his brow. I've seen it before. It's only there when he's in deep concentration about something, and it frightens me. I'm afraid he's thinking this isn't going to work. Or maybe he doesn't want to try.

I reach up and place my thumb on top of the contracted muscle to smooth it. "I only see this when you're thinking hard about something. What's on your mind?"

I'm scared of what he's going to say, but he gives me a crooked grin and I'm relieved before the first word leaves his mouth. "Say my name."

I don't know which one to go with. He hasn't asked me to call him anything but Lachlan and I don't want to overstep his boundaries. "Lachlan."

He shakes his head as if to say tsk tsk, wrong answer. "Say my real name."

Oh. "Jack."

His face becomes serious. "Both of them."

My heart is pounding. This is huge, according to his mother. He would only ask me to do this if he loved me. "Jack Henry."

He closes his eyes as though he's savoring the sound of it coming from my mouth. "Say it again, Laurelyn."

I hesitate and he opens his eyes to look at me. That's when I choose to say it again, at the moment his eyes meet mine. "Jack Henry."

He kisses me and I feel his mouth move into the shape of a smile. "That's who I am to you from now on. No more Lachlan. No more pretending."

CHAPTER FORTY

JACK MCLACHLAN

I've shut the door on Lachlan Henry forever. He no longer exists. Only Jack Henry McLachlan resides here, and I like it. For the first time in more than four years, it feels good to be me with a woman. And not just any woman. Laurelyn.

"Now that I know your real name, which I think you'll agree is the single-most important piece of identifying information, do I get to know everything else?"

She wants the rest of my story.

"You know my name. You've met my family. What else would you want to know?"

"We're as close as two people can be, so I want to know everything."

Things feel really good between us the way they are. Am I ready to tell her more?

"You don't have to worry, Jack Henry. I'm not going to stalk you the way Audrey does."

I hear her say my name and I'm a goner. I'll tell her anything she wants to know. "I have a condo here in Sydney. It's home when I'm not traveling, which isn't very often, because I own too many vineyards to stay home for long."

She takes a minute to process this information. "You own them all?"

"Yes. Avalon is my latest purchase."

She wasn't expecting that. "How many total?"

"Too damn many." And that was the truth. I was stretched too thin across New South Wales and New Zealand. I was following in my father's footsteps and also making steps of my own. I shouldn't have purchased Avalon. I don't have the time it requires to make it successful, but I can't regret it. It's what led me to Laurelyn.

"So does that mean you're rich?"

"Yes. I told you I was when we met."

"You've told me a lot of things but I've assumed most all of it lies."

"A lot of it has been, but it's all part of our game, baby."

"And now our game has changed."

Yes. Indeed, it has. In more than one way.

I'm rubbing my hand over the satin gown covering Laurelyn's belly and I feel the metal piercing through her navel. I really want to push her gown up and kiss her there, but I don't. She's not comfortable being intimate in my parents' house and has already told me no once tonight. I don't want an encore or a reminder of our earlier quarrel.

Since we aren't pretending anymore, I might as well warn her about Margaret McLachlan and what she's up to. "My mum wants you here so she can work on you."

"Work on me? How?"

"She wants me to have a wife, and you're the closest thing she's seen. Ever."

"Oh." I'm not sure if her surprise is at Mum's intentions or because I bring it up. "I guess she didn't get the memo about our agreement."

"She'd shit if she knew what I'd been up to."

"But didn't you tell her I was leaving permanently next month?"

Permanently. What a shitty word. I hate it as much as no. "She knows but doesn't care. She's determined."

"Maybe we should roll with it. You know, make her happy."

Hmm. It isn't a terrible idea and getting her to back off for a while would be nice. "I'll do it if you're sure you're up for it."

"Puh-lease, like you and I don't know how to pretend."

Of course, I wake before Miss Sleeping Beauty. She's so peaceful, I want to let her sleep longer. Besides, she'll need her rest for what's ahead of her today. Margaret McLachlan can be exhausting.

I'm wearing sleep pants only, so I put on a T-shirt before going downstairs. I'm the first one up, as always. I'm even awake before baby Mila.

I make a cup of coffee, but opt to wait on breakfast until Chloe's up. I'm certain she'll have some new dish she wants to try out on us.

I fetch the newspaper and sit at the bar. I start at the back—because it's my routine—and resist the temptation to thumb through for the photo I'm certain will be there. I turn the page a second time and there it is, just as I knew it would be. We made the news, baby.

We're in the "My Sydney" section. Laurelyn is beautiful in the photo, even if it's only newspaper quality. I scan the small caption beneath and laugh. "Multimillionaire bachelor Jack McLachlan at the Sydney Opera House with mystery woman."

Mystery woman. She's definitely that. I really can't believe anyone cares about this kind of shit. Except Audrey. She thinks she successfully sent Laurelyn on her way, so she's going to flip out if she sees this. It might be wise to have Jim tail her for a few days so I know her whereabouts. I'll need to call him later today.

I hear someone come into the kitchen and I know it's Mum without looking. She's the only other early riser in the family. "Good morning."

"Morning, Mum."

She waits for her cup of coffee to finish brewing. "Have a good night?"

Damn, I think the old girl is asking if I had a naughty with Laurelyn last night? I lower the newspaper and glance at her over the top. "I slept fine."

"And Laurelyn?"

This is too bloody much. "She's still sleeping."

She's not done, not even close. "I thought I heard something come from your bedroom last night—like maybe you raising your voice to Laurelyn." She's giving me that look, the same one she gave me the night of my birthday party when she thought I left a sick Laurelyn home alone. It tells me I better not have screwed this up with her.

I'm in a shitload of trouble. I feel like a toddler about to be disciplined. I lift the paper up so I don't have to look at her and return to reading. "Don't worry. We're fine."

That's all I give her because that's all she needs to know.

"Jack Henry, you shouldn't have shouted at that sweet girl like that. I didn't teach you to disrespect women like that."

I couldn't argue with her because she was right. I hate that I yelled at Laurelyn. "I knew it was wrong the minute it came out of my mouth. I told her how sorry I was and she forgave me. We're fine, so stop worrying."

"Women hold grudges. She might have told you that you were forgiven last night, but now she's had time to think on it. You'll be lucky if she speaks to you today."

I hope Laurelyn gets up soon, but judging on the time, it will be another couple of hours. "She doesn't play games like other women. If she says she forgives me, then I'm confident she does. You'll see when she gets up."

"Yes, we'll see, son."

Luck is on my side. Laurelyn gets up early. I'm still reading the paper when she comes into the kitchen. She walks up behind me and puts her hands on my shoulders. I peer at her over my shoulder. "Good morning, love." Is she going to think the endearment is too much?

She leans around and kisses the side of my face. "Good morning, darling." No, she's good with it. My mum is all detective-eyed, analyzing Laurelyn's interaction with me following the lovers' spat.

She sits on the stool next to me at the bar. "I wasn't expecting you up so early."

"I couldn't sleep after I woke and you weren't there." Oh, she's laying it on thick for dear ol' Mum.

I turn to the social page to show Laurelyn our picture since I don't have to keep her in the dark anymore. "Look, we made the news. You're a mystery woman."

She leans over my shoulder for a better view. "Hmm, at least it's a good picture and I'm not making some kind of goofy face." She bumps my shoulder with hers. "Which was a real possibility since I wasn't expecting a total stranger to shove a camera in my face."

I sense Mum's scrutiny. "This is new for Laurelyn. We don't attract this kind of attention in Wagga Wagga."

"Yes, I'm sure you've enjoyed being innominate in a small town. I know how you love your privacy." She has no idea. Laurelyn's eyes meet mine and we smile at our private joke.

⚬⚭⚬

DAD DOES WELL, SO HE IS DISCHARGED HOME AND WE SPEND THE NEXT TWO days with my family. Laurelyn and I play the part of being in love for my mum, at times making a game of it to see who can be more convincing. It's fun and I'm surprised by how natural it comes for me. Sometimes it's unintentional and I wonder if it comes as easy for her.

It's her second day with my family and she has already found a comfortable place among them. She and Chloe are almost the same age and have a lot in common, but she connects most with Emma. I think it's because she plays with the girls and they have taken a special liking to her, which is unusual. Mila doesn't like anyone. Especially me.

She's on the floor with the girls and I see the way my mum watches her. Her natural ease with my brother's children doesn't escape her attention.

My mum is sitting next to me on the couch. "I don't know how she won Mila over. That kid doesn't like anyone." I think I could be a little jealous. "She likes Laurelyn better than me and I'm her uncle."

"Laurelyn's mother material. Mila senses that about her." We watch them play a few more minutes and Mum leans over to whisper in my ear. "If you don't do something about it, she's going to make a wonderful mother for some other man's children."

I've watched the way my family has interacted with her for two days and realize my mistake. I shouldn't have brought her here. They're all falling in love with her.

CHAPTER FORTY-ONE
LAURELYN PRESCOTT

WE'RE DRIVING BACK TO AVALON AND I'M THINKING HOW I'VE ENJOYED THE last three days with Jack Henry's family. We've spent the last seventy-two hours pretending to be head over heels in love. It was so easy to play the part, I have to ask myself if I was pretending at all.

I'm curious to see if we revert back to our former selves now that we're away from his family or if we'll continue our romantic façade. I'm too afraid to ask because the answer—either one—scares me.

He reaches for my hand and rubs his thumb across the top of my hand. "You're quiet."

I can't tell him what I'm thinking. He would freak out. I think. "You have a great family. I'm glad I got to meet them."

"They think you're pretty great too. Especially Mum. She was in heaven seeing us together." He squeezes my hand. "Thank you for helping me make her happy."

"My pleasure." And it was my absolute pleasure.

I go to sleep in the car and it's late when we get to the vineyard. Mrs. Porcelli is already gone for the evening, but we find she has left us a welcome-home dinner on the stove. I've never minded cooking or cleaning, but I must admit that walking in to find a home-cooked meal after a five-hour drive is a definite perk of living with Jack Henry.

He brings our bags in from the car and drops them in the laundry room before he joins me in the kitchen. I lift the top of the casserole dish to see what we have. Hmm, maybe it's some kind of chicken casserole? "Smells good. Are you ready for dinner now?"

I feel him behind me and his hands are creeping under my cotton dress. "I'm ready for dessert now."

Mmm... I love me some him.

He goes straight for the kill, sliding his hand down the front of my panties. "Jack Henry, we just walked through the door." I check the clock on the stove. It's only a quarter past five. What if Mrs. Porcelli is still hanging around?

"It's been a week," he groans in my ear as he teases me with his fingers.

"It's been three days," I correct him as I drop my head back against his chest. But it could be three minutes and I think I'd want him again.

He slips a finger inside me and then another. "I can't help myself. It feels like forever since I've been inside you."

I feel his rock-hard erection grinding against my bottom while he slides his fingers in and out of me. The way his hand is positioned, his fingers are rubbing my sweet spot and each stroke brings me closer to orgasm.

"Come for me, Laurelyn, and say my name when you do."

Now, I'm grinding down on his hand and I'm saying his name in my head over and over until I fall over the edge into pure oblivion. "Jack Henry," I cry out with the familiar spasms I've come to love so much.

I recognize the sound of a tearing wrapper so I know what's he's doing. I feel his fingers loop around the waistband of my panties and he drags them down my legs until I step out of them. "Hold on to the countertop. We're not going to make it to the bedroom."

I wrap my hands around the edge of the solid granite in front of me and he uses his knee to push my legs apart. One of his arms loops around my waist and yanks me so that I'm bent just the way he wants me. I feel him there, against my wet core, and then he pushes inside me with a force reflecting that of his pent-up sexual frustration.

I cry out at the surprise of the sudden intrusion and he stills. "Too rough?"

It only takes a moment for me to adjust to this position and then I'm rocking against him wanting more. "No, don't stop."

We synchronize our rhythms and he pounds into me over and over until I hear my name. That's when I know he's slipped over the edge. So I follow him.

TWO WEEKS LATER

I wake at four in the morning with lyrics racing through my head. I almost leave the bed to go to the piano, but I don't. I can't stand the thought of losing one minute of lying next to Jack Henry.

After he's gone to work, I scramble to the piano to play the tune that danced in my head all morning and struggle to remember the exact words I was sure I couldn't forget.

I jot down lyrics telling my story—how I wonder who will take my place after I'm gone and how I am secretly desperate for him to ask me to stay because I love him so much. I struggle because my hand isn't fast enough to get the lyrics down as they flow from my head.

I put the words to music and sing them aloud, adjusting the melody for the best sound. I raise the key to test the tone of the chorus.

As I sing, I have that feeling you get when you're being watched. Since Mrs. Porcelli often listens to me play, I look toward the doorway expecting to see her, but it's not. It's Margaret McLachlan.

My heart jumps into my throat. I immediately think something terrible has happened to Henry and she sees the fear in my eyes. "Nothing's wrong, Laurelyn."

I bring my hand to my chest, as if to calm my erratic heart. I get up from the piano and she meets me halfway for a hug. "Jack Henry is out on the vineyard. Should I call him?"

"No. I didn't come to see him."

I'm confused by this and I gesture toward the couch. "Come sit with me. Would you care for some coffee?"

"No. I'm fine, thank you." She takes a seat on the sofa and I sit on the edge of the chair across from her. It seems the appropriate place for me to be—on the edge of my seat—because I'm dying to know what has brought her to Avalon.

"I'm sorry. I would have called, but I had no way of getting your number unless I asked Jack Henry, and I don't want him to know I'm here to see you."

This is news I wasn't expecting. "You're here to see me?"

"Yes, Laurelyn. I know you're only here for two more weeks and I have something I want to say to you."

I clutch the cushion of the chair to hold on so my ass doesn't fall off into the floor. "Okay."

"I know my son very well, and Jack Henry loves you. I see it in his eyes every time he looks at you." Is it love she saw or was it the façade? "He wouldn't have brought you to meet us or into our home if he didn't. Trust me. That's not something he does lightly."

She's smiling. "So now, I'm going to be a very forward and meddling mother. Do you love my son?"

Wow. I'm taken back by her question, but I know the answer without thinking about it. I should be guarded and not willing to confess it so easily, but I want nothing more than to scream it from the rooftop. "Yes. I love Jack Henry very much."

She smiles even bigger and pats the cushion next to her. "Come sit next to me."

I get up from the chair and do as she asks. She faces me and takes my hands. "Believe me, he's going to be a stubborn jackass when it's time for you to leave in a couple of weeks. He isn't going to want to put his heart on the line and ask you to stay, but he will be sick with himself if he lets you go. Because you love him, you have to spend the rest of your time together showing him why he should ask you to stay."

Whoa. I'm not sure, but I think Margaret McLachlan is advising me to get it on with her son. Does she think I haven't already been doing that?

How do I make her understand about our agreement without telling her? "We knew we'd only be together for three months, so we agreed from the start that our relationship wouldn't become serious. I don't think he's changed his mind about that."

She squeezes my hands. "Hon, it doesn't matter what you agreed to.

If you love each other, that changes everything. Trust me. Nothing else matters. And a little nookie to change his mind never hurts, either."

Yep. That's exactly what I thought she was suggesting.

CHAPTER FORTY-TWO

JACK MCLACHLAN

IT'S ONLY ONE WEEK UNTIL LAURELYN LEAVES. IT'S TOO SOON AND I WANT more time with her.

I'm neglecting my work at Avalon because I'm desperate to spend every minute with her. I can't get enough of her and this morning is no different. That's why I've come back to the house to see her after being gone for only an hour.

I open the bedroom door expecting her to still be asleep, but she's not, and I hear the shower running. Maybe I'll slip in and join her.

As I'm thinking it over, I hear a smothered version of "Sex on Fire" by Kings of Leon playing somewhere in the bedroom. I follow the sound until I find a ringing phone inside Laurelyn's purse. I reach in and take it out to see the caller ID in case it's an emergency from home. At least that's why I tell myself I do it.

It's Blake Phillips. Again.

This time it's not a missed call notification I see. It's a photo of Laurelyn with her lips pressed against a man's cheek. They look like a happy couple. Maybe even in love.

I contemplate what to do—answer or let it go to voicemail—and my curiosity wins out. I slide the bar over and have no idea what to say because I'm in the dark about who this man is. I put Laurelyn's phone to my ear and listen without saying a word. A moment later, I hear his voice. He's a Yank—of course. I would expect him to be. "Laurelyn. I know you're there. I hear you breathing."

I continue silent, waiting to hear some clue as to what kind of relationship she has with this man.

"If you're not ready to talk, please listen." I wait and hear nothing. I think we've been disconnected, but then he continues, "I miss you, Laurie. We had a great thing going and I know we can get it back. Baby, no one knows about us. I convinced Mitch and the guys you just needed a little time to deal with the stress of the music industry, but they're not going to wait forever. You need to come back to Nashville so we can push this record deal through. You need to come home to me."

I'm still not positive who Blake Phillips is, but I'm getting a much clearer picture. He's the one before me, the one who hurt Laurelyn.

"Laurie, I know you miss me."

I've heard enough. "Laurelyn can't come to the phone right now."

There's a moment of silence before he asks, "Who is this?"

"Jack McLachlan. I'm Laurelyn's boyfriend, her Australian boyfriend. Because that's where she is—in Australia with me. Not in Nashville with you."

"I need to speak with Laurie as soon as possible. Please, tell her to call Blake."

"She doesn't want to talk to you and you're out of your fucking mind if you think I'm telling my girlfriend to call her ex-hole. I'm sure you understand." I press the end button because we're done here.

Laurelyn is mine. Not his.

After I end the call, I thumb through photo after photo of Laurelyn with this guy and see the proof of her happy life before me. It's unsettling, even painful to see.

I hear the shower cut off and try to decide what my approach will be to asking Laurelyn about her relationship with this guy. I'm sitting on the side of the bed when she comes out of the bathroom wearing a towel wrapped turban style around her hair. She's as naked as the day she was born.

She's startled to see me and lets out a girlish squeal as she uses her hands to cover herself. She realizes it's me and grins as she drops her hands from her naked body. "Shit, you scared me. I thought you were gone for the day."

"I was, but I came back for something." I wish I hadn't. I don't want these feelings I have.

Laurelyn grins as she walks over to her lingerie drawer. "What's going on? You're acting weird."

I watch her step into a pair of white lace panties and pull them up. She reaches for the matching bra and slips her arms through it before fastening the clasp between her breasts.

I decide I'm done wondering. "Tell me who Blake Phillips is."

She pales as she freezes in place. Her words come out as a whisper. "Why would you ask me that?"

I don't like the way she's affected by a question about him. "Because he called while you were in the shower."

She busies herself with adjusting her bra to avoid looking at me. "You answered my phone?"

"The 'Sex on Fire' ringtone sort of caught my attention. I answered it because I want to know who the hell Blake Phillips is and what he wants with you."

She stares blankly at me. I'm not sure if it's because she doesn't want to tell me who he is or because I'm acting like a possessive Neanderthal. "I'm not used to this, Laurelyn. You know everything about my previous relationships. Everything! Including what a stretch this is for me, and I know so little about yours. I want to know who he is to you."

I'm almost certain she's going to tell me and then I feel a pang of fear. Maybe this isn't something I want to hear, but it's too late. "He was my record producer."

I toss her phone toward her onto the bed so it lands screen side up featuring an affectionate picture of them together. "Does everyone kiss their record producer like that?"

She shuts her eyes and turns away from the phone. "Blake and I were spending a lot of time together while we were working on my album. One thing led to another and we started seeing each other. He told me it wouldn't look good for him to be in a relationship with someone he was representing, and I believed him. It sounded like a legit reason to me, so we agreed to keep our relationship secret to protect our careers. I later found out he wanted to keep us secret because he was married with three kids. I was devastated. And I walked away from all of it. Him. The record deal. The music career I'd worked so hard for. Everything."

Now, I really hate the motherfucker. "When did it end?"

"Early December." That was only a couple of weeks before she came here—not near long enough for her to be over him if she was in love with him.

"How long were you together?"

"Three months." Almost the same amount of time she's been with me.

I lean over with my elbows on my knees and my head in my hands. "Do you love him?"

She doesn't answer right away and my throat tries to eat my heart. "There was a time I thought I did, but that was before I knew the truth." I want her to reach out and touch me as a sign of reassurance, but she doesn't. "I loved a lie, and the truth shattered anything I felt for him."

I want to look up at her, but I can't. I'm afraid of what I'll see. "So, you feel nothing for him now?"

"No. I can't love a lie and that's all we were." Her words are sobering. Hadn't I asked her for a relationship based on a lie? He tricked her into being his dirty little secret, and I outright asked her to volunteer as mine.

I lift my face to see her standing in front of me, but her eyes avoid mine. That's when I know it. I'm a motherfucker just like Blake Phillips.

I slide off the bed to my knees in front of her and wrap my arms around her legs. "I'm so sorry for not treating you the way I should have, Laurelyn."

She strokes her hands across the top of my hair. "What are you talking about? You've never treated me poorly. You spoil me rotten."

I gaze up at her from where I'm on my knees. "I asked you for a relationship based on lies. I kept you as my secret from the world until I decided I needed you when Dad got sick. I'm no better than he is."

CHAPTER FORTY-THREE
LAURELYN PRESCOTT

JACK HENRY IS IN FRONT OF ME ON HIS KNEES, TALKING ABOUT THINGS THAT aren't true. He presses his face against my stomach and I twirl my fingers in his hair. "No, that's not true at all. Don't ever compare yourself to him."

I take his hands and tug on them. "Get up from there."

He stands and reaches for my face. "I'm so sorry."

I don't understand what he means. "Stop this. You've never hurt me the way he did."

He's stroking his thumbs over my cheekbones. "I'm sorry for all the secrecy, for making you feel like you weren't important enough to know the real me. But I'm most sorry because I have fucked you—I don't know how many times—and never made love to you."

I realize I'm crying when he uses his thumbs to catch tears as they roll down my face. "Please, don't cry. I never want to be the one to cause you tears."

He leans down and tenderly presses his lips to mine. I open my mouth and he slips his tongue inside to meet mine for a familiar yet new sensual waltz.

We've shared countless kisses. They were almost always heated and demanding, but this one is entirely different. It tells me things he can't or won't say because it goes against everything he intends for our relationship.

Jack Henry cares for me. If his kisses don't tell me, his touch does. His caress is so tender. He handles me as if I'm a precious, delicate treasure.

We move onto the bed and his mouth feathers kisses lightly down my chin and throat. His mouth continues traveling lower as he puts his fingers inside one of the cups and finds my nipple. He rubs and rolls it, causing it to stand at attention for his touch before he pulls my bra down and takes it in his mouth.

I love the feel of his tongue against my sensitive nipple and something between a moan and the sound of his name escapes my mouth as I lace my fingers through his hair.

When his mouth leaves my breast, he unfastens the bra clasp and frees me from my lace entrapment. I grasp his shirt over his stomach and push it up because I want to feel his flesh against mine. He grabs it by the neck and pulls it over his head in one swift motion before he lowers his head and takes my other nipple in his mouth.

It doesn't matter where he makes contact with my body. Each touch sends a wave of sensation directly between my legs, and I grow wet for him.

His mouth glides lower down my belly and then to my hipbones. He kisses each of them and everything in between before he pulls back on the waistband of my panties to bury his nose inside. I hear him inhale deeply. "Mmm, you smell so good."

Kneeling between my legs, he grabs the waistband of my panties and pulls downward as I raise my hips. He lifts my feet off the bed to free the lace from my ankles and then tosses them to the floor next to his shirt. I sit up to slip my loose bra from my shoulders and add it to the growing pile of clothes.

I'm naked as he kneels between my bent knees beholding my bareness. He puts his palm on my chest between my breasts and slowly glides it down. "You are so perfect. So beautiful."

He's being so sweet, but I can't stop my thoughts from jumping to what he said. He thinks he's no better than Blake.

The notion invites my ex into my head. I don't want him there so I put my hand over my eyes, as if that will help block him out.

Jack Henry knows I've gone somewhere else and reaches for my hand. "Look at me, Laurelyn. Leave him out of this. Only think of me." I open my eyes for him. He kisses the inside of my right knee as he looks up. "See me." He kisses higher inside my thigh. "Be here with me."

I throw my head back against the pillow and groan because I know what he is about to do.

He flattens his tongue against me and licks straight up my center. "Ahh!" I groan. Nothing feels better than his mouth on me. He licks several more times and I already feel the onset of my orgasm starting. It isn't going to take long for him to push me over the edge. I bite my bottom lip as my breathing increases and I feel the waves quickly rising to the surface as he maintains the slow, torturous rhythm of his tongue.

"Mmm, I love the way you taste." His words vibrate against me and then he stiffens his tongue and pushes it in and out of me against my upper wall, hitting that sensitive spot. I lift my head from the bed to see him buried between my legs and the sight makes my orgasm come on fast and furious. I have no control as I pant and fist his hair in my hand, pulling harder than I should. "Ahh, Jack Henry!"

I lift my hips to bring myself closer to his mouth. I feel the shudder of contractions building deep in my womb and I pull his hair. I go stiff and arch my back from the bed as Jack Henry makes me come undone.

When it's over, I fall back against the pillow to catch my breath and feel the tiny post-orgasmic quivers again. He scales my body and kisses his way up until he hovers above me. I feel the roughness of his jeans against my skin and remember he's still dressed from the waist down.

I reach for the button on his jeans and give it a jerk before I slide his zipper down. I put my hand inside his boxer briefs to stroke him. "I want you inside me."

"No more than I want to be inside you." He rolls off the bed and my eyes never leave his glorious body. I watch as he kicks off his shoes and pushes his jeans and boxer briefs down at the same time, causing his erection to spring free.

He bypasses his usual stop at the nightstand drawer and crawls back onto the bed. He lowers his body between my legs and stares into my eyes. Everything between us is different. Our eyes share a silent conversation our mouths don't dare interrupt. I understand what he's asking without words. He wants to be closer. Skin on skin, nothing between us.

I tell myself it isn't irresponsible to forgo a condom because it's what we both want. We're both clean and the risk of getting pregnant is almost zilch since I'm on reliable birth control.

He swallows hard as he gently presses himself against my slick opening and waits for my answer. It's his way of asking before he enters my body, and I give him permission by pushing my hips against him. He slides inside my slickness and squeezes his eyes shut as he hisses, "Laurelyn, you feel incredible."

I tighten my walls around him as he moves in and out with methodical slowness. I savor the full sensation of Jack Henry inside me unsheathed for the first time. I watch his beautiful face dancing over me and I've never felt closer to anyone in my life. Ever.

He is gentle with me, as if I'm a virgin. The affection I have for him is overwhelming, and hot tears roll down the sides of my face as I own the feelings I have for this man. I love Jack Henry McLachlan.

We're heart to heart and he fades into me until I don't know where I end and he begins.

"I'm getting close and I want to come inside you." He keeps moving as he talks and I wrap my legs around his waist, my head spinning with the ecstasy of his words. I forget who he is, who I am, and what we are to each other.

I want him to mark me, to make me his. I lock my legs around him and squeeze. He couldn't free himself from my tight hold if he tried. "I want you to."

He pushes harder inside me. I can't see his face because it's buried against my neck, but he's close. I know he is about to fill me with a part of him.

It's in this moment I know without a doubt that Blake is my past. Jack Henry is my present, and as much as that pleases me, I want him as my future. The feelings and emotions he stirs inside me make it impossible to contain the way I feel about him. I lock my arms around him and squeeze my legs tighter as he groans and spasms inside me.

"I love you, Jack Henry," I whisper against his ear as he empties himself into me.

I love Jack Henry McLachlan. And now I've told him. And I regret saying it the moment the words leave my mouth. Words of love aren't what he wants to hear from me. He doesn't feel the same. This isn't what he signed up for, and I've probably just ruined the little bit of time I have left with him.

I am a foolish, foolish woman.

His face is still buried against my neck so I can't see his reaction. And I don't want to. I feel him breathing heavily against my hair. I think he's contemplating his next move, so I give him the easy out I owe him.

"Let me up." I push him off me without meeting his eyes and dart into the bathroom so he can dress and leave without feeling obligated to talk about what I said.

I wonder if he'll ask me to leave when he comes home from work. My back is against the door, my tear-streaked face in my hands. Maybe I should save him the trouble and just leave on my own.

CHAPTER FORTY-FOUR

JACK MCLACHLAN

I LIE ON MY BACK AND LOOK AT THE CEILING. WELL, FUCK ME RUNNING. Laurelyn loves me. I wasn't expecting to hear that. I'm not really sure how I feel about it.

Our days are winding down and I've been thinking a lot about how I'm going to feel when she's gone. I admit I'm confused by the emotions I have. I've never grown attached to any of my companions in the past, but I've known from the beginning that everything about Laurelyn is different. She means something to me—more than any of the others ever did—but does it equal love? I have no idea.

A part of me wants Laurelyn to leave so I can go back to my life before her, but then there's another part that wants to beg her to stay forever. As hard as I try, I can't decide which is stronger.

I feel a terrible ache in my chest when I think of her leaving. Is that what love feels like? I hadn't thought so, but then I hear her say she loves me and I feel more confused than ever.

I sit up on the edge of the bed and ponder what to say when she comes out of the bathroom. Several minutes pass and I realize she has no intention of coming out while I'm still here.

I knock on the door. "Laurelyn, will you come out so we can talk?"

"I really don't want to. Please, don't make me." She sounds nasally, so I know she's crying. It's almost more than I can stand because I want to be the one to wipe away her tears, not the one to cause them.

"I really think we should." I reach to twist the knob but already know it will be locked. "Please come out."

Another minute passes before I hear her unlock the door. She opens it and stands wrapped in a towel, her eyes downcast refusing to meet mine. I reach out and tilt her chin upward so I can see her eyes, but she closes them and locks me out.

I asked her to come out so we could talk, but now I don't have a damn clue as to what I should say. I feel something genuine for her, but I don't know what it is. I can't say I love her, so I do the only thing I can to show her how I feel.

I untuck the towel from under her arms and it falls to the floor. I put her arms around my shoulders and pick her up. "Wrap your legs around me."

I put my hands under her thighs and carry her back to the bed. I lay her across the mattress side to side and creep over her on all fours. I take her chin in my hand. "Look at me, Laurelyn."

She hesitates and then opens her eyes and stares at me. Tears roll down her temples and I lean forward to kiss them away. I wish I could say I love you.

I can't give her my heart, but there's one thing I can give her.

I lower my hand and feel that she's drenched with my body fluid all the way down the insides of her thighs. I run my fingers through it and rub it into her skin as if to mark my territory. I'm shocked to find how much I like having that part of myself on her. And in her.

She is mine, at least for a little while longer.

I enter her slowly and within seconds, her hips are meeting me stroke for stroke. I want to be gentle because making love to her is new and I like the way it feels, but she has other ideas in mind. Using her thighs, she coaxes me to move faster as I slide in and out of her. She reaches for my neck to pull me down against her and whispers in my ear. "Harder!" I give her what she asks for and when I feel her contract around me, it pushes me over the edge. I push deep inside her one last time as I erupt.

What is it about coming inside her?

I push her hair from her face and she watches my eyes. I see fear as she asks, "Are we okay?"

I lower my mouth and softly kiss her lips. "We're so much better than okay." I give her an Eskimo kiss and then sit up to check the time. Shit! I really need to get back to work.

I get dressed while she watches. I sit on the edge of the bed to put on my shoes and she crawls behind me to slide her arms around my waist. I lean my head back against hers. "I'm never going to make it back to work at this rate."

"I'm going to let you go in a minute. I just need to savor this moment for a little while longer."

Why would she need to savor the moment? Is she going to leave me because I didn't tell her I loved her?

I spin around and push her down on the bed. I imprison her with the weight of my body and pin her arms over her head. I watch her eyes when I ask, "Are you going to leave me?" She swallows hard and doesn't answer. "Don't you even think about not being here when I come home this afternoon. I'll come for you and drag you back by your hair like a caveman."

This brings a smile to her face and I can't resist kissing her one last time before I leave. "I'll probably be late getting in tonight since I need to make up the work I've missed this morning. Be here when I come home tonight."

I still have her hands pinned over her head. "I will."

"Promise me." I don't know what good I think a pledge will do. If she wants to leave, she will.

"I promise."

My guts tells me she was about to run, so it doesn't matter if she promises me or not. She will run if the notion strikes her, so being away from her today won't be easy for me. I won't rest until I get home and find her still here.

⚙️

I send my fifteenth text to Laurelyn today and await her response. I'm probably annoying her, but she needs to understand how much I want her to stay with me until she goes home next week. I'm not ready to say goodbye. At least not today.

My phone beeps with a response.

Here waiting 4U

I'm able to relax because that doesn't sound like a response from a woman who has run away.

When I get back to the house, I almost race through the door to get to her. I'm eager to see proof she isn't gone. "Laurelyn, where are you?"

"In the kitchen." Relief. That's the only word to describe how I feel at the moment. I can breathe again.

I go into the kitchen and find her standing in front of the stove. "I let Mrs. Porcelli go early because I wanted to cook for you. I hope you don't mind."

I come up behind her and put my arms around her waist. I kiss her neck and peer over her shoulder to see what she's cooked. Hmm. Lasagna? My favorite. I wonder if she knows that. I'm reminded of the night we ate at the Italian restaurant in Auckland for her birthday. "Smells delicious."

"My lasagna has been known to bring men to their knees."

"Baby, it doesn't take food for you to bring me to my knees."

She faces me and puts her arms around my shoulders. "Is that so?"

"True story."

"Good. I like you on your knees."

The second the words leave her mouth, I see her remembering our morning. After the touchy incident following the Blake Phillips conversation, I decide it's best to change the subject. "Can I help you with anything?"

We both know what I'm doing, but she rolls with it. "As if you'd know what to do."

"I'm not totally helpless in the kitchen. I think I recall cooking brekkie for you one morning."

"I'm not sure a bagel with cream cheese counts as cooking breakfast, but regardless—I'm good. Why don't you go choose a wine for us?"

I kiss the side of her face. "That I can definitely do."

I go into the cellar and choose a merlot. As I walk back to the house, I hear myself whistling "Private Dancer" without thinking about. Damn, she's always on my mind, even if it's my subconscious.

I hear Laurelyn talking to someone when I return from the wine cellar. I walk into the kitchen and she turns to see me standing behind her. She's upset and that's when I know it's him. He's called again.

I take the phone from her hand and hit the end button. "Don't take his calls again. He upsets you and I don't want to spend what little time we have left with him on your mind. I want to be the only one you think about. Agreed?"

"Agreed."

I want her to forget his call, his face, his name, so I pull her close for a kiss. "Now, do you think you can make it through dinner without him in your head, or do I need to take you to bed and give you a reason to forget all about him?"

"Although I love the idea of you taking me to bed, he's already out of my head. He was the second you kissed me."

"Good."

While we're eating, I can't stop myself from watching the way the candlelight dances on Laurelyn's face. God, I'm going to miss her when she's gone.

She notices me watching her and a smile spreads across her face. "A penny for thoughts?"

I reach for her hand and squeeze it. "I was just thinking about what I'm going to do after you go home. Damn, I'm going to miss you."

She pulls her hand from mine and begins to clear the table. Her eyes are dodging mine. "You'll do exactly as you've done all the other times. You'll move on to the next town and find number fourteen."

I can't imagine there being anyone beyond number thirteen.

CHAPTER FORTY-FIVE
LAURELYN PRESCOTT

THE TIME HAS COME. I'M LEAVING TODAY, BUT JACK HENRY HAS NO IDEA. HE believes we have twenty-four more hours together. Why have I lied to him? Because I can't bear to see him be all right with watching me walk away forever when I'm not at all prepared to do so.

He's sleeping next to me. He takes a slow, deep breath and like clockwork, I hear a quiet snore every other breath. It's his breathing cycle and after sleeping next to him for three months, I've come to predict it. To expect it. To love it. I don't want to know what it's going to be like not hearing it once I'm in my bed at home, so I decide I won't. I go to my purse and take out my phone to record his sounds. It's silly, but at least I can have this part of him with me after I'm gone.

When I finish, I sit in the chair in the corner of the room and scan through the pictures of us on my phone. I have come to love these images of us together. I decide I won't give them up, either, so I silence both phones and go through the photos texting each one to my personal phone. He'll never know I did this and even if he figures it out, what's he going to do about it? I'll be over nine thousand miles away.

When I finish transferring all the photos to my phone, I sit and watch this man I've come to love. I have no idea how long I sit staring at him. I only know I won't get to do it again after tonight.

I curse the glowing time on the clock—4:36. I realize the time I thought would never come has. The flames burning from both ends of our candle are meeting in the middle this morning. My three months with Jack Henry has dwindled to less than three hours and is about to be snuffed out.

I pull my legs up and cradle them as I begin to cry. I'm forced to cup my hands over my mouth to muffle the uncontrollable sobbing. I hear him toss in the bed and I cup my hands tightly so he won't hear me, but he does anyway. "Hey, what are you doing over there?"

I take a deep breath and my chest vibrates. The light from the cracked bathroom door is minimal in the corner where I'm sitting so he can't see my face. I work to disguise the nasally sound I'm certain my tears have caused. "I'm memorizing everything I don't want to forget after I'm gone."

There. I said it. It's the reality we've been ignoring. This is me giving him the opportunity to talk about me leaving. Say something. Anything. Please.

But he doesn't. "Come back to bed."

"Okay. I just need a minute in the bathroom."

I splash my face with cold water and then hold a cool cloth over my eyes knowing it won't help with the swelling by the time he gets up for work. He's going to know I've been crying and there's nothing I can do about it.

When I get into bed with him, I slide over and put my head on his chest. He wraps his arm around me and rubs it up and down from my shoulder to my elbow. "Everything okay with you?"

"Yeah."

"It doesn't feel okay."

I agree. Nothing about this feels okay. I can't tell him that, so I do the only thing that will. I roll to my stomach and rise to my knees. I hitch one leg over him until I'm straddling him and then my body covers his as I drop my mouth to kiss him.

We're both still naked from our earlier romp. I feel him grow hard below me as I slide back and forth over his growing erection. My intention is only to tease him and myself, but then I feel him angled perfectly to slide inside me. I push him inside just a little, dying to slide his full length all the way in.

We've only gone without using a condom the one time last week when I told him I loved him and it was the best ever. I felt so close to him and I want that again before I leave. I need it one last time.

His hands are on my hips and he doesn't push me away so I slide his length inside me a little more. "Laurelyn…"

"Do you want me to stop?"

He doesn't answer me immediately. "No, I don't want you to ever stop."

I lace my fingers through his and use them as leverage as I sink his remaining length inside me until I'm completely full. I love you so much, Jack Henry.

I hear a deep groan from him and the sound alone is such a turn-on. Knowing I'm the one who makes him come undone gives me a kind of pleasure I've never known.

He flexes his hips up every time I slide down. "Oh, that feels so damn amazing, Laurelyn."

I would do this everyday if it were up to me, but it's not my choice. It's his. And he's choosing to let me go.

Now his hands are on my hips and he encourages me to move up and down faster under his splayed hands. "I'm close, Laurelyn." His fingertips are digging into my skin. "Is it okay to come inside you?"

"Yes."

His fingertips close around each of my hipbones and he pulls me down hard against him. He makes his come sound that I love so much because it always has my name behind it. "Ooh, Laurelyn."

I feel him twitch inside me and I know he has just filled me with a part of him.

When he releases my hips, I collapse against his chest and his arms wrap around me. "God, I'm going to miss you."

And there they are. My walking papers. I no longer hold out hope he will ask me to stay, and I feel the tears. Thank God I turned off the bathroom light when I came out so it's dark and he can't see me. And I won't see the love he doesn't feel when he's holding me.

I feel the stream slide down my cheek.

"What is that?" He slides his hand between us and feels the wetness. "Are you crying?"

"No." Yes.

"You are crying. What's wrong? Did I hurt you?" He slides up in the bed, although I'm on top of him. I feel him reach for the lamp on the nightstand, but I grab his hand to stop him.

"No. I'm not hurt. I'm fine." Yes, I'm hurt but not the way you think.

I lace my fingers through his so he won't try again to turn on the lamp. I don't want to attempt to explain this.

He doesn't say anything else about it and neither do I. I spend the next two hours lying next to Jack Henry with my head against his chest. I'm listening to his heartbeat—another thing I'll never hear again.

He kisses the top of my head. "Mmm. I'm going to be late if I don't get ready for work. I'd hate to get fired."

"Yeah, that's a mean ol' mister you work for," I laugh, but even I hear how phony I sound.

The sun is up and I watch Jack Henry walk naked to the bathroom. Damn, I'm definitely going to miss seeing that every morning.

When he's ready for work, he comes over to kiss me like he has every morning that I've been in his bed, but this time is different. "I'll see you this afternoon, baby."

I kiss him like it will be the last time I ever see him. Because it is. I clutch him in my arms. This is our last kiss. Our last embrace. Our last everything.

"You're squeezing me like this is it." Can he read my mind? Sometimes I wonder. He kisses my forehead. "Are you sure everything is okay?"

I nod because I'm so unstable. I'm about to burst into tears and I have to keep it together just a little bit longer.

"I'll try to come in early so we can do something special tonight."

This is it. Here it comes.

I watch Jack Henry walk out of my life forever as he leaves the bedroom. And that's when it all sinks in. We're over. Forever.

CHAPTER FORTY-SIX

JACK MCLACHLAN

At twelve o'clock, I decide to call it a day because I'm getting nothing accomplished. All I can think about is Laurelyn and how she's going to walk out of my life tomorrow. It's all I've thought of for a week since I heard her say that she loved me.

This has been the shortest three months of my life. My chest quite literally aches with the thought of never seeing her again. We agreed on three months, and our time together is up. I promised her the time of her life, but I'll be damned if she didn't turn it around on me. I'm the one who had the best three months of my life, and there's no hope for ever topping it.

I love her too much to let her leave and I need to tell her right this minute.

"Harold, I'm taking the rest of the day off."

"Yes, sir. Have a good afternoon."

Within minutes, I'm at the house and Mrs. Porcelli greets me in the kitchen. "Mr. McLachlan, would you care for some lunch?"

"Has Laurelyn had lunch yet?"

She looks peculiar. "She left this morning not long after you went to work."

She didn't say anything about needing to go into town. "Did she say where she was going?"

Mrs. Porcelli hesitates. "She told me she was going home. I thought it was strange you weren't going to the airport with her, but I didn't think it was my place to question it."

No. She's wrong. That can't be right.

"Laurelyn!" I run toward the bedroom and nothing seems out of place, but it's too clean and in order. Laurelyn isn't this organized. Something of hers is always tossed on the chair in the corner, but it's free of clutter. I open the top drawer of the chest where she keeps her intimates and find it empty.

Please, don't let her have left me.

I go to the closet and everything hanging there belongs to me.

Why have you done this, Laurelyn?

I take my phone out of my pocket and dial her number. I hear my personalized ringtone and I follow the sound. I find her phone next to her Martin on the coffee table in the living room. There's an envelope lying next to it with my name written in her handwriting.

This is bad. Very bad.

I hold the envelope without breaking the seal. She's gone and she left this ink on paper here in her place. These are her final words to me. I open it and remove the folded paper.

My beautiful Jack Henry,

This has been coming for three months and I'm no better prepared for it today than I was when we met. If anything, I'm less prepared. I didn't love you the day I met you, or even a month later. But somewhere between hello and the goodbye I'm unable to bear, I fell desperately in love with you.

I know you don't feel the same. That's why I told you I was leaving tomorrow instead of today. I couldn't bear to say goodbye and see how little you were affected by watching me walk out of your life forever. Because it is forever. I promised I wouldn't contact you and I won't. You kept your promise to me. This has been the best three months of my life and I'll never be able to top it. You made my every fantasy come true and that includes finding the love of my life. Now, it's my turn to keep my promise.

I love you, Jack Henry, with every fiber of my being. Forever.

— LAURELYN YOUR AMERICAN GIRL

No! I thought I had more time to tell her, but she's gone. She's really gone.

And then it strikes me that she might not be. Her plane might not have left. When she wrote the letter, she expected me to find it hours later.

I race toward the garage. I get into the Sunset and drive faster than what's deemed safe toward the Wagga Wagga Airport.

I arrive in record time and don't attempt to find a parking spot. I abandon my car at the front entrance. To hell with it. They can tow it.

I race toward the first open counter. "I need help. I need to find out if a plane leaving for…" I stop to think. Damn. Would she fly home from here? No, Wagga Wagga is too small to have a flight to LAX. She would have to connect in Sydney. "Sydney."

She's clearly annoyed by me. "Sir, we have several flights to Sydney every day."

"It's an emergency. Can you check to see if all of them have left?"

She sighs. "I'll check for you, sir. Any particular carrier?"

"No."

She's in no hurry as she clicks her mouse, and I think she's doing it to piss me off. "They've all left for today, sir."

"What about returning flights to LAX out of Sydney?"

She sighs heavier. "I'll have to check, sir."

She clicks several times. "There are two flights to LAX today. One left at seven this morning and the other is scheduled to leave at three o'clock."

Damn! That's in two and a half hours. Even driving wide open in the Sunset, there's no way I can make it to Sydney in that short amount of time.

I find my car still parked at the front where I left it. There's a security guard standing behind it jotting down the plate number. He sees me coming his way. "Is this your car?"

"Yes."

"You can't leave it parked at the entrance, sir."

I wave him off. "I'm leaving now."

"Good thing you came when you did. I was about to have it towed."

I didn't give a roo's ass and I almost told him as much. Any other time I would, but right now I didn't care enough to tell him anything.

I get into my car and drive away from the airport. I don't make it two miles before I'm on the side of the road thinking of anything I can do to get to Laurelyn, but I'm totally blank.

I can't stop this from happening.

Think. Think. Think. Okay, as much as I hate to admit it, Ben Donavon is my only answer. He might not know how to get in touch with Laurelyn, but he can put me in touch with his sister.

I grind my teeth as I drive toward his apartment. It's going to hurt like hell to ask for his help, but I'm willing to walk through fire to get to Laurelyn.

After I use the intercom to let him know I'm here, he buzzes me into the building. I knock on his door and wait. When he opens it and sees it's me, he cocks his head to the side and shifts his jaw. He is going to enjoy the hell out of this and that pisses me off.

"You already know she's not here, so what do you want?"

It kills me to depend on him as my only link to Laurelyn. Literally, I'm having chest pain because I'm lowered to this level. "I need to know how to reach Laurelyn."

He narrows his eyes at me. "You've got to be kidding me." He's smirking and shrugs. "I wish I could help you out, bro."

He's enjoying this way too much. "Okay, let's not pretend like you're not loving this."

The little fucker laughs. "I'm not pretending. I am loving this shit, but I still can't help you out because I don't have her number."

"Then I need Addison's."

He's smirking bigger now. "Sorry. I'm not giving you my sister's number."

It'll be a miracle if I don't choke this little bastard. "You know I only want it so I can contact Laurelyn."

He crosses his arms to let me know he doesn't plan on giving in. "If Laurelyn wanted contact with you, she would have given you her number, so I think that means she's dropped you."

I feel panic coming on. If he won't give me her number, how am I going to find her when I don't even know her last name? I debate asking him and decide to eat shit if it means I find out. "What's her last name?"

"Laurelyn's?"

He's shaking his head at me, judging me. "Dude! You just fucked her for three months and you don't know her last name?"

"It was part of an agreement we had," I spit out through a clenched jaw.

"I don't know what the two of you agreed on, but apparently she left here keeping her end of it, so I suggest you respect her enough to keep yours."

I watch the door slam in my face before I kick the hell out of it. Fuck! What do I do now?

I walk like a zombie to my car. I get inside, but I don't drive away. I sit there. Thinking.

Shit, I'm so stupid.

She tried to tell me she loved me and I wouldn't listen. I refused to see I might love her in return because I was too unbending. I thought I had something to prove by not falling in love with anyone. Ever.

But I did fall in love with her, and now she's gone.

CHAPTER FORTY-SEVEN
LAURELYN PRESCOTT

I FEEL ADDISON SHAKE MY ARM. "WAKE UP, LAURELYN. YOU'RE FREAKING me out."

I feel myself snubbing. At least that's what my mom calls it when you're crying so hard that your chest forcefully heaves so you can catch your breath.

I open my eyes and she's staring at me. "You were crying in your sleep. Hard."

I sit up in the uncomfortable airplane seat and warm tears roll out of the corners of my eyes. I suck back the snot threatening to drip from my nose. Then I remember. I was dreaming of Jack Henry.

"What's wrong with you?"

"Nothing's wrong. I'm good."

She gives me her I know better than that look. "You're a damn liar. I know you're torn up about leaving him."

I stare out the window. I don't want this. I don't want to talk about it. Him. I want to forget the whole thing ever happened.

"I thought fucking Lachlan would get Blake out of your system. I wouldn't have encouraged you to go for it if I'd known you were going to fall in love with him." His name isn't Lachlan. It's Jack Henry.

"I didn't fall in love with him."

"You're full of shit and it's not an attractive look for you."

"You've swallowed your vocal cords because you're talking out of your ass."

She sighs. "At least I can admit I love Zac and it's killing me to leave him."

I should be a friend and offer to talk to her about the man she loves, but I don't. "This is a long flight and I'm not doing this with you."

I get up from my seat and walk toward the back of the plane so I can get away from her. I go into the tiny bathroom and lock the door. I look like shit so I splash my face with water, but it doesn't help. Water won't wash this away.

I've known pain my whole life, but this is a new kind for me. It isn't born of something wrong or ugly. This pain is conceived out of beauty—my love for Jack Henry McLachlan. I embrace it. I clutch it as tightly as I can with both fists because I never want to forget the love I have for him. Loving him will forever be my Beauty from Pain.

ABOUT THE AUTHOR
GEORGIA CATES

Georgia resides in rural Mississippi with her wonderful husband, Jeff, and their two beautiful daughters. She spent fourteen years as a labor and delivery nurse before she decided to pursue her dream of becoming an author and hasn't looked back yet.

Sign-up for Georgia's newsletter at www.georgiacates.com. Get the latest news, first look at teasers, and giveaways just for subscribers.

Stay connected with Georgia at:
Twitter, Facebook, Tumblr, Instagram,
Goodreads and Pinterest.

THE Beauty SERIES

MEN OF LOVIBOND

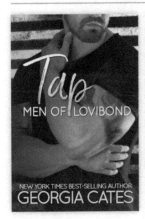

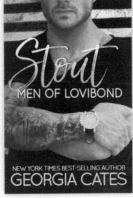

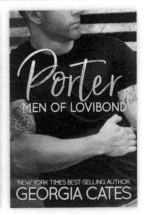